IN THE SHADOW OF THE PYRAMID

by H. W. Moss

NetNovels
Publishing Co.

© Copyright 2015 by NetNovels

ISBN 978-1-942924-01-2

Cover & Typography, Bob Bohle
Production & Layout, Layla Lyne-Winkler
Graphics, Laurent Cito Reboul/Smile Productions
Proofreader, Kate Nolan

First Edition, March 2015

Published by NetNovels Publishing Company
3311 Mission Street
San Francisco, CA 94110

Published in the United States of America

In the Shadow of the Pyramid by H. W. Moss

"The way it reads is not the way it was written."

K. Moss

This book is dedicated to our father,
who stuck around long enough to read the first draft.

TABLE OF CONTENTS

One	The Excavation	9
Two	The Whaling Ship — March, 1849	17
Three	An Old Boot & A Box Of Square Nails	29
Four	Rites Of Passage	33
Five	Getting An Historical Perspective	39
Six	Life Aboard Ship	45
Seven	The Plan	55
Eight	The Hotel's Own Emperor	69
Nine	A Rude Awakening	81
Ten	A Golden Talent	99
Eleven	The Morning Meeting	115
Twelve	Bummer & Lazarus	133
Thirteen	The Right Price	145
Fourteen	The Bet	161
Fifteen	A Day In Court	181

About the Author

CHAPTER ONE

THE EXCAVATION

A battered Dodge pickup turned down Merchant Alley and stopped beside the marble clad facade of a modern office building. A vacant lot covered with a pile of rubble, mostly broken chunks of concrete and bent rebar, lay on the other side of the contemporary structure.

Across the alley was an open pit half a football field in length and four stories deep. The driver of the Dodge switched off his engine and the vehicle backfired loudly. One piston caught in after-burn while the other five ran to catch up, the motor wheezing like a tired old horse before it quieted.

The driver's door opened after a moment of silence and the lanky man behind the wheel stepped down. "Be still Boomer," Don Worthy said pointing a finger at the windshield and using a slightly menacing tone in his voice. He squinted over the hood of the truck as if it were capable of acting on its own volition.

To prove it could, the truck gave out a final rumble and shook with the agitated rattle of a castanet.

"I'll get you a tune-up just as soon as Gus gets out of jail," Worthy said soothingly. "I promise." The engine gave one more sigh before it fell silent. Worthy waited some seconds before he decided it was the last gasp, walked around the front bumper toward the chain-link fence that surrounded the excavation. He gripped the fence high up and it seemed at first as if he intended to climb over. Instead, he bent at the knees and hung like a monkey behind bars, nose poked through a link, eyes peering intently between the holes in the barrier.

It was midafternoon on Black Friday, the last weekend of the month. Don Worthy knew the union construction crew knocked off early that day, but he stared in silence until he satisfied himself no one stayed late. He returned to the truck, popped open a tool carrier behind the cab where he rummaged around until he produced a large bundle of keys attached by a thick wire ring. Then he marched over to the padlocked gate.

For several moments Worthy attempted to match keys and lock. At last, he inserted one that fit perfectly. The lock sprang open.

"Not bad for a novice," he muttered as he unwrapped the chain from the post and swung the gate open. He returned to Boomer. Front door open, he leaned inside without sitting in the driver's seat and gingerly turned the key in the ignition. He listened as the engine cranked. It would not start. He turned the key off, frowned, tried again. The starter motor operated and forced the flywheel to spin, but the engine would not catch. Worthy jumped inside and pumped the gas pedal, cranked the engine again.

"You're starting to piss me off," he said with rising inflection in his voice. This time the truck did not even back-fire. It just coughed and choked on the fuel in its system. "Gus gets out of jail in two weeks," Worthy said with promise. The motor spat exhaust through its carburetor. "Tune-up in two weeks." The engine rumbled to life. "That's more like it."

Worthy backed the vehicle up and aimed toward the open gate. Why walk when you can drive? He wore a self-satisfied smile. As soon as he cleared the opening in the fence he set the emergency brake, let the engine idle and returned to swing the gate closed. Rewrapping the chain around the post, he was careful not to snap the lock shut.

"Have to remember which key that was," he said to himself as he settled into the seat behind the wheel. Boomer's engine ran smoothly which surprised him. He hoped it would not find out he lied about Gus being available in two weeks. More like two months if the county considered good behavior toward early release.

Don Worthy guided the creaking old Dodge down a wide dirt path cut against the side of the immense excavation site. This was the only entrance into the pit, a temporary path that dropped at a sharp angle like a switchback mountain road that had only one switch. Worthy wondered if his brakes were as tired as the engine but decided not to dwell on that thought.

The bottom of the pit was muddy in places. He maneuvered Boomer around several large pieces of heavy equipment — a steam roller with stegosaurus spikes on its weighted front canister and a back hoe that had been shut off in mid rise -- taking care not to scrape the truck against their metal sides and giant tires. A crane, not yet one story tall and still well below grade, was being pieced together in the northern corner of the cavernous hole. The construction crew used it to hoist long, wide steel plates into place flat against the earthen wall. The plates would become support for a wood frame into which cement would be poured to form a foundation, subbasement and multiple level parking garage well below street level of the completed high-rise.

Worthy was impressed. "Hundreds of underground parking stalls, layer on layer," he said to the crisp, cool air. He drove Boomer beside a Dynapac bulldozer, its open scoop lying in front of it. Worthy imagined it to be a captured wild animal staked to the ground about to be flayed before it was carved to pieces and carted away by primitive hunters.

The excavation site covered half a city block and was so large he drove Boomer around on the flat floor like a racecar driver tearing up the road. After one quick tour, Worthy parked the truck with its grill aimed at the upward incline he had just driven down, set the emergency brake and switched off the ignition. He was a few feet away from the tread marks his arrival left in the soft earth.

This time the truck did not backfire or after-burn. A remarkable silence surrounded Don Worthy as he sat in the cab and leaned out his open window. He lived in a city that was never asleep, was always noisy and alive with an ethnic soup created by several hundred thousand people eating and defecating, breathing and perspiring and all the while constantly traveling, moving between places where they did these things, starting and turning off diesel engines, making tires squeal, horns honk, radios blare, alarms sound and who raised their voices loudly above their own deafening mechanical roar so they could be heard.

Finding such solitude as he now had demanded Don Worthy's attention. He was introspective enough to know this was an illusion that could not long be sustained so he took a deep breath and exhaled slowly, smelled the aroma of freshly dug earth clinging to the air. The moment passed and he opened the door with a sigh. He stepped down and leaned toward the open cab.

"All out," he said sharply. Then he clicked his tongue in the roof of his mouth a few times making a sound like a cricket, whistled once long and loud. "End of the line. C'mon, c'mon, snap it up there. Let's go."

A few polite seconds passed before a small furry head appeared on the floorboard under the passenger seat. The cat looked quizzical as it tried to make out its surroundings. Worthy slapped his forehead in mimed dismay but left the door wide open as he made a tour around the truck to the passenger side where he opened that door.

The cat took the hint and leaped to freedom. Its paws stuck in the ooze and he shook them individually as he walked.

"Very good, Mac. I'm pleased you could put in an appearance," Worthy said sarcastically. He slammed the door, went back to the driver's side and slammed it closed as well. The sound of metal hitting the frame rumbled around the bottom of the well before fading into sky. Worthy heard the echo as if from inside a bell or deep in a ravine.

There was a brightness, a tang in the air that magnified sound. He yelped just to hear it. He popped a finger in his cheek. He made a farting sound. Then he became suddenly serious and stood at attention. He raised the flat of his right hand to his forehead and saluted smartly.

"We got work to do, boy," he said to the cat which had turned to investigate a dirt clod. "Find me something I can sell at the market and I buy you nice hunk of fresh fish. Deal?"

Worthy made another mock salute into thin air. "Yes, Sir!"

He bent down toward the animal and stared the creature straight in the eye. "We're looking for a flea market special down here. Unnerstan? He'p me, MacArthur, he'p me look 'round this here hole Mister Mac."

The cat shook a paw which made the pebble caught between his claws take to the air. Then Mac turned his back and wandered away from the crazy man.

Don Worthy was used to such disdain from humans. Perhaps it was his peculiar calling which caused almost everyone he met to eventually turn and walk away from him. Scavengers, it seems, do not get high marks for social interaction.

Worthy frequented junk piles, dumpsters, and digs like this to pick up items he could sell at the open air market or hawk from out the back of his vehicle. He held a perennial garage sale on the sidewalk near his apartment though he had no garage of his own. He knew all the "antique" stores that were interested in "found" art. He resold discarded copper wire from union electrical jobs, telephones and chairs left over from office moves, carpet and linoleum when it was in decent condition. His most recent discovery was old bricks. He collected braces of these which he cleaned of their mortar and sold at a significantly higher price than new ones would fetch. Used bricks were prized by home builders and renovators over new ones for aesthetic reasons. They became decorative fireplace frames inside, added a tastefully textured look to an exterior.

He did not understand this at all because, for the most part, old bricks were old. They were already in a state of crumbling decay but, still, he went along with a trend as long as it proved lucrative for him.

The excavation where he was trespassing began with a demolition two months ago. Worthy retrieved several lengths of conduit from the alley of the office building up above and picked up half a pallet of bricks lying around this very site. They were the residue of an old hotel that had stood on the corner of Sansome and Clay since the quake of 1906. The building weathered nearly a century of neglect and numerous sordid tenants but at last fell victim to the vicissitudes of finance and the demand for office space. It was shattered by the wrecking ball.

Worthy remembered the structure with an anonymous sort of regret. There were so many buildings that had met a similar end in the recent past that it made little sense to be emotionally attached to any of them. He accepted their passing philosophically, more concerned with his own future than that of an inanimate object, let alone an un-reinforced brick hotel. He would grieve for his truck before he concerned himself with a building brought low by progress. Besides, their passing meant new projects which gave him an opportunity to live off the leavings just as he had for the last twenty years lived off their predecessors.

Worthy looked around at the dirt which had turned to clay at this level. Tooth marks in the light ochre ground revealed where the 'dozer driver had been working. The machine was settled directly inside two curved black formations, one behind the machine and one in front, which might be geologic and which the driver had scrupulously avoided. Instead of crushing them outright, the machine had raked the top of both arcs flat, then scooped six inches of yellow earth from inside each without hitting them.

He walked over to stand inside the deepest part of the excavation, next to the bulldozer, within the framed confine of the two curves. They had the bend and shape of Indian bows and ran exposed along the surface for 30 or 40 meters on either side of the digging tool.

The arcs piqued his curiosity and, as Don Worthy ambled over to the nearest one, he pulled a small Swiss Army pen-knife from his pocket. He knelt beside the belt of black which was wider than the spread fingers of one hand, pressed the point in and felt the material yield. He dug a bit of pulp from the spongy surface. Charcoal burned long ago. The discovery made Worthy laugh.

"The driver thought he was going to have to call for help," he said to Mac who had wandered over to investigate. "He avoided hitting these because he was afraid to bend the blade. He probably didn't climb down to look at them, thought they were rock formations. He's gonna be surprised come Monday to find out they're only made of wood. And rotten wood at that!"

Worthy straddled the one black barrier and bent to examine its inside more closely. He scraped off a thin layer of clay, carved his knife into the coal-like surface which revealed a white sub-surface. He poked at this but the blade was unable to penetrate.

"Oak," he said with such conviction it rang like a gong against the dirt walls. "Dense, first growth stuff. Don't see much of this now a'days."

A fragment pried loose where the point struck. He held his knife blade up to examine what it retrieved. Stuck to the tip was a square peg. One side was dark and cracked, the other the lighter color of the natural wood. He rotated it in the now fading late afternoon sunlight.

The darkest side of the peg, the side that had been lying on the surface, was as black and foreboding as a starless night. He pressed a fingernail into it and it dented. He rolled the caked powder under his fingernail against his thumb and sniffed.

"This side's been burned," he said to no one in particular, not even his cat. "Now what do you make of that?"

Don removed a cigarette from a half-empty pack and cast about for a place to assume his thinking position. He considered the yellow machine where it lay with extended scoop. He had wandered far enough away from his truck that the nearest comfortable raised spot was the red plastic seat of the bulldozer.

"They must've knocked off work about the time this got uncovered," he mused and waved his arm toward the two belts of wood on the surface of the fresh dig. He began to feel like a sleuth, an archeological explorer. In his excitement he forgot that night was about to sit on his shoulders and he should probably start heading home. He wandered over to the earthmover and clambered up its side. He slipped into the contours of the curved plastic seat, leaned on the steering wheel and struck his lighter. He sucked the flame onto the tip of the tobacco stick.

"So why in hell are there swaths of charcoal at the bottom of a twenty-five foot hole in the middle of San Francisco?"

MacArthur delicately picked his way through the wasteland of small rocks and clods of clay until he stood looking up from the foot of the machine. His human companion had found a clean place to sit. He mewled.

"C'mon up, you whiner," Worthy said exhaling smoke. "There's nothing to eat here, your food's in the back of the truck so don't keep that noise goin'. C'mon, boy, jump."

The cat leaped onto the earth mover's lowest foot rail, recoiled to spring again, obviously planning to complete his jump into Worthy's lap. Just as Mac fell back to leap, the huge machine gave a shudder and began to shift out from beneath them both.

"Jesus, Mac," Don shouted, "What the hell'd you do?" Worthy tumbled from his perch reaching frantically for anything secure, the lighted cigarette crushed between his fingers as he grabbed one of the 'dozer's steering levers and held on to it with all his strength. There was a moment of weightlessness as the heavy machine dipped backward and slid into the ground amid the loud sounds of splintering wood beams.

The cat, already airborne, changed direction in mid-flight. Mac chose to reach for the solid floor that came up to meet him rather than claw for Don's back.

The lights went out for Don Worthy. For an instant he thought he was unconscious or dead. He held the lever tightly in his grip which confirmed he was alive, up to the moment without pain. He felt around in the darkness and realized he was wedged in an area below the 'dozer driver's seat. A mournful cry reached his ears. He glanced skyward to see faint light and the outline of his cat dangling from an open ceiling. What had been the bottom of the pit was now the roof of a musty smelling cavern.

The machine gave one more lurch and Worthy was certain it was about to fall over the edge of a cliff. But it was just settling to rest with its front end pointed toward the heavens.

Overhead MacArthur cried loudly as he dug hind feet into empty air. Worthy saw the cat get a rear claw on the ledge and then the entire rear paw. The animal scrambled over the thin lip of roof. Don decided it was time to make the same run for safety and began carefully to extricate himself from his position on the metal floorboards.

There was no more movement, no earth tremors as he worked his way to the front of the machine. The scoop, larger than two bath tubs, had become hung up on broken timbers near the surface and was pointed away from the hole that Worthy had fallen through. The earthmover now looked even more like a trapped animal lumbering in its death throes, trying to untangle itself from a well-laid snare.

Worthy used the machine's outstretched arms connected to the scoop as a walkway to safety. He climbed these until he was able to reach his hands up to the floor that was now a ceiling. He hoisted himself back up onto the excavation site.

He did not look for Mac until he stood securely back on solid ground a full minute. The cat was nowhere to be seen until Worthy's gaze followed the line of the ramp he had driven down into the pit. The animal was half way up the dirt trail and making excellent time toward the top.

"Come back here, you coward!" Worthy yelled at the fleeing tail. But Mac never wavered in his flight. Worthy watched him scramble through a hole in the fence and disappear. Eventually the cat took cover under a block of broken concrete that was part of the pile of debris in the alley.

CHAPTER TWO

THE WHALING SHIP — March, 1849

Captain Henry Cleaveland could trust only three of his 32-member crew implicitly. He knew without doubt that if he dangled by a line from the bowsprit, these three could be counted on to pull him to safety. They were, after all, his sons.

The young men and six other children were birthed in the master bedroom of the Cleaveland's rambling white clapboard residence in West Tisbury, Massachusetts. Theirs was a seafaring family which traced its lineage from one of the first whaling men to settle Martha's vineyard, Eustice Cleaveland, Henry's great grandfather. Captain Henry was proud to have three of his boys with him on the voyage, but his thoughts rarely strayed in their direction; they knew their duties and he had his own concerns to occupy his time.

Captain Cleaveland and his crew were nearly 12,000 miles from their Atlantic seaboard home. They anticipated a three or four year voyage and were already nine months out, traveling the whale route, roughly following the contours of the continents of North and South America aboard the *Niantic*, a three mast sailing ship. *Niantic* flew a complete compliment of 37 sails which, when full of the wind, drove the sturdy oak hull in a slow, steady glide over the world's seas. A wide ship and strong, she registered in at 413 tons and was thought by both captain and crew to be capable of breasting the highest waves, the fiercest storm Cape Horn could throw at her.

Launched in 1831, *Niantic* was born to the China trade. In '40 under the command of Captain Richard Doty, she was trapped inside the port of Canton, blockaded by the British during the Opium War. Freed three months later, she made a safe journey back to Sag Harbor, New York, where she was dry-docked the better part of a year.

By June of '44 *Niantic* was no longer being used to carry spice and tea. She had been refitted as a whaler and placed in the command of Captain Slate. In his hands, her last voyage consumed 35 months at sea as she hunted sperm whales off New Zealand. Slate returned her to Sag Harbor laden with ten thousand pounds of whale bone and 2,400 barrels of whale oil. The bone would be used as stays in ladies' corsets, as the spokes of umbrellas or in jewelry. The oil would be used to light lamps or heat cooking stoves.

Now *Niantic* was under the able guidance of Captain Cleaveland, having again come out of dry dock and repairs in Warren, Rhode Island. She headed for the Pacific Northwest where gray whales were to be found now that right whales near shore and sperm whales farther out had been decimated by over fishing.

Pods of gray make their way down the western edge of the world from their summer home in Alaska on a 6,000 mile journey toward breeding grounds in Baja, Mexico. *Niantic* would follow and stalk the sea mammals until her hold was again full, then the return voyage would begin. Perhaps one season would be enough with many gray coming her way in which case they could return home early; perhaps it would require all three seasons to fill the hold. It had not been good hunting thus far. During her three-quarters of a year outward journey, *Niantic* sighted nothing larger than a dolphin.

The crew was mostly made up of Hawaiian sailors, the dark skinned island laborers called Kanaka and a few Irish. None were particularly concerned about the voyage now that the dreaded Cape had been rounded and they were on their way to the hunting grounds although there had been talk among them that such a long trip with nothing to show for it so far boded poor whaling to come.

The Captain was not unaware of the superstitions the crew whispered to one another at night. However, he remained confident they would take their fill in record time now that they neared spawning waters.

Before continuing northward, Cleaveland decided to put in at Paita, Peru, to replenish supplies depleted on the journey. He sent one of his boats over the side to purchase stores and receive news from the outside world and was studying a chart which was spread on the table in front of him when someone knocked on his cabin door.

"Enter," he said without looking up from his work. A white clay pipe with a long stem rested in the palm of his left hand. He puffed at it without raising his arm from the table.

"Mail packet caught up with us at Paita, Sir," Second mate Sylvanus said as he tossed a full sackcloth onto the Captain's table. Sylvanus waited patiently at ease while his father opened the bag and extracted several bundles, sifted through a number of letters and opened one that immediately caught his eye.

"Well that's a fine howdydo!" the Captain's deep voice burst out. "Remember Rowland, Syl? Capt'n Rowland Macy? Says he's quitting whaling and thinking of opening a dry goods store. Invites me to do the same. Become a partner. Wouldn't that be a sad end of me?"

The Second said nothing. He decided he could safely nod his head in assent.

Cleaveland picked up another batch of mail which bore the postmark of the Hawaiian Islands and was tied together by a piece of hemp twine. Idly he handed it over to his son.

"Give these to the Chief Kanaka, whoever he is this time 'round," Cleaveland said.

"Yes, sir!" The young man began to take his leave.

"Stay a moment, Second," Cleaveland said as he closely studied another letter he had just opened. "Seems we have something here from our American Consul in Panama, fellow name of Nelson." The Captain read a moment to himself. His face grew pinched and he looked thoughtful. At last he glanced at his crewman. "Send in the First. I have something to discuss with him."

Sylvanus exited with a muffled, "Aye-yi, Captain."

Two knocks on the cabin door signaled the nearly immediate response to his command. An older version of the young second mate with the same ruddy complexion, more weathered, his shoulders broader, entered at the Captain's acknowledgement.

"The Second says you want to see me, Sir."

"Sit down James Freeman. I have need to discuss a new business with you," the Captain said with a wide smile and a familiarity to which the First was unaccustomed.

Captain Cleaveland rarely allowed personal relations to enter his conversation when at sea. His sons were the First, Second and Third Mates and properly addressed as such whether becalmed or in the midst of the strongest gale. A man's courage, the Captain believed, was tested as much by how well he responded to the chain of command as it was by how well he behaved under the awesome power constantly exerted by an unforgiving sea.

There were moments, though, when he took his sons into his counsel. At such times Captain Cleaveland adopted a conspiratorial tone toward the young men for it was the closest Cleaveland ever managed to get to his offspring. This was his way of metaphorically placing an arm around their shoulders and asking for their opinion. That was how he felt now with James Freeman standing opposite: Fatherly.

But the Captain always maintained a certain distance, never became too familiar with either his sons or the men under his command. In fact, Captain Cleaveland did not believe people should touch one another, not even affectionately, so he never shook hands in either greeting or farewell. Nor, if truth be told, did he ever actually listen to anyone else's thoughts on the subject at hand. When anyone expressed an opinion, even if he elicited it from them, he heard them out but did not heed them. His mind was usually completely made up by the time his sons were invited to join in conversation and he did not really believe anyone else had better insight into life in general nor life at sea than he.

When he made up his mind to do something, as he had just done with the Panamanian Consul's request, there was nothing anyone could do to alter it.

The eldest, but not the brightest, son was James Freeman. As First Mate, he was often taken aside early in the planning stages for any change of course or new port of call. It fell to James to keep his brothers on the same tack, they in turn to keep the rest of the crew in line with the Captain's orders.

"It seems a good wind has come to fill our sails," the Captain began by way of preamble using one of his many seafaring aphorisms.

"Begging the Captain's pardon, but we are at anchor," James Freeman replied with self assurance. He had never been a particularly imaginative child; he was less so as an adult.

"It warrant meant to be a literal statement, a figure of speech merely," the Captain said reasonably. "Consider what I am about to propose as manna from heaven if you will." The Captain squinted at the man opposite. "Ye have been keeping up with your Bible studies since we set sail, hayan't ye?"

"Why, of course, Sir."

"Good. Yer mother would be pleased to learn that. I shall write her saying as much on your behalf. Now then," he took a puff from his pipe. "I have here a request we take on an unusual cargo and I want your assistance." He passed the letter from Consul Nelson across the table to James Freeman. The Captain remained silent for a few moments until the First Mate finished reading which took considerably longer than his father.

"As you can see, we are asked to become a passenger carrier." The Captain paused to allow this to sink into his son's less than acrobatic cranium. "I believe there is an honest dollar to be made for our shareholders as well as for ourselves."

And he meant this with all the integrity in his soul, for Captain Cleaveland was the consummate Yankee capitalist. He had always been a seaman, but his trade had not always been in whales. At one time he dealt in humans. As master of his own vessel, Cleaveland gambled it against high odds for a higher return — and lost. The British took both ship and cargo, a consignment of Africans he was taking directly to market in the Americas, when he was boarded a day out of Nigeria. He had injudiciously chosen that moment in history when Britain no longer respected slavery as an institution even though her former colonies continued to do so. The Captain's own attitude was to abhor slavery on Sunday, to sell it where legal on Monday. He remembered with relish two highly successful trips prior to the losing venture and longed to possess, not just be the master of, his own ship again.

Although commander of the *Niantic*, he did not own the vessel. Cleaveland worked for the benefit of a stock company in New York. He held no shares, but all profits were divided and it was true that when he did well for the owners he did as well or better for himself. That is why Nelson's letter was so compelling.

"I am informed that there is a great crush of humankind sleeping on the beaches of Panama," Cleaveland intoned. "Seems they are all of a desire to be in San Francisco."

"Yessir," the First Mate responded. "I had wind of this while collecting stores in the town, Sir. There were Spaniards as asked me if our vessel were for hire or for sale. And sums were mentioned. But it never came to my mind you would consider missing a season at the whales, Sir."

"Well, I have considered it and we shall. For when we arrive and there are, as this Consul Nelson describes, but as few as half the quantity of men on the beaches with the desire to book passage north, then we shall make a season of whaling in one boatload." He allowed time for this statement to hit home with James Freeman. "Therefore, I propose we refit for cabin class on the top deck and arrange pallets for steerage on the mid and lower decks. This should be done almost as it were for the Afrikerns as you recall."

"I do, Sir."

"Good. Yes, I b'lieve we can outfit to transport near as many whites as heathens once were quartered if we employ the decks. Below, however, let there be the breadth of a hand more room between bunks. They are likely at least to be Christian and entitled to some creature comforts."

"Yessir, Captain," James Freeman saluted.

"Money will put feet on a duck, lad," the Captain concluded in a more pedantic tone. And although James Freeman had heard this aphorism many times over the years, yet it was still lost on him. He squirmed whenever two incompatible images tried to fit themselves into his brain.

"Change your port of call when the counting house moves, that's what I say," Cleaveland finished. He favored giving his son little homilies at moments like this. James Freeman, on the other hand, was sensitive only to the Captain's tone, not the content or meaning of his words. He had grown up being stung by similar words from his father and disliked being addressed in this manner.

Captain Cleaveland, meanwhile, was completely insensitive and unaware of the effect the nuances in his voice had on the lad. He considered the subject closed, their discussion complete. He was quite pleased with himself and his decision.

"We'll not be whaling, then, Sir?" the young man asked with a certain amount of annoyance and incredulity in his voice. Was he missing something valuable in the conversation? James Freeman clearly understood the worth of hunting whales. How had that changed in the course of their stay at the port of Paita?

"There will always be whales to harvest, me boy," Cleaveland said with exasperation. This mellowed somewhat when he realized James Freeman had little or no grasp of how the winds of change operated. "The Lord shall provide for that. But there will not always be men sitting on beaches willing to pay a fare to reach San Francisco. 'Tis a small port with but a few luckless souls living nearby. It's inhabited by un-converted Indians and men who've run from the sea. I believe you shall find it a wearisome place. As will the others of our crew."

After a few seconds of silence, the Mate realized there was no more to be said. "Will that be all, Sir?"

"For now, James Freeman. I need your youngest brother Daniel Athearn in here directly. He can reckon and sum better than you and I put together."

It was of some concern to James Freeman that he and his father could somehow be "put together" like rigging through rings, ballast arranged below decks or links in a chain.

"We must needs charge our passengers enough to make the journey worth our while." The Captain ended the conversation with a long pull on his pipe which crackled as it fumed smoke.

The First's exit was followed closely by another knock on the cabin door. "Come in Third Mate Daniel Athearn Cleaveland," the Captain said without glancing up from the charts lying on the table before him.

After the door was closed behind him, Daniel Athearn was surprised to hear his father's cryptic opening remark: "We shall now count sleeping quarters as compared to pounds of whale blubber."

§

The *Niantic* was stripped of her casks and harpoons. Only two of the four fat rendering kettles originally on deck were retained. These two were converted to mess kettles for the journey north which the captain reckoned should last no more than two months. Round trip should take no more than twice that, in fair weather under full sail. Cleaveland, the pragmatist, anticipated a six-month voyage there and back and so informed the largest merchant in Paita, A. Rudent & Son, who agreed to warehouse the excess equipment. A. Rudent also assisted in communicating with Nelson in Panama, with Cleaveland's wife and the New England ship owners.

A. Rudent sent a letter up the coast ahead of the sailing craft on one of their merchant steamers. This letter was from Cleaveland and asked Nelson to act as agent in arranging passage for the beached band of men for which Nelson could expect a rich reward, depending, of course, on the total number of passengers induced to pay the fare.

Mail to New England only left Paita twice a year so the letters addressed to Mrs. Cleaveland and the Captain's company waited in A. Rudent's offices nearly a quarter of a year before they were sent. The letter to Mrs. Cleaveland was typically distant and brief. It told, among other things, how well her sons were doing, that "they were active and gentlemanly" and each maintained weekly Bible study.

A third letter, dated March, 15, 1849, was addressed to Messrs. Burr and Smith, owners of the vessel, whom Cleaveland believed might be moderately interested in learning the status of the voyage and the fate of their investment.

"Dear Sirs," the Captain wrote. "I arrived here with the *Niantic* on the 8th, ship in good order, crew all well, no oil. My intention was to recruit with vegetables and go to the North West coast but in consideration of the great demand for ships to take passengers from Panama to San Francisco, being a great number at that place, per advice of the last steamer which touched here the day before I arrived, and a great prospect of doing first rate for all concerned, I think it my duty to prepare the ship with the utmost speed and lose one North West season. So in 10 days, I shall leave here for Panama with prospect of remitting from there some $20,000 or $30,000, and sincerely hope it will meet with your approbation. Shall take light freight enough from here to Panama to pay our expenses."

The letter continued: "I have been offered here $20,000 to go on the voyage and return to this port which would occupy six months. Should I meet my expectations I want to keep the ship going as long as it pays well. Should there not be business I must go on with whaling again. Please advise as to sale of ship should there be a great offer. Please write by first steamer in care of the American consul at this place and also at Panama. Assist my wife to forward a letter by the same.

"Am very respectfully," he concluded, "Your servant, Henry Cleaveland."

It is somewhat remarkable that a letter actually reached its destination in those days. Cleaveland's correspondence would itself take a desultory course to New York, traveling first to Brazil after lying in Paita more than four months, stranded for want of any ship making a return trip around the Cape. It eventually found its way onto the counting house offices of Mister Burr and Mister Smith nearly a year after being penned.

They were to immediately write in reply: "Do not abandon pursuit of whales this season at all cost. Do not sell the *Niantic*. Do not accept passengers in Panama."

That, of course, is a letter which never made it into the hands of its intended recipient.

§

Gold fever is an insidious disease. It infects the mind leaving the body relatively unscathed. This has the effect of lulling a victim into believing there is no malady at work. The ailment can be a protracted illness lasting a lifetime, or it can run its course in a brief period, sometimes consuming but a few months of an otherwise un-ravished existence. The fever usually manifests itself after a failed immunization. Inoculations against the illness are frequent, common, and take many forms. Some people grow out of the time in their lives when danger of succumbing to the condition is most likely, during their youth. Men who acquire a wife and child while relatively young are often saved from the worst ravages of the disease. Those who find their lives fulfilled and fruitful, who are content with their lot, these are often passed over by the dark cloak of illness. No one, however, is certain they are immune until tested; and such a test can provoke an incurable onslaught of the malady.

The best defense against gold fever, of course, is never to face exposure. If the disease does gain a foothold, it spreads as surely as any bacterial growth, geometrically increasing until it decimates entire populations. It can spread to infect a village, a city, a region or even a country.

How many of us truly have a lifetime inoculation against the desire for instant wealth, the promise of riches beyond measure? If the spark is there, a flame can be fanned. Folk tale and legend become palpable, translate themselves into a frenzy of energy ready to be burned in the search for the Seven Cities. Buried treasure and Inca jewels, giant pearls and diamond mines, golden fleece and holy grails, mineral deposits, a king's crown and scepter, all have been hunted with equal zeal.

Curiously, the complaint appears to be sex-linked. Very few women succumb to gold fever. It is mostly the young men from good families, educated, enterprising, articulate youths approaching their lives with good prospects, who are most susceptible to the promise of a short-cut to prosperity. The youngest child, the last where the eldest has been assured of a patrimony, where there is no room remaining in the nest and the law of primogeniture is strictly enforced, the child who has few options to consider and who hears of an alternative to entering a monastery, this is the most likely candidate for contagion.

It does not matter the character of these men, whether good or evil, nor their religious background. Totem worshiper or animist, Christian or Jew, Hindu and Muslim, all young men are prey to the promise of riches without toil. In the case of the California Gold Rush, the entire world was stricken with the sickness in 1848 after one nugget smaller than a thumbnail was taken from a creek near Coloma, California.

Coloma is little more than 100 miles inland from the western seaboard of the Pacific Ocean by raft or side-wheeler. Easily accessed by steamship up the natural fresh-water delta that flows westerly out of

San Francisco Bay into the wide Pacific, Coloma's proximity to Sacramento and thence to San Francisco made it an overnight celebrity. More than a hundred years later, however, few remember its name. Rather, it is the owner of the mill on whose land the pebble was found, not even the finder, who has become part of the lore of the Gold Rush that began January 24, 1848.

John Sutter never benefited from the discovery and died a pauper. His life and business were destroyed by the hordes of prospectors from around the globe who gravitated to his land following that fateful discovery.

The final jumping off place for victims of the fever was the port of San Francisco. Until 1847 this was a small pueblo community originally named Yerba Buena, Spanish for "good herb." The name was changed, but the village was still under the colonization laws and the protection of Mexico and many settlers were former American citizens. Edwin Bryant was alcalde, roughly equivalent to a mayor, with a constituency that was comprised of Mexicans, Indians and a growing number of western pioneers.

This city's port was a shallow anchorage called Yerba Buena Cove. The cove was a vast mud flat which no deepwater vessel could enter. Years were to pass before the flats were dredged and an embarcadero created. In 1847 this protected bay had fresh water entering it from the east by way of the Sacramento River. Mountain rains coursed and mingled in the delta with the salt of the sea where it entered the bay.

In order to reach Yerba Buena Cove and the growing city of San Francisco which was the last leg of the journey toward the gold country, the demented patient had to travel from a point of origin some many thousands of miles distant. Only one ocean separated the Asian from the western seaboard, but the Pacific was the widest in the world. Yet it was possible for someone in China to make a single long sea crossing directly to the West Coast. A remarkable testament to the strength and endurance of the human spirit is the fact that many Chinese in boats not usually thought capable of making an ocean crossing did, indeed, manage this perilous voyage.

The European or Slav who became infected with the fever had first to land in America. That voyage typically took an entire month, often three, at the whim of the winds. They then faced one more obstacle standing between them and the gold mines of the west.

From the Eastern seaboard one still had the difficult choice of how to cross 3,000 miles of unsettled continent. This could be accomplished either by land or by sea, but both passages were full of hazard and both required tremendous stamina as well as courage to accomplish. Many land crossings were aborted midway. Many ended early — as soon after breasting the west side of the Rocky Mountains as possible. Sacramento was to be settled by travelers who simply did not have the gumption to go another ninety miles.

For any who chose the sea over the deprivation of inland travel, the terror of the Cape was well known. Sailing around Cape Horn was one of the most dangerous sea passages in the world. Many were the vessels sunk off the treacherous rocks of Tierra del Fuego. It had taken Magellan, the Portuguese explorer in service to Spain, and his fleet more than a month to negotiate a mere 350 miles through the straits that were named after him.

To make matters worse, the equator must be navigated twice in order to pass through the Straits. The Cape is bordered by baffling winds, known as the doldrums, that can becalm a ship and keep it in thrall for weeks at a time.

There was one shorter route the victim of gold fever could take in order to cut travel time and avoid the Straits and the Horn entirely. That was to cross the Isthmus of Panama on foot or horseback. The Caribbean and Pacific Oceans are within 20 miles of each other on this connecting link between continents. Taking passage to Chagres on the eastern side of Panama, men who were otherwise level-headed but now were afflicted with the disorder, made the crossing through a tropical jungle to beaches on the western side of the country. There they waited for a steamer or a sailing ship on which to complete the longest but relatively safe final portion of their pilgrimage.

What they usually forgot as their eyes clouded over with the imaginary glint of yellow was the lack of a prospect for booking passage where no passenger ships traveled. Few gold seekers who contemplated Panama even gave a thought to how unlikely the possibility of obtaining transportation was once they reached the other side of the isthmus, they were so blinded by their illness.

Some who crossed this land bridge did so in the erroneous belief that they could complete the rest of the trip on foot, hiking to San Francisco. That would be a distance of 4,300 miles across what may well be the most arid and hostile terrain in the world.

Cleaveland set sail in his newly outfitted ship seven days after sending his letters. Two weeks later he dropped anchor within sight of the white Panamanian beaches. Even from where his vessel bobbed on the water, it was possible to see with an unaided eye that the sands were littered with human beings.

Thousands of men were camped unable to proceed, frustrated in their search for wealth. Many were afflicted with dysentery and other tropical diseases with the death toll among them rising. Few were pleased with their less than civilized living arrangements. Those who had brought money were willing to pay almost anything to get on with their quest.

Captain Cleaveland had judged well the desperation of these men.

CHAPTER THREE

AN OLD BOOT AND A BOX OF SQUARE NAILS

Don thought at first the city had suffered its long forecast and much dreaded earthquake. But when he was secure above ground he looked around and realized only the bulldozer had moved. It lay at an angle sunk almost completely below grade, a carcass more than half in its own grave.

Worthy dusted himself off and checked for broken bones he might have missed in his panic to reach the surface. Nothing to report, SIR!

He attempted to snap off a salute and winced in pain as his back creaked and told him he might have injured it after all. He was sore in several places. His left elbow had banged against the rear firewall and the floor when he tumbled and now he rubbed the joint ruefully. All in all, though, he felt lucky to be alive.

"Yes, sir. Thank you, SIR!" he said with as much enthusiasm as he could muster.

He did not bother looking for Mac. Worthy put out a bowl of dry food near the truck, clicked his tongue, whistled, and coaxed for a few seconds. The cat did not appear and eventually he decided he had better things to do with his time.

Worthy rummaged around in Boomer's cluttered back bed until he found his strongest rope and a powerful battery powered trouble light. He tied the rope to the truck's bumper, checked the light to be sure of its brilliance, then changed into work clothes: a jump suit with the name of a bar stitched on the back. He stalked over to the hole that engulfed the sunken machine.

Evening arrived and a chill was in the air. It was getting dark in the pit by the time Worthy tossed the rope over the edge and tested its firmness before he began lowering himself hand-over-hand. He clambered down onto one of the arms of the metal scoop which he could see without the aid of the flashlight. He snapped on the light, looked toward the ground in the beam. He judged it to be only about a ten foot drop. Rappelling off the metal edge of the bulldozer's side, his toes touched a solid floor. When he was steady on his feet, he shined the flash around and realized he was in a large open space.

He landed near a wall where the rear end of the bulldozer had come to rest. The machine was securely settled, its hind treads lofted from the floor of its underground resting place by several large splintered pieces of wood which had fallen with it.

Worthy sprayed the sunken room with light and was immediately disappointed. He did not know what he had expected, but the buried chamber was very nearly empty. With the exception of the earth mover in outstretched supplication, his light played off the wall and moved around to reveal a spacious but vacant hold. The area was remarkably dry, though wine cellar cool, and he shivered as he pulled gloves from his back pocket and shoved his hands into them.

Worthy's first hesitant steps were guided by the glow of the flash. But as his eyes became accustomed to the dark, he became careless. He was gazing at the sloping walls when he placed a foot on something insecure that moved out from under him and he nearly stumbled. He aimed the beam, realized he had slid on a leather boot so desiccated by its long hibernation it was no longer pliant. He picked it up to examine and it retained the shape bent into it by age.

His light showed the floor on which he and the 'dozer rested was comprised of wood planks that formed a catwalk along each side of which ran two arrays of rock. The stones had been neatly placed in straight rows and ran the length of the cavern.

This puzzled Worthy as he paced the floor and touched the walls and the curved wood ribbing that framed the structure. Perhaps because the image was so out of place — and out of time, he realized — he did not at first recognize the rocks for what they were. At last he put it together as it dawned on him that this was the interior hull of an old ship. It was only part of a ship, however, and probably just that much which would have been below the waterline near where the keel joined.

This became obvious when he considered the oddly sloped floor and how the near end of the large open space tapered toward a point. The stones were clearly ballast which reminded him of his navy days and the labor crews he had been forced to join as an ordinary seaman. During his four-year career he must have helped arrange tons of concrete blocks in the holds of modern warships. In times past, before malleable cement, sailors used rocks to keep the boat steady and upright in the water.

Worthy chose a direction and began walking. The light struck a flat surface he took to be the stern. Within thirty paces he was able to reach out and rub his gloved hand on the aft, a boxed square of joined wood planks, leaving a smudged trail in his palm's wake. The space was large, but nothing compared to the hulls of contemporary ships.

An eerie feeling crept up his spine and for a moment he had to hold back the claustrophobia and panic that surged within him. He imagined the spirits of men long dead inhabiting this place. He took a few deep breaths, expecting and dreading a sepulchral wraith to appear at any moment, but no skeletal hand reached out and no smoky form made its presence known. His heart pounded in his ears before he overcame his fear of ghosts. Then he had to convince himself that real live poisonous creatures could not possibly inhabit the place. This stood to reason, he considered, since he had only discovered it moments ago. Buried for decades without air, food and no water meant nothing bigger or meaner than a worm could possibly be alive down here.

With these concerns under control, Worthy's scavenging instinct took over. He began to search in earnest for whatever might be lying around.

Almost immediately he found a wooden case under a shroud of dust and cobwebs in one corner of the wide stern. He scooped away the crud and peered inside. A dozen bottles stood upright in the yellow light. Here was something with which he was familiar. He plucked one out and held it up front of him. An amber liquid sloshed around. The cork was intact with a layer of wax sealing it. The label was melted by time refusing any efforts which might identify the contents.

Carefully, Worthy lifted the entire box which remained intact. He carried it over to where the rope snaked down the side of the digging machine and continued his search. Aiming his light beneath the planks, Worthy found a pistol, cap and ball type, and two rifle stocks.

The pistol's mechanism was rusted into one unit, hammer and trigger solidly joined to the body. Still, it was an interesting artifact and he included it in his growing pile. He walked to the forward end of the hull where he discovered a box containing square metal nails rusted into a lump. There were other oddments lying about on the floor, but these were mostly broken bits of porcelain and another boot. Perhaps it was the partner of the first one he discovered.

In all, not a very rich treasure chest even by his meager standards, he thought as he surveyed the collection.

Worthy tied the rifle stocks to the rope and began the process of delivering everything he found up to Boomer. It took him three trips, but the truck bed was so full he considered tossing out several boxes of computer paper to make room. In the end, he placed these on the front passenger seat and determined to deposit them in an alley later. He smiled at the irony, comparing the things he had recovered which might be a century-and-a-half old, with the modern trash he usually accumulated. He briefly considered leaving what felt like 30 pounds of the square nails, decided he could break them apart and sell them ten cents a piece.

The clock in the truck, like the air conditioning and heating system, did not work. He had no idea what time it was when he finally cranked Boomer's engine and his cat came out of hiding. Mac had been tempted back by the bowl of food which was now empty. The animal yawned and stretched and held its head out to be scratched as if nothing unusual had occurred. Mac gave every indication of having fallen asleep in the cab rather than of cowering in fear.

Don Worthy did not even take the trouble to unload when he arrived home. He was dog tired and lucky to find a parking space less than a block away. With Mac at his heels he strode through the front door and headed directly to the refrigerator.

It was empty save for a box of Mac's food.

Worthy poured some of this in a bowl which he left on the floor, considered eating a handful himself. His stomach growled in rebellion. Going through his cupboards he eventually found a can of tuna which he opened and forked greedily into his mouth.

The only clock in the house was on the kitchen wall. Don was surprised to glance up at it and see that it was well after midnight. He had spent nearly six hours poking around the construction site and inside the belly of the ship.

He turned out the lights and went immediately to bed.

CHAPTER FOUR

RITES OF PASSAGE

Consul Nelson was a corpulent fellow who affected a white suit with a wide cummerbund across his middle. The tropical fare seemed to meet with his digestive system's approval. When Sylvanus first saw the man, he feared the Captain's launch that was to carry them back to the *Niantic* might capsize well before they could get from shore to ship.

"Captain Cleaveland sends his greetings and wishes me to conduct you to his quarters," the Second informed the guest when they were at last safely topside.

Nelson followed with a quizzical good nature. His eyes nearly bulged from their sockets which Sylvanus thought might be due to the gross size of the body attempting to squeeze these grapes from their pouches. In reality, the man absorbed every aspect of life aboard the schooner, took in the number and racial background of the crew, the care with which the ship was stowed and the potential space available for passengers. He smiled inwardly at the thought that many more might be transported than he at first dared hope.

Nelson was ushered into Cleaveland's cabin only to find the man pouring over several sea charts laid out in front of him. Sheets of paper covered in calculations written in longhand were scattered about. Cleaveland's long-stem pipe crackled as he took puffs from the heated bowl without lifting either his head or his hand.

Cleaveland at last glanced up from his studies and smiled broadly. Rising, he extended his free right hand in greeting. It was gloved. "Delighted to make your acquaintance, Mister Nelson." The Consul gave his own hand in return. Cleaveland shook it but stepped back a pace, the extended arm still in his grasp. He looked critically at the unusual uniform his guest wore.

"Tell me, sirrah, is this the attire our country's administration requires of you?" Cleaveland asked with innocent candor. His guest resembled an overgrown school boy wearing a younger brother's breeches. The suit was no match for his girth and the material, though new looking, gave the impression of being on the verge of bursting its seams. In addition to the waist band, Nelson sported a top coat and vest made of two different types of material. But it was not the apparel so much as the hash on the man's chest which caught the captain's attention. Cleaveland observed an unfamiliar band of ribbons and medallions across both sides of the breast, each side three rows deep.

Nelson was nonplussed and responded with an easy grace. "As a matter of fact, no. I outfitted myself when first I arrived. The locals respect pomp, you see," he fingered a piece of red and gold brocade as he spoke. "This latitude is not at all like our western territories where I understand once you get past Chicago it is a mixture of rugged individualist meeting the barbarian. But in this clime, not so sir, not so. Here it is a matter of clothes making the man, indeed, sir."

Cleaveland declined further comment and seemed oblivious to the blusterous response his question provoked. Yet his undemanding sensibilities were astounded by the pretentious apparel. Not particularly satisfied with the explanation, he said, "We have outfitted the ship for passengers, as you requested."

Nelson turned to business. "I would like to know," he glanced toward the scattered sheets of paper, "have you an accounting of available berths? We must work out a few details before I can lend authority to the transfer of men." His attitude was officious but reserved. It was obvious to the Captain that Nelson was openly hinting at some sort of partnership arrangement.

Cleaveland was not willing to give up certain details of his ship. He was also somewhat reluctant to divulge how he and Daniel Athearn had worked out prices for berth space, and instead parried the Consul's opening remark. He asked the method Nelson proposed for ferrying men to the *Niantic*.

"It is true there are no wharves in Panama," said the Consul. "And you will have to lie several miles off shore from the beaches. However, the natives have a canoe which is quite sturdy called a bungo. They have agreed to make enough of them available to us if we scratch their palm." He made a pinching motion with his left hand in his open right to emphasize his point. "If you get my meaning. I shall see to that, have no fear."

"In your hands. When do you propose to begin?"

"Tomorrow sunrise, if that is convenient. You should be able to sail in less than a week's time. I wager you will be back in six months for another load. There seems to be no end to the men who will cross over."

"And can you tell me one thing more, Mister Nelson?" Cleaveland inquired of his guest.

"If it is within my power, certainly."

"Can you explain what the devil it is that draws these men to this forgotten corner of the world?"

It came as a great surprise to Consul Nelson that captain and crew alike were as untouched by gold fever as if they were new born babes. Their voyage had begun just as James Marshall plucked the nugget from the stream in California which ignited the spark that changed the course of world history and until this moment they had not discussed with anyone news of the discovery.

Nelson, never at a loss for words, did his eloquent best to spread the infection.

§

The small native craft were able to transfer men even though the much vaunted bungo Nelson had praised and put so much store in proved nearly worthless as either cargo vessel or ferry. Too many people and the canoe capsized easily. Occupants frequently abandoned all possessions in order to save themselves. The waters were not without shark. Ultimately, it was *Niantic*'s whale boats which found their lives renewed as they were pressed into service bringing passengers aboard.

The captain and Daniel originally set the fare at $75 for steerage, $125 for cabin class accommodations. To their minds, there was little difference between the two, but it became evident that a distinction lay in the minds of their charges.

These prices had been arrived at while under full sail to the stranded travelers. The rates were deemed fair in that a total complement of passengers at those prices would produce revenue equal to an entire season of extraordinarily good whaling. Captain and son determined the ship could sleep 200 comfortably. If twenty percent of these decided to travel in the best accommodations available, thereby paying the extra rate, *Niantic*'s total income would gross $17,000. That did not include Nelson's cut or the graft the natives asked.

Even before sailing from Paita, Cleaveland feared Nelson's description of hundreds, perhaps thousands of men stranded on the beaches would prove false or highly exaggerated. When he saw the quantity that had, in fact, made the trek only to find themselves without means to continue, Cleaveland's next concern was whether there were more than a handful able to pay the price he demanded to board. It turned out, however, that Consul Nelson had pre-arranged all available stowage on a reservation basis. Not knowing in advance precisely how many sleeping places were available or even the price that would be charged, Nelson over-booked by half.

Each man came aboard carrying a chit bearing the Consul's signature. During his initial visit, before abandoning *Niantic* for the security of his tropical domain, the Captain was pleased to offer Consul Nelson five percent for every chit.

"This by way of compensation, you might say, Mister Nelson."

The Consul was pleased to decline the kind offer. "I should point out not incorrectly that the American government is my employer." Each man nodded deeply and sympathetically in the other's direction. "However, I should be pleased to send these émigrés to you for a settled amount of seven and a half percent," the fat man said agreeably.

Cleaveland thought this a reasonable commission and said as much.

Not until much later, when the voyage was well under way, did it become clear in conversations with the passengers that Mister Nelson had also charged each bearer of his signature an additional ten percent of the value of the ticket in order to book passage.

There was such a quantity of men coming aboard and no lack of them on shore, it behooved Third Mate Daniel Athearn, who had inherited his father's Yankee business acumen, to suggest the price of passage be increased two fold. Those already billeted were assessed the additional amount. If they did not have the fare they were ordered to return to shore. When that occurred, the larger portion of their money was returned, but not all of it.

Cleaveland rarely accepted anything other than gold or silver coin as currency. The paper dollars of the eastern seaboard were worthless until the ship returned to home port. But as long as the specie of any country weighed in properly, it was accepted.

The rare exception was when Cleaveland allowed family heirlooms, a watch, ring, or other jewelry, to pay the fee. He would study such an artifact, consider it against others with which he might be familiar, and place a price on it. This price was invariably much below the seller's own estimate of value and arguments were frequent. That was one reason why Cleaveland added a surcharge on top of the cost of passage for accepting a trade instead of coin. Another reason for the surcharge was his complaint that, by accepting such objects, it turned him into a jeweler when, after all, his calling was the sea.

There were those among the pilgrims who were destitute after they paid the toll. More than half had nothing left but the scant possessions they carried with them. If Captain Cleaveland had not included rations as well as sleeping accommodations in his flat rate, many would have starved.

In addition to the increased fare, the Captain and his son made another change in their original plans. They determined the ship could comfortably hold many more than the 200 they at first considered. When it became apparent the passengers were willing to accept closer quarters, the number who would be billeted in *Niantic*'s hold and on deck increased to 248.

There were far too many more on shore who could afford the conditions imposed and the duty charged. Little protest was heard. Ultimately, the ship's manifest recorded 246 passengers although there were independent counts of as many as 289 in addition to Captain and crew who made the voyage. Any money earned over and above the estimates of a good season of whaling remained within the Cleaveland family.

The Captain gave up his own quarters and moved in with his First Mate for the duration. This was hardly an altruistic act on his part. He was paid handsomely for the private room by one of the more wealthy travelers who also had a slave attendant.

By the time they weighed anchor and began the long voyage north, five hundred more men had hiked the overland trail. They were among the ill-tempered crowd that stood on shore and watched the wide square fantail of the *Niantic* recede toward the horizon.

As for Consul Nelson, it took him nearly three months before he found another captain and crew willing to accept passengers from his shores.

Thus, at night during the early summer of 1849, thousands of fires dotted the Panamanian beaches like a thickness of stars compressed into one small area of black sky.

CHAPTER FIVE

GETTING AN HISTORICAL PERSPECTIVE

The first thing Don Worthy did when he woke up every morning was hack and cough until a congealed ball of phlegm cleared his throat. Then he crawled out of bed wrapped in a bathrobe faded a dingy blue, shuffled over to the toilet and spat.

The next thing he did each morning was reach for a cigarette.

He rested before figuring out what to do after that. Usually he placed his bathrobe covered butt on the armrest of his leather couch and sat there smoking until a three inch ash grew. He used a cupped hand to catch it. Sometimes his stomach gave him his next instructions. Sometimes it was his bladder. More often than not, Don Worthy got up from the arm of the couch because the ashtray was across the room and his hand was filled with gray.

He did not get out of bed each morning in order to go to work because he did not have a job. Neither were there appointments on his calendar. Left to his own design, Don Worthy would as soon lie between the sheets with a comic book.

There was, however, a negative need which drove him from his bed into the bright light of each day. He felt the absence of money. He squirmed uncomfortably beneath the thumb of this acute pressure near the end of every month. In response to this force, he shambled over to his kitchen area with the plan of forcing a cup of coffee down his throat.

Worthy was not good with money and it never seemed to stick to him. His attitude was that money is something some people have and others want. When he had it, he gave it to others. The landlord was one of the others who regularly received. Worthy was a funnel, a conduit or pipe through which paper and coins passed. He was unaffected by this process, a catalyst who watched but remained unchanged by the flow of currency.

It was nearing the end of the month and rent would soon be due. He could go a few days, even a couple of weeks into the month before threatening phone calls began arriving on his machine. But rent money, like money spent on cat food, gasoline, soda pop, or cigarettes, was something Don had to have in certain amounts at certain times on a regular basis. He would have been quite happy to do without money at all and often bartered an item for a pair of jeans or a shirt at the flea market or garage sale. It was a fact of his life that Don Worthy always had something to trade to someone.

Since he was nothing more than a passage way for money, Worthy felt it was important not to spend much time acquiring something only transitorily his. Therefore, he did his best to find money without actually working for it.

The kitchen clock told him it was 11:39. Saturday morning, not yet noon. What do you know? He was up early. Sunlight streamed into the kitchen and refracted off millions of flecks of dust. Cold, worn linoleum crinkled under his toes. He started the hot water for coffee. At his feet, a warm bunch of fur stretched, spread claws, arched its back before nudging Worthy's ankles.

"Bowing before the Food God, I see," he commented dryly as he reached for the refrigerator handle. "You shall be rewarded." Don pulled a five pound sack of kibbles from a bag he kept in the vegetable crisper. It was the only safe place. His cat had learned how to open every other cupboard and drawer in the loft apartment they shared.

"There's black and white tufts of fur all over the house," Worthy scolded the patiently waiting animal. He held back the bowl. "What'd you do, have a fight with yourself again?" He placed the bowl on the floor.

Water boiled and Don splashed some into a cup. He added two heaping tablespoons of instant coffee crystals, another two heaps of white sugar and stirred. The smoke from his second cigarette curled around his forehead as he lifted the cup to his lips. MacArthur began to chomp and crunch the multi-colored pellets. Don knelt beside the animal and stroked the fur behind its flea collar.

"You want to live here, ol' buddy? Youse wanna have a nice warm place to dump? Well, we gotta get some dough togedder or you an' me is gonna get the boot." Worthy chuckled and took another puff. The landlord was an Italian with a New York accent. Worthy was fond of giving vernacular renditions of the old man at parties.

He continued to stroke the cat behind the ears. When he thought the animal was not paying attention, he snatched one of the hard bits of kibble right out of Mac's mouth. The cat made a halfhearted attempt to bite it back, disdainfully returned his attention to the bowl when Don dangled the yellow-green kernel out of reach in front of him.

"C'mon Mac. Go for it Mister Cat. Here kitty, kitty, kitty. Come on. Don't be such a spoil-sport," Don teased between cigarette puffs. But the cat was as put off by the smoke as by the dull game. MacArthur refused to play. Realizing this, Don studied the bit of compressed fish meal as if there was meaning in its form.

Then he popped it into his own mouth.

§

The truck had not been running right for a month. It coughed and sputtered just like Don when he awoke.

"You can make it, Boomer. One more week." Don rocked back and forth in his seat as he churned the engine. The starter motor was all that gave any sign of life. Worthy pumped the pedal madly.

The vehicle was full of rubbish Don intended to sell at market. Don, of course, did not think any of the material he was hauling was trash. Other people might. But after all, those were the same people who had thrown it away in the first place. As far as Worthy was concerned, there was gold to be found in the trash heaps of San Francisco.

Which reminded him of the discovery he'd made yesterday.

There is a special section of the San Francisco Public Library devoted to the history of the City. It is at the end of a long hallway in the east wing of the third floor of the main branch. Patrons asking to look at materials in the San Francisco Room are issued white gloves. This is done in hopes of reducing wear and tear on many of the one-of-a-kind pieces in the collection.

Display cases line the walls to the entrance of this special collection. At the far end was a case with former Police Chief William J. Quinn's 1930's cap and uniform enshrined. His seven pointed gold star shown bright against the dark blue breast.

The story of the Panama Pacific International Exposition is told here in pictures and souvenirs. The Exposition opened in 1915, timed nearly to coincide with the opening of the Panama Canal in 1914.

Cases of memorabilia chronicle the history of the clashes between organizing labor and organized police; the World's Fair of 1939 and the island created in the middle of the bay to house the fair are documented with abundant photographs. The opening of the Golden Gate Bridge is shown in photographs and the story that it was believed impossible to build is retold on these display walls.

"Sunny" Jim Rollins, mayor from 1912-13, later governor of the state, smiled brightly from a large photograph mounted above the entrance to this room.

Don Worthy had no time to read the cards or admire the police uniform. He was at the library with what he thought was a brilliant idea. It had taken him until late afternoon to get out of the house, but now he was armed with a plan.

He went straight to the main desk where a matronly woman wearing thick glasses asked if she could be of any help.

"I need information on a ship. It was beached in San Francisco. I guess it got built on top of instead of being removed."

"Do you know the address?" she asked without batting an eye.

Worthy thought his search would be difficult, his request seemed so absurd. But the librarian did not see anything strange in it.

"Well, let's see. It was on the corner of Sansome and Clay streets," he said.

She disappeared into the back room. When she returned she had two card files in her hands.

"Sansome and Clay," she repeated while she flipped cards. "Here we are. That would be the *Niantic*. It was turned into a hotel. And the Historical Society gave it a plaque. Looks like it was destroyed in the fire of 1851."

Worthy was impressed. He asked if he could read several of the referenced articles and was handed a stack of magazines. The librarian directed him to a book shelf where, she said, the City's history reposed.

She disappeared again. When she returned she asked for his library card and issued him his requisite pair of gloves before she handed over more folders.

"By the way," he inquired before she turned to help someone else, "were there any other ships that were landlocked like that?"

"Lots of them. Could be as many as nine hundred buried in and around the Financial District. The *General Harris*, the *Apollo*, and the

Georgian to name a few. Those were just the best known. It was common practice to pull them onto a lot at high tide and turn them into warehouses or stores."

Worthy pondered this information for a moment.

"You see, ships got double duty in those days," she continued. "They might get hauled onto shore or sunk in place where they were moored if the water was shallow enough. Then they were made over into shops or maybe a hotel like this one was. In fact, the city's first prison was a ship that was in the China trade called the *Euphemia*. She was purchased by the city fathers and used as a floating jail, tied up permanently alongside Long Wharf. The *Sara Sands* was an iron steamship. They beached her at what is now Battery and Vallejo streets and turned her into a cheap lodging house."

"Do you think any of them have any value? I mean, if you were to dig one up, would anybody want it?" he asked.

"I'm sure there are historical museums that would like to have an original Gold Rush era ship, but there wouldn't be much of one left if you were to dig it up. I mean, between the fires and the worms, all you'd find would be rusty nails and ribs that'd crumble at the touch. Even the *Sara Sands* or one like her would just be a pile of scrap metal today."

"Does everybody know about these ships?" The idea was still novel to him.

"I don't know what you mean by that, young man." She looked miffed. "Everyone here in the San Francisco Room does."

He spent several hours reading the history of the Barbary Coast. One thing he learned was that all the ships that might have been in use on land at the time were thought to have been completely destroyed in the fire of 1851.

There were no adequate records on exactly how many vessels had been reused as buildings in San Francisco's early years, but there were hundreds of ships to choose from. The crews of these vessels frequently jumped ship when they reached the entrance to the gold fields and as many as 1,000 seaworthy craft were abandoned in this manner.

It was easier and cheaper to haul a boat onto a vacant lot or simply to sink it on its shallow water lot than to build a legitimate structure in its place.

Don read that the City was ravaged by five major fires between 1849 and 1851. Two large fires are said to have been responsible for destroying more than half the downtown area. Yet even as smoke from the ruins around them rose to the heavens, workmen were fast at work rebuilding what had been destroyed.

He learned The Niantic Hotel had several incarnations. After its original oaken ship frame and decks were destroyed in the fire of '51, it was promptly reconstructed as a real building. This structure was replaced in 1872 with a more modern edifice. At that time workmen discovered the hull of the old ship, exposed by the excavations for a new foundation. This rated a few lines of type in the *San Francisco Daily* which mentioned that "the keel must have been fully twenty feet below the present level of the street, showing the amount of ground made over it in twenty-three years."

Then, in 1907, a third building was erected on the site and a bronze tablet placed on the side of the structure by the Native Sons of the Golden West. The tablet bore this inscription: "The emigrant ship *Niantic* stood on this spot in the early days when the water came up to Montgomery Street."

It was clear to Don the old hull had never been fully excavated. It was still there, still solid, beneath the current street and sidewalk level and it was into this he had fallen last night.

When the buzzer sounded and he was told the library closed at five, he was startled to see how quickly the hours had passed. He armed himself with copies of the articles he thought most important and went back to his apartment. He had a lot to think about. And he had to figure out how he was going to do something with his discovery before Monday rolled around.

CHAPTER SIX

LIFE ABOARD SHIP

Captain Cleaveland set their course south by west from Panama. He was quite pleased with himself, and with good reason. The Purser, Third Mate Daniel Athearn, tallied the Captain's share of the passenger's fares at more than $18,000.

Total booked receipts were $49,150. Nelson's commission lessened this by a little more than seven percent, but it was still a worthwhile venture, this hauling of human cargo. The Captain realized he had guaranteed his ship an amazing amount of income compared to the fluctuations of the whaler's trade. And it was legal income at that.

Cleaveland generously subtracted $27,000 from the total. He planned to send this amount by overland mail to Burr & Smith as soon as they reached port. He also deliberated making at least two more trips of equal worth before heading back to Massachusetts, there to purchase his own vessel again or even the *Niantic* from her owners if they would entertain his offer.

From his helm he surveyed the entire ship. The deck crawled with humankind. It was rare for *Niantic* either as whaler or spice ship to have this many free men aboard and topside. During his slave trading days, Cleaveland took care to keep the chattel in dark holds below deck where he knew they could not attempt to leap overboard and swim toward safety, real or imagined.

Cleaveland looked down upon the groups of men, some eating, others playing musical instruments, some merely reclining along the gunwales gazing at open sea. They were a motley bunch from many lands, their variety of apparel and language unappealing to the New Englander. He preferred the steady solitude of the sea and the security which rank provided to the teeming mass of humans who littered his deck. He was even more contemptuous that they all paid dearly for the privilege of being aboard his ship.

Captain Cleaveland thought every one of his passengers a fool.

A burly dark skinned man, one of the Kanaka sailors, was reassigned from harpooner to assistant cook. He stood ten hours stirring and stoking the fire beneath two 200 gallon kettles set up on the aft deck, dishing out meals to organized gangs of gold seekers.

One passenger, Dan Nason, returned for a second portion and was rebuffed. A hand darted out, snatched an ounce of meat right from under the Kanaka's nose as he was distracted with Nason.

"They say the gold flows from the hills into your hands if you but wait at the bottom of a sluice," said Dr. Stanton with conviction. "I believe you want a bag to cart it away with."

"Well, I have a bag big enough," said Nason who laughed and held up the only thing he owned in the world. It was a canvas sack that once hung from his shoulder. Nothing was safe from the moist air of the hold, not material or men. The sack's strap mildewed and broke a week into the voyage.

Another crew member named Kiki represented the islanders. He spoke and negotiated with the Captain who considered Kiki to be their leader. More privileged than the rest of the crew, Kiki was allowed to make his own work schedule. Thus, the massive man was able to overhear these stories as he leaned into the wind from the sea, his dark sun-burnished arms overhanging a nearby rail.

Two dozen men were clustered on the top aft deck where they finished consuming one of two daily meals. They were within earshot of both Kiki and the cook but spoke openly as if the islanders were not there. The men were gathered around a tub set up between the giant kettles, a large metal bowl that was originally meant to hold rendered whale parts. It now contained their daily ration of meat. A pail next to this held coffee.

For the duration of the voyage the men would meet like this. They would eat together, afterward smoke the few tobacco leaves they could purchase from the crew, tell tall tales of castles built glittering and bright with the gold they would find.

Captain Cleaveland long ago learned to delegate authority. He divided his passengers into a dozen groups, each with a leader responsible for keeping order and bringing the men on time to their meals. The diet consisted primarily of cured meat, cut in strips or sometimes chopped for easier chewing. It had a leather-like texture. This was supplemented with boiled beans and rice. In addition to coffee, the balance of the fare was comprised of sweet potatoes, tea and duff.

Duff was particularly unpleasant stuff. It was not hardtack, the English contribution to biscuit making. It was not bread. It was a flour or corn dough, whichever was in supply, raised over night with yeast caught from the air and boiled in canvas bags. The only way to make it palatable was to cover it with molasses.

"No sir, that weil not dew," rang the voice of a young man with a bright red beard. He had traveled from Glasgow and been stranded on a beach with no one to curse but himself for more than a month. He was not about to be outdone by a transplanted Englishman. "Y'ell be needing twa' these to carry ye an' yer gold from the hills!" He held up a bagpipe with the confidence of an auctioneer.

The Scotsman blew into the mouthpiece and began to pump his pig skin. Wood pipes bristled flaccid on one side until his breath filled the bag. A flat tinny honk began to drone, became sustained in the air as the piper began his cadence, a steady rhythm to which anyone could slap his hands in time.

A fiddle from amidships joined the bagpiper's easy sway. Two men began dancing, arms hooked, around and around making as much noise with their boots as the bagpiper and fiddle player. Their appointed hour for mess was almost over but the men took time to convince each other they would be great benefactors toward mankind when they returned home with their riches.

"I shall have an estate," offered McCollum. "One that will grow pheasant and hare for everyone to take."

"I'll have ten such estates," boasted Johnson in return. "And you will never see me give away a pheasant. I won't need to give anything away. For everyone on my fief will have their own field and their own bird. I'll see to't."

The music played. More webs of fantasy were spun. One had a girl to woo. He would place a ring on her hand so heavy it would cause her to sink to the ground.

"I shall buy all the women in town!" shouted one jaded youth who refused to be outdone.

"And I the whole town shall buy!" yelled another. "Half of it will be given to the women I may wive," he crowed.

The noise from above drifted below to the interior of the ship. It was heard as a thump-thump-thump for the most part, but it eased the monotony of weeks of sailing. Initially, there was great relief for finally having boarded. Each man was sure he was on the way to riches beyond measure. When not playing music or eating, the men wrote in their diaries, talked, played cards.

Captain Cleaveland had strict rules regarding gambling: there would be none. The hands of cards were merely won or lost without a pot.

Many of the hundreds of passengers were musicians. Their fiddles and pipes were frequently danced and sung to as the stories of how each planned to spend his wealth was told and re-told. Many of these grew more elaborate, larger and wilder with each hearing.

"I shall buy half of Louisville," shouted James Raverty. He was the son of a poor dirt farmer who lived near that city. Raverty lay swaddled in *Niantic*'s makeshift sickbay from which he overheard the music and the boasting. After the men abandoned the deck above and made room for the next group's turn at the tubs, Raverty's ears continued to ring. He was delirious, his uneasy dreams haunted by his quest and the reason he was so far from home.

He lay directly below the mess area on an open deck below the poop, which had been transformed into a kind of hospital. Lying here were the more seriously ill of the travelers. All day they were bombarded with the tales, hour upon hour, as each shift made its way to the feeding troughs.

Those like Raverty who were physically ill had little to comfort them. There was no medication other than a damp rag for the sweating brow, and not much hope except a break in their fever.

One passenger within hearing distance of the boasts was the acting nurse, a man with nothing but practical experience to draw upon and an infinite amount of patience. He made a clucking sound with his tongue and raised a hand to touch the sick man's forehead, then shook his head grimly after he felt the heat.

"End oy shall buy as many a bee kin be kept in a hoive," nodded Peter O'Donnellan who bent over Raverty. "For honey y'know is da sweetest treacle cn swab yer t'roat."

O'Donnellan wrung water from a rag and brought it to his friend's brow. The man writhed as if struck a blow. O'Donnellan held Raverty in strong hands and prevented him from hammering his head against the deck. If only there were honey now to succor those parched lips, to soothe that horribly red throat and a dram of whiskey to help the man sleep.

"Oi den't know why does not comb the doctor Stanton to see to ye, James Raverty. But is sorry ay yam tuh see yuh thus. Hol' still now." O'Donnellan wrapped the towel about Raverty's head. The Irishman had begged brandy and other strong spirits from Captain and crew. If the Captain was to be believed, there was none to be had aboard, not grog for the crew nor laudanum to counter pain. O'Donnellan himself was a Pioneer which meant he foreswore ever a drop of liquor, but for Raverty there was nothing else that might hold back the consuming fever.

It was frightening to touch Raverty's brow, his fever was so high. The man lay sweating like a piece of smoking meat. O'Donnellan looked up. He was not without a sense of irony for, above them, men appeared to be dancing on Raverty's grave.

It was not as if Raverty were being ignored by the ship's surgeon, Second Mate Sylvanus. But there was little that could be done no matter who of captain or crew became stricken. Sylvanus was a surgeon in name only, it being a nominal rank aboard ship, and he was equally without medicinal aid for any who fell ill. If it came to the need for someone to staunch a flow of blood or cut a limb from the torso, then the ship's physician might be able to provide the saw and afterward catgut to stitch the wound closed. As for "ship fever" or any other of the agues the tropical jungles and beaches may have imparted, everyone was equally powerless to offer relief.

Niantic was becalmed several times. Cleaveland decided to go below the equator to find the Trade Winds, then he headed north at 110 degrees longitude. This maneuver eventually caused them to be off course by 1,200 miles although still on the same latitude with San Francisco. Before they reached the coast, however, the winds played fickle.

"We rolled for days like a log without sufficient air to cause a ripple," Nason wrote in his diary. "There is a great uneasiness manifested and something foreboding in every face."

Thoughts of gold gave way to fears of being marooned in the doldrums around the equator. Then, one month out of Panama, on June 4 James Raverty died.

"This morning after breakfast was served, he was brought out from under the poop deck," Nason wrote, "and sewed up in his hammock. With a fifty pound bag of sand at his feet, and at the tolling of the bell the passengers assembled on the deck, rigging, and yards, in every place where they could witness the unusual occurrence of a burial at sea."

The Episcopalian Reverend Mr. Mines read the service. Afterwards, Captain Cleaveland ordered the ship scrubbed from stem to stern. Lye soap was distributed and pumice stone was used with water to sand the surface of every piece of exposed wood in the poop area. He feared the cholera. There were no other deaths aboard *Niantic* that voyage though this was hardly due to the disinfectant properties of pumice stone. Almost as if they had been appeased by an offering from the mortals floating in their wooden craft below, the winds began to blow favorably again. Yet it took another month before the ship hove within sight of their destination.

Sixty-five days after leaving Panama, Captain Cleaveland moored the ship in deep water off Clark's Point in San Francisco bay. They were not the only boat floating there. At least 750 other vessels stretched in several rows for a mile to Rincon Point from *Niantic's* anchorage. This was a giant ghost navy, rising and falling with the tide.

"It does seem strange, now, don't it," Sylvanus said to his older brother. "All those ships and some of 'em whalers, but none with a crew. I doubt we'd see as many a ship in Boston Harbor after the season has changed."

Niantic had not time to send a party ashore before they were greeted by emissaries. A punt with two men aboard came within hailing distance only hours after they dropped anchor.

"Din't waste no time, did they?" remarked First Mate James Freeman as he made a reply to the visitors. "Come aboard, then," he called down to the greeting party. A rope ladder was thrown over the starboard side and the two easily worked their way to the main deck.

"John H. Jenkins, at yair sairvice," said the one who appeared to be in charge of the expedition. Jenkins doffed his flamboyantly large floppy hat toward James. "Oid lyke tuh have a waird w' y'r Cap'n. In proivit if ye will."

The Captain's quarters had been returned to Cleaveland. He was still in the midst of putting his personal articles back in order when Jenkins was ushered into his presence.

"Sir," Cleaveland said with some lack of conviction in his voice. "How may I be of service to you?" He did not offer his hand.

"Oi represents the only organized bidness as yew needs to work wif in all of the town o' Saint Francis." Jenkins winked. He winked again. Clearly, he suffered a facial muscle spasm which gave him a conspiratorial air to which Captain Cleaveland took an immediate dislike. It

H. W. Moss

may have been no fault of Jenkins, but he probably should not have been the one sent to do business with new arrivals.

"We's uh Sydney Ducks and so called for our 'aving come by way of Australier to this beau'eful country. An' fur the raison as we needs to 'ire some bright men to carry on our trade, we wants ter 'ave first crak at i-rin some o' dem wha' yew brot wit yuh."

Interpreting what he heard, the Captain paraphrased Jenkins' flinty speech. "As I understand it, you wish to employ some of the passengers before anyone else offers them a job. Is that correct?"

"At's rye. An' fer yer trouble convey'in this offer to 'em wit as much cornwiction as yer able, I be aut-orized to adwance a certain sum."

Jenkins concluded his speech by producing a small, soft deerskin pouch from his shirt pocket which he handed over to the Captain. It was heavy for such a small size. Cleaveland pressed a finger into the bag, removed it covered with a fine yellow powder.

The Captain's opinion of just how foolish his passengers were was changing. It looked as if they were in the land of plenty after all.

"Do you have terms? Can you fix a sum of money for their day's labor?"

"Oi yam able t'offer eight dollars a day payable in gold dust onct a week."

That was an incredibly high daily rate of pay, even by Cleaveland's recently jaded sense of worth. He determined to convey the offer to the men. They could choose to accept or reject as they saw fit.

"I shall do your bidding, Mister Jenkins," Cleaveland said with sincerity.

There was a great deal of joy from the looks on the faces of the men who heard this proposal. They felt all their trouble getting here justified, the hardships quickly forgotten when such extremely good pay was immediately offered for their services. Not a few were pleased to take Jenkins up on the terms he quoted, signing their names for a year of indentured service.

However, those who still had coins in their kits felt no need to take the first opportunity that came their way. At least half the passengers abstained, even for the unheard of sum of eight dollars a day! Jenkins saw to it that all who accepted were ferried off the ship immediately, another boon to being in his employ.

Afterward, the deck nearly empty, Jenkins stood making no move to follow his new employees. His business was concluded as far as the Captain was concerned. Finally Cleaveland asked if there was anything else the man wished to discuss.

48

"As a mat'er o'fack."

Jenkins informed the Captain an insurance policy was often issued to a new ship, even if it was planning to remain only a day or two. Cleaveland insisted there was no need for any such coverage and Jenkins insisted there was.

"Yew an' yer crew," twitched the little man, "wants ter be sure the canwas o' yer riggin' doan catch fire. Or the wood o' yer 'ull doan explode. Don'tcher?"

The suggestion that a calamity if such proportions was even remotely possible sounded perfectly ludicrous to Cleaveland. It even smacked of a veiled threat and he told the man as much. Then he suggested Jenkins leave immediately before he took his comments as menacing and had him bodily thrown off his ship.

"Oil tell yer what, Cap'n. Oi unnerstan how yer feels. Tonight you watch that air ship to windward." Jenkins pointed at a schooner that lay fifty yards distant. "The same sor' o' sujestion ware made to the Cap'n o' that wessel. He come in abou' a week ago. Said he'd be gone in a day's time as well. Only thing is, he ain't. Now oi has this pre-monition an' oi ent likely bean wrong predictin' in the past, so you watch the future unfold tonight. An me or an'odder Duck will be payin' yez an'odder wisit tomorrey."

Cleaveland was so incensed by the man's arrogant attitude he nearly had him tossed overboard on general principles. That night the schooner which had been pointed out to the Captain erupted in flames just as Jenkins predicted.

The next day, true to his word, Jenkins and another man arrived at the *Niantic*. Captain Cleaveland paid Jenkins $500 on this visit and felt lucky to have given so little for so much security. During the course of that second day, a dozen men left the ship and discovered their labor in extremely great demand. These were the men who declined Jenkins' offer, selected instead jobs of their own choosing from many offers made them ashore. The men who had become indentured laborers in that first pass with Jenkins learned quickly the going rate for their work was ten dollars a day and rising.

At eight dollars, a man could barely put food in his mouth in this boomtown far from the niceties of civilization.

The Captain prepared to return to Panama for more passengers. He addressed the crew, reminded them to do their duty and return to the ship. But a prophetic log entry that second day in port was short and to the point.

"Five of crew deserted," Cleaveland wrote for the first time. He would make many such entries before himself abandoning the lost ship.

On shore, the Sydney Ducks turned out to be the worst criminal element in a city without law. They had, indeed, come by way of Australia where they were originally transported from other parts of the British Commonwealth. But even their former continent, itself comprised of the cast-offs of the empire, could not put up with them. The Ducks left Australia individually or in groups, under duress or of their own volition, though the former circumstance prevailed, with clouds hanging over them for criminal offenses ranging from barn burning to back stabbing. Collectively, they were probably the most vicious group of people ever to come to the gold fields of California.

Niantic was given protection from the Ducks by the Captain's extortion payment. But she never again returned to the open seas.

CHAPTER SEVEN

THE PLAN

Worthy rolled a nice fat joint and licked the glue on the paper's edge. He lit the cigarette with an eighteen inch match usually associated with a fireplace. Thick smoke curled in the air as he took a deep drag.

"S'good herb," Don managed to say through pinched lips as the smoke filled his lungs. He passed the cigarette to his companion, a short fellow with blond hair who wore thick glasses.

"Thanks," the other man said as he took the stick of marijuana. He made a small inhaling noise compared to Worthy's deep lung filling pull.

"Come on, come on, Benny. I told you this is good shit. But you gotta take a solid hit. Take a big toke. 'At's the stuff," his voice trailed off as Benny complied. "Say, Benny. I gotta ask you something." Don became more relaxed. "No offense, but do you wear your suit every day? I mean, even on Sunday?"

"Well, I hadda go to a meeting," Benny replied somewhat defensively as he exhaled. "And you wear suits to meetings. Don't you wear a suit to meetings?"

Don laughed which caused the last of the fumes to explode from deep within his lungs. "I don't even own a tie. And I guarantee I haven't worn a three-piece suit since my First Communion."

"Your first what?" Benny asked with what seemed to be genuine interest.

"Never mind. Never mind." They sat on the living room couch in Benny Rossen's modern well appointed apartment. Don invited himself over after he phoned to see if the attorney had a few minutes. Now Don licked a finger and touched it to the run that had gone up one side of the joint.

"Did you know you can get about a pound of salt out of four gallons of sea water?" Don asked offhanded. He intended to lead up to his real reason for visiting Rossen at a gradual pace.

"News to me," the attorney replied as he accepted the joint between thumb and forefinger.

"Well, you can. However, what I wanta talk to you about is a special type of law, Benny. You a sea lawyer?"

Benny was quiet. He appeared to be deep in thought. At last he spoke. "I'm a sea lion," he said with a perfectly straight face. Then he erupted in gales of laughter. "How's that? Almost a seal! The Great Seal of California, will that do?" He slapped his thigh and bent double at the waist, his head between his knees. "Arf, arf," he barked between gasped breath and gales of laughter.

A full minute passed before he calmed down enough to allow Don to comment wryly: "Knew it was a bad idea getting you stoned." Worthy sounded exasperated. "Now listen to me, Benny. I need your help on this. Seriously. Okay?"

"Try me," Benny said perfunctorily. He sat stock still in the couch, his back straight against the cushion, the perfect imitation of a schoolboy being good.

Last night Worthy had been unable to sleep and spent the whole of his time lying in bed preparing his argument. He developed what he thought were sound, logical answers to every question he was able to pose for himself. He was ready to take a position from several perspectives, but he was also on uncertain ground and he knew it. He convinced himself from the little he picked up of international maritime law while doing naval service that he had certain rights, but convincing a lawyer to help him fight for those rights was a totally different story.

Benny Rossen was the only lawyer with whom Don Worthy had ever felt comfortable. He was also the only attorney Don knew in real life. Benny had been assigned by the court to defend Worthy pro bono after a debris box incident landed him in jail.

Fiercely independent, having to rely on someone, even a lawyer, went against Worthy's grain. He rarely asked anyone's opinion and, if he wanted to do something, he just went ahead and did it. Dumpster diving was a perfect example. It was a fine point, splitting hairs actually, when he was told the debris box was on private property instead of a public street, or that climbing into it was regarded as trespassing and taking any of its discarded contents was considered theft.

"But it's been thrown away! It's just trash!"

It irritated Don to rely on others. However, he did have enough sense to know when he required expert opinion. This did not make it any easier to bring his plan of action to Rossen even if the man was the single source he had in the legal department.

Worthy made up his mind. He needed a legal way to accomplish his goal. The set-up was important and much as he hated to admit it, he had to get help. Initially, all he thought he was looking for from Rossen was the language with which to phrase his actions for an immediate confrontation with the builders, the Boesk Corporation.

But that changed the more Worthy lay in bed and thought about it. The only certain thing in Don's check list of "what ifs" which he worked out was that the parent corporation responsible for developing the corner lot and the ship he fell into Friday night would have its own set of hired guns on the job as soon as he told them what he was doing. Preparing for that eventuality, he envisioned an audacious plan that involved Rossen and, before he visited his lawyer, he put in a call to his old girlfriend, Christine. He got a promise out of her to be available later that night to drive him somewhere. He'd been purposely cagey about exactly what time, where and why.

"Lemme ask you about abandoned ships, okay Benny? If you found a boat that had been abandoned on the high seas, you'd be legally allowed to claim the right of salvage, wouldn't you?"

"That is correct, sir," the little guy said as he took another hit.

"What if it was abandoned on dry land? Like maybe it got buried before anybody could pull it out of the way of a landslide or something. Can you still claim the right of salvage?"

"Now how the hell should I know the answer to that? All I remember of Admiralty law you can put in a toothpaste tube. I'm a criminal attorney, not maritime. 'Fraid I don't know all there is to know about every law on the books."

Don chuckled good naturedly. "Now I know you're stoned, Benny. That's the first time I ever heard a lawyer say anything as honest as that!"

"'Sides. Sounds more like a trick question for law school students, not something that would really happen."

Worthy sat silent in his thinking position. His mouth stopped moving. He still wasn't stoned and thoughts raced around his mind.

He was a regular dope smoker and had taken so many psychedelics over the years, sometimes he never did get high no matter how many joints he smoked.

"So what's the story?" Rossen prodded. "Care to tell me so I can at least consider your latest hare brained scheme?"

Worthy had no one else he could bring into his confidence and reveal his discovery to, so he opened up. He explained how he had fallen into the hulk of a hundred-and-fifty year old boat in downtown San Francisco. He elaborated on the find enough to describe the interior and concluded by admitting there was nothing of value aboard.

They passed the joint as he talked. Don remained convinced he was unaffected by the drug throughout their conversation. Meanwhile, Benny melted deeper and lower into the couch until he had all but slouched onto the floor. When the attorney gave signs of disappearing into the carpet, Worthy picked him up, straightened him out and propped him up again.

"So I ran down to the library yesterday afternoon and learned all about the buried ships in San Francisco's business district. There are probably still a dozen down there. 'Cept this one got uncovered last week and I found it before anyone else did. Now my question is: do I get to claim the right of salvage?"

Interested in unusual points of law, Benny followed the story and asked an obvious question: "Why would you want it?"

"Historical interest if nothing else." Don presented a defensive posture. "There has to be a value for something like that. Somebody will pay something for it, all I have to do is find that person. Besides, how many three-masted schooners are there left today?"

"Plenty. Believe me, there are lots of them on the East Coast. I know. My father bought one at auction once. But he got a whole one. Sounds to me like you have part of one."

"The Maritime Museum will want it. The California Historical Society. The Sons of the Pioneers..."

Benny was remarkably coherent and interrupted him. "That was Roy Rogers' singing group, Don."

"Well, somebody will want the damn thing." He fell silent. "Don't you think?"

Benny shook his head negatively. "And where would you put it even if you were able to dig it out?"

Rossen was incredible. He shot down Don's arguments with amazing accuracy. "All right, so howsabout the possibility there's a body buried under it."

Benny became more attentive and sat upright. "Do you have reason to suspect someone died on the construction site and there's a cover up?"

This conversation was suddenly too serious for Don who never became earnest about anything. Not even rent money.

"Well," Don said with obvious unwillingness to speak frankly, "not really. I don't have any proof. But I bet there's more down there than anyone wants to admit. I bet if you investigated you'd find plenty wrong with the operation."

"Evidence, Don. Hard evidence and I can help you."

"Well, have you ever wanted to do something because it's the right thing to do? Something bigger than you? Like, my father always wanted me to be a lawyer or at least a real estate broker. I feel like my father would of wanted me to do this. Maybe you did what your pop wanted when you went to law school."

"Not me," Benny volunteered as the joint came his way again. "My old man wanted me to be a fighter like he was. There was more money in it in his day. He was a middleweight. Did all right, too."

Worthy rolled his eyes at the ceiling, but the gesture was lost on Rossen.

"You really make me feel good saying that, Don. The cockles of my heart are warm."

The guy was getting tears in his eyes, Worthy thought.

"Too much to smoke," the attorney said as he rubbed a finger to wipe away a tear. Don agreed silently.

"Seriously, Benny, I gotta know how to play this. I could lose a lot if I get it wrong."

"I have no idea what you are playing. Marbles? Maybe jacks or skip rope. You have to tell me before I can help. If I can help. Exactly what are you trying to do?"

"I want to buy time."

"You want to buy time," his attorney repeated. Don nodded. "I know a television and a radio station that could use your patronage. Is that why you came here tonight? To buy a TV commercial?"

"Cut the crap, Benny. I have a bigger problem than that. And I think I have a case."

"Sure you have a case. Everyone has a case. But is it worth paying for a law suit? That's what you have to ask yourself."

Worthy began to think he had come to the wrong person.

"Look, Benny. I know you think I have a wire loose or something, but hear me out on this. I found a sunken ship. It could be a treasure ship. It could be full of dead men and bottles of rum. But whatever it is, it's planted right here in the center of the city and I can't get at it or keep it without a little legal help. Now tell me about the law when it comes to salvaging a ship, okay?"

"I thought you said you investigated inside and found only junk?"

Don became agitated. "Come on," he whined. "I just want some advice."

Throughout his entire academic life, Benny Rossen had no problem achieving excellent marks. He had an eidetic memory which rarely failed him and when called upon he could quote entire passages of material he read only once. With just the hint of a reference, Rossen could dredge up whole pages and read them in his mind's eye. He was also good at paraphrasing. He could do this during an exam although his style became cramped when he had to use a pen. He was at his best in extemporaneous speech. Without the pressure of a test, Rossen was virtually an encyclopedia of legalese. He made an effort to put things in lay terms when he responded to Worthy's request.

"Salvage is not pay," Rossen began. Worthy started to raise his hand to speak but was cut off. "Now hear me out. You have to understand why salvage exists in the maritime industry before you can use it in court. And you probably cannot invoke it as a protection." The dope had the effect of assisting Rossen's memory and he began to wax loquacious. Worthy assumed a comfortable position on his end of the couch and clipped the roach to a tweezers on his keychain.

"The point of a salvage operation is to remove liability from someone who might screw up what they're trying to save. Or kill someone they're trying to help. It guarantees the salvor a portion of the value of what's salvaged. This is separate from other types of situations on land where you might rush in and become 'an officious intermeddler.' Like at a fire. Then you'd be a volunteer. As a volunteer you're liable if you damage someone's property or hurt the people you're trying to help. On land, there's no equitable recourse for such a helper, or meddler. At sea, they change the rules. You get me?" Rossen asked with a bright smile.

Worthy thought he did and said, "Yah. Sure I do. You break it you bought it. Right? But if it's on a boat, you get paid for it."

"You are partly accurate. You only get paid if you successfully save the property that has been abandoned at sea. And if you save humans while others are saving property at the same time, you are entitled to a fair share of any award made to the property salvors." Benny paused to be sure Don followed the legal reasoning. "You realize there has to be some value to the property in the first place. Otherwise there's no moiety."

"What's that?" Don asked.

"A share in the proceeds," Benny replied. "As for the question of where the vessel was at the time of salvage, we in the U. S. have taken a more liberal view of the definition of littoral rights and what types of property are subject to salvage than the English, for instance. I vaguely recall a case where a ship was judged to be subject to salvage even though it was on dry land in dry dock."

The attorney reached for a book on his shelf. He turned to the index, thumbed to a page near the center. "Ah, hah!" he said so vehemently Don jumped. "Not bad. Gilmore and Black, The Law of Admiralty, chapter eight. The Jefferson case. However, I'll need time to research this notation. There's not enough here. I dunno, Don," he said looking up with a finger marking the page, "you may really be on to something here."

Worthy squinted at Rossen out of one eye. He went dredging into the cluttered file drawer in his head that doubled as a brain. "As I think about it," he winked at Rossen, "the reason the captain goes down with his ship is so that nobody else can claim salvage. As long as there's a representative of the owner still on board, it's not abandoned. Is that right?"

"That's sort of correct. But remember, this comes from my third year in law school and I read it a long time ago." Rossen accepted the proffered roach clip. "Thanks."

"So can I salvage the thing or not?" Don asked impatiently.

"In all candor, probably not. But you can, as you suggest, gain some time by asking for an injunction. I just hope you have a sympathetic judge."

"Isn't that true everywhere?" Worthy asked with a tinge of sarcasm.

"No, I mean seriously. The judge has to think there's some merit to the plea or he won't even listen to you. Pass the joint."

Worthy slapped his chest with both palms as if looking for it in his shirt pockets, patted his pants and finally he looked squarely at Rossen. "You have it, dummy."

Smoke rose from a small area on Rossen's shirt front where the roach had fallen. He looked down at the rising wisps of grey and then back at Worthy. "You're right. I do have it," he said matter-of-factly.

There was a delay of perhaps a second before Rossen leaped to his feet and began vigorously swatting his necktie. "Ow. Shit, that hurts!"

He jumped from one leg to the other as Don watched amused. "Ow. Damn! What a crummy way to end a day."

"Hey," Don remarked, "it ain't over yet."

§

After they worked out the details, Benny fired up his computer and together they wrote an injunction enjoining the construction company from further excavation for seven days.

Worthy convinced Benny to visit a judge that night by offering him one more joint. By the time they smoked it to a nub, Rossen was certain the laws of the sea applied to the reclaimed tidelands of the bay. Worthy listened to one side of a telephone conversation as Rossen called Judge Tarera at home, then began to describe the situation. He marveled at how well the man could argue when he believed in his case. Don swore if he ever got busted for anything bigger than trespassing in a trash can, he wanted Rossen to defend him.

Rossen sat down at his computer and printed the legal document the judge would have to sign. However, not until an hour later when Rossen returned with the autographed paper and a stop work order, did Don Worthy himself believe he would actually go through with his surprise attack on the construction industry in San Francisco. This was all new to him and not really his type of fight. He was not the sort to stand in front of the machine and tell the driver to stop. Crossing guards intimidated him. For the most part he was speechless when confronted by the combined efforts of architects, engineers, developers, contractors, the heating, venting and air conditioning people who raise and lower the curtains on corpopulate America.

Don displayed more initiative than usual by putting the rest of his plan into action immediately after he saw the legal wheels begin to grind. He felt a sense of urgency, a need to get started or else he might never make his stand.

The judge reduced Rossen's request to five business days in which to either prove the injunction should be made permanent, or abandon the project. In his statement to Tarera, Rossen explained how he relied on the historical value of the object in question, rather than its salvage value.

Tarera squeezed a Hearing to Show Cause onto her calendar for the following Friday morning. Rossen interpreted the injunction to Don, explained that "permanent" did not mean forever, merely until excavation and removal of the relic was complete.

Furthermore, Rossen cautioned, there was not much likelihood the case would be continued beyond five days although there was always a slim chance Tarera might grant an extension.

"How long that would be is anybody's guess. If she grants it." The attorney had a silly wide-eyed expression on his face. Don interpreted this as elation mingled with surprise. "I did it," Rossen said in a self-congratulatory tone as he settled in his favorite chair. "I got an injunction out of Tarera. Amazing." He waved the few sheets of paper in the air like a captured flag.

Don ticked five days off on his fingers and turned to Rossen. "I don't have much time if the hearing is Friday." Rossen smiled foolishly in response, nodded his head yes. "In that case, I have to start right now. Lots to do." He shook the smaller man by the shoulders. "Benny, listen to me!"

Rossen wiped the grin off his face and become serious again.

"The way I got it figured is this," Don began when he was satisfied he had Rossen's attention. "I'm the captain of that vessel. If that's true, I can't abandon it like they did over a hundred years ago or I won't have a claim. Zat right?"

"Sounds correct to me."

"Then I gotta get onto that boat tonight and stop them from doing anything else with it tomorrow. Soon as they figure out what it is down there in the ground, they'll cover it up again. I guess I'll have to wait out the time it takes for you to get the case prepared for the judge." He took Rossen's right hand and shook it firmly. "I can't take the time now to talk about how I'll be able to pay you, but I'll make it up to you, Benny, believe me."

With that, Worthy left Rossen who was in surprisingly good humor considering he had just been told he would probably not get paid.

Don drove straight home and set to work. He emptied all Boomer's contents onto the driveway next door. The truck expelled material he did not remember picking up and many objects he swore he'd sold months ago. He began to refill the bed of the vehicle with arm loads of supplies from inside his home.

It was getting dark by the time he decided he had packed everything he would need for a week in the wild. This included a camp stove, folding shovel, cooking utensils, cutlery for one, a cup, a plate, a bowl, two Jerry cans holding ten gallons of water, a large sack of dry cat food, seven complete changes of undergarments, two pairs of jeans, four shirts, a Dopp kit, snake bite and sewing kits, portable potty (the "Heeeere's Johnny" logo prominently displayed in large letters), a folding card table and two aluminum folding patio chairs, a two person tent, plenty of dehydrated food including such delicacies as chicken Kiev, beef stroganoff, salmon Almandine — all left over from previous camping trips — half a dozen bottles of California chardonnay, three novels he had been trying to finish for a year including Lowry's "Under the Volcano," a deck of cards, four cartons of cigarettes which was his entire supply, one full carton of paper matches and the *pièce de résistance*, a cellular telephone in a blood red leather briefcase.

Worthy discovered the phone a month ago when it was discarded by a new vice president at one of the city's major banks. The man revamped his entire office in elegant excess after the corporate overthrow of its previous occupant. Allowing no trace of the former V.P. to remain, the cell phone was tossed out due to the new officer's overzealous penchant for self-indulgence.

Don unplugged and pocketed the base though he had no idea where he would find an electrical outlet. Boomer's cigarette lighter did not work, nor did he have an adapter. Other than hoping to be out of the hole before the fully charged battery ran out, he had no plans to use the charger. He touched the O button to learn the time and listened patiently. The phone worked perfectly and he could care less where the bill was being sent as long as it was not in his name.

He delivered all these things to the construction site where he picked an area to create his camp. In the truck bed under everything, at the last minute he found a ten foot piece of rebar with one end bent into a handle which was a ground penetrating tool he had been using for years. For no good reason he could think of, Worthy carried this along with his rucksack to the campsite.

It was nearing eleven when he drove Boomer onto the back lot of his apartment building. He intended to leave it parked there for the entire week rather than on the street. He called Christine from inside the cab.

"Just a small favor. Nothing Roger will get upset about. All I need is for you to drive me some place and drop me off. In your car. I'm leaving Boomer in back at my place."

Don and Christine used to live together but broke up last year. She had begun dating an old friend of theirs. Don still called from time-to-time and she was willing enough to do small favors for him. Friends, she still wanted to be friends. His request seemed innocent and relatively simple on the surface. She agreed to pick him up within the hour.

He was waiting for her outside his apartment building with a knapsack over his shoulder and a porta-pet box at his feet.

"Is Mac in there?" Christine asked as he climbed into her old Peugeot sedan. The sunroof was stuck permanently open and Don playfully reached toward the stars.

"Moonroof still works, I see." He leaned over and pecked her on the cheek. "Thanks. I needed the lift."

She put the car in gear and began to drive. "Where we going?" she finally asked. He directed without telling her the ultimate destination. As she followed Don's instructions through the Stockton tunnel, she became testy when he put her off the third time she asked.

"I want to know what you're up to Mister Don Worthy! And where am I taking you and your cat? Have you finally been evicted? Did your landlord decide he couldn't put up with late payments every month or what?"

"I need you to keep a secret," he said after a few moments of silence. She was one of his oldest friends and although they once knew each other as lovers, that had been over since the day he packed her belongings into the back of his truck and drove her to the YWCA. It took her six months to forgive him for that. Ultimately, she gave him a call and apologized for the tantrum she threw when he would not take a job her brother offered him. He had been equally contrite about making her leave so abruptly.

"I'm going to tell you this because I kind of want a back up. I need to let someone besides my attorney know."

"That little creep Rossen?" she cut him off before he could finish. She was openly hostile toward the man ever since she hired a friend recommended by Rossen to handle her divorce. She still believed she should have received the taxi permit, not the house, in the settlement. No amount of financial reasoning could change her opinion on the subject.

"Despite what you may think about how your case turned out, you'll have to accept the fact I've retained him for this and it is BIG, Christine. I mean, BIG in capital letters. I'm taking on a national corporation. And I need to know you'll help me if I have to call on you. Okay?"

This was the closest Don Worthy had ever come to saying he needed someone. To him, it was not meant to be a statement of his love for her, but Christine turned toward him when he made this pronouncement. She was visibly overcome.

"Oh, Don. That means so much to me." She swerved into the southbound lane as she said this.

He made a grab at the wheel which he held steady for a hundred feet. "I'm going to explain, but you have to promise to drive carefully for the next few minutes if you expect me to tell you what I'm doing." Together, they guided the car into its proper lane.

"I promise, I really do. I do."

"Well, remember how important I told you this is. And you're only the second person in the world to hear about it. So it's critical you promise not to tell anyone else, got it?"

She promised silence, sealed her lips with a finger. He explained how he intended to salvage a boat buried on the site of a new high rise construction project in the Financial District. She tried to interrupt him when he said "salvage," but he continued non stop to the end. He told her enough of the story to prevent her from asking any more questions before they turned into the alley behind the project. He planned for her to drop him off and go home, but she insisted on seeing where he was spending the night. Reluctantly, he agreed.

"We walk slow and quiet from here," he whispered. She nodded agreement. It was so dark he had difficulty making out his feet in front of him. He led her by hand through the fence and along the perimeter of the excavation. The lights of the city were bright enough to guide them once they were out of the deep shadow cast by the buildings in the alley. He kept his flashlight off until they were over the sloping lip leading into the pit, then lighted their way once he was sure no one else could see the beam and give away the fact they were trespassing.

"It's all right to talk now," he said with the path illuminated in front of them. There was a mewled cry from the cat carrier.

"Don, this is scary," she said and drew nearer. "It's like going into a cave or something. Are there bats down here?"

"Not to worry. No bats. No problem."

At the bottom of the pit, he marched her over to his camping gear. He picked up a butane lamp, pumped the handle and lit the wick. With his other hand he pulled a cigarette out of his shirt pocket and touched the last glow of the match to the tobacco. Meanwhile Christine set Mac free.

"Are we supposed to be here?" she asked with disbelief in her voice. It reminded her of their camping trips to Yosemite.

"That's the beauty of it, my dear. I'm as legal as a meter maid. Rossen saw to that. For about a week, I can squat here and nobody can kick me out. This is where I aim to stay 'til Friday at least."

He went to his makeshift pantry, a half dozen boxes on the ground beneath the card table, and extracted one of his bottles of white wine.

In a paper bag he found two Styrofoam cups and an Ah So two-prong cork puller. He shucked the wine's lead cap as if it were a paper wrapper, lifted it off in one piece without tearing it in the slightest. He poured wine into both cups, held his in the air. "A toast, my dear, to the archaeological find of the century," he said as he tapped his cup against hers. After a sip, he held the lamp in the air and guided her over to the half buried bulldozer. "See that hole? It's a sunken ship. What I was telling you about. I claim the right of salvage."

She never did get a chance to ask him why he was doing this and what he expected to gain from it. That was because he carefully steered the conversation away from those issues. He did tell her he thought the historical society would place a high value, maybe as much as ten thousand dollars, on an authentic Gold Rush ship. He picked the number out of the air and mentioned the box of nails, the old boots, the pistol and the box of bottles he'd already found and left at home.

The wine was gone in less than an hour. By then she knew almost everything about Don's discovery including the history of the *Niantic* and how this was just one of an armada buried in the reclaimed earth of San Francisco. She grudgingly admitted that Benny Rossen appeared to have done the right thing. Don had a legal niche on which to plant his bedroll.

He toyed with the idea of inviting her to spend the night, eyed his sleeping conditions and thought better of it.

At last she said, "I better get going." She stood up from the camp stool and leaned in his direction. He took the hint and embraced her.

"It doesn't have to snow for me to get the drift," he said as he kissed her long and hard. "Things aren't all that good with you and Roger, I take it?"

"Don't even go there."

He escorted her back to her car, arm in arm up the path and through the fence. "Just don't tell anybody about this unless I call and ask for help, got that?" he reminded her through her open roof as she started the engine.

"Promise," she said. She blew him a kiss as she drove away.

CHAPTER EIGHT

THE HOTEL'S OWN EMPEROR

Less than a year after *Niantic* the whaler turned passenger ship and sailed into port never to have crew enough to sail out again, she was hauled at high tide onto a vacant lot a hundred yards from the marshy bay. Most of her keel was sliced off and thirty men rolled her on logs and pulled with rope and chain to drag her, dripping and barnacle encrusted like the sea animals she once hunted, into position. The stately old lady lumbered slowly into a trough dug specially for her the day before, ten feet deep and as long as she was wide.

"She settled in almost as if going peacefully to sleep," one of the men who had been hired for the day, a German from Gottingen over whose shoulder ran a thick length of rope, remarked as he wiped sweat from his brow.

Niantic was braced upright with a bulwark made partially from her own masts and partially from the largest stones to be found and gathered from nearby construction projects. Dirt was packed around her to keep her from listing left or right. The nautical terms "larboard" and "starboard" would never again apply to this schooner. *Niantic* was at her final rest.

Her many sails were sold at auction and fetched a higher price than the ship herself. Canvas, even the wind-worn and many times patched material *Niantic* once proudly wore, was in short supply as were almost all other products of the civilized world. Her sails were made into miner's shirts and breeches, her rigging re-used as rope to tie down cargo or to pluck, as the German and the men on his crew had, other ships from the sea.

One enterprising tailor, a Bavarian immigrant, bought some of this sail cloth. He used rivets instead of thread to fasten the pockets of the canvas clothes he made because he heard many complaints from miners who said conventional weaves just would not hold a pocket full of gold nuggets. The clothes this man made sold well.

An entrance was cut in the ship's side between the main and second decks. A stairway was built from there to reach the ground. The once proud ship's hull was mired in earth that was often under water. In a few months, however, other lots were built upon, more ships were drawn from the sea and planted in the land between soggy soil and shore until it became clear a barrier wall of some kind was needed to prevent the tide from rising to the land's new level. There were no monies available from public funds so the local owners agreed to pay for the project.

Until the seawall was built, squatters purposely scuttled ships on a water-logged lot in order to claim the ground beneath the vessel. Over the coming years dredging in the bay gradually pushed the land further and further out over the mudflats. This reduced the need for the multitude of wharves which had sprung like a tree's root system leading out to deep water.

People and horses walked now where clam and oyster were once harvested by Indian, Mexican, and American settlers. The mud flats of Yerba Buena cove disappeared as planks and then equally muddy streets took their place. The long wharves, which once stretched for miles over the flats to reach ships, were turned into thoroughfares. San Francisco real estate, not unlike much of the land in Holland, was taken inch by inch from a usually unforgiving sea.

New businesses opened their doors daily. Some were housed in edifices of brick, but these were the exception. Lumber to build houses had to be imported and, with gold competing for their attention, laborers did not come cheap. Construction costs usually exceeded most reasonable rates of return for such an investment with the result that in those first years, hastily erected buildings fashioned from wood milled for that purpose were not as common as structures created from re-used ships like *Niantic*.

These old vessels were given new life, but often only briefly. Fire resistant while at sea, in their new incarnation planted along wood streets that had themselves once been wharves made every dwelling and many roads vulnerable to the least conflagration. In large part, the city was a giant collection of tinder boxes waiting to be torched.

Meanwhile, the stream of pedestrian and horse drawn traffic increased in direct proportion to the rush to the hills for gold. The population swelled from a few thousand before the Gold Rush to an estimated 55,000 in 1855. *Niantic* became for a time a warehouse, then a retail store and, finally, a hostelry. The land surrounding the hotel was reformed almost as if San Francisco were in the throes of geologic upheaval. The street level rose as mud was dredged and brought ashore in order to accommodate the demands brought on by an increase in shipping. The dredging, in turn, drew more ships. Within two years the roadway was elevated to the point where the steps in front of the boat that had been turned into a hotel were removed.

City administrators began to be elected who would spend taxes on public works. The street in front became well traveled. Ultimately, a real sidewalk was installed and for the first time pedestrians were able to walk without soiling their shoes.

Like a fertile cultivated field, rows of wooden structures sprouted. Civilized touches included public drinking fountains and horse watering troughs. Brick making eventually became common and bricks became the material of choice for the new mercantile class responsible for developing a multitude of commercial projects. More land was reclaimed from the sea and more lots prepared to take improvements until the entire expanse of shoreline along the embarcadero came to resemble the cities of the east.

The Niantic Hotel sat barge-like on a busy corner in one of the many business districts that sprouted up in San Francisco. Her name became an anachronism that required a sign explaining to her guests and the public that this was the former schooner *Niantic*, having come all the way 'round the Horn in 1849. Both she and the world surrounding her altered so much that in less than three years she no longer very much resembled an ocean-going vessel.

The hotel was among the cheapest in town. Its rat infested interior was dark, damp and musty and never quite free of a strong fish odor that had crept into its pores during years at sea. The odor dismayed even the most seasoned traveler. Those who worked there grew accustomed to the stench but kept sachet or nosegay close at hand.

Fires frequently engulfed this ramshackle community. The largest was that of May, 1851, which destroyed half the downtown city center. It was popularly believed to have been set by the Sydney Ducks who, it was said, torched a chandlery in order to create a diversion while they looted the bank next door. It was just bad luck that brought the wind off the bay when it did.

A vigilance committee caught a fellow named John Jenkins with his hands on the safe. A week later, Jenkins earned the dubious distinction of being the first person hanged from Portsmouth Square by the vigilantes under the generalship of Sam Brannan.

But the fire was a blessing in disguise. The surface superstructure of the original *Niantic* was destroyed along with most of the San Francisco waterfront as air was sucked under the hollow planks of the streets in an enormous bellows created in some angry god's annealing forge. Niantic was rebuilt of brick but with no foundation. It would have required too much effort to actually dig out the old hull so the builder sealed the openings at either end and used the lower deck as a naturally flat surface on which to begin construction. He covered this with earth and brought in ten more feet of top-soil which was spread evenly before the first floor beam was in place. More earth was moved to form an outside buttress for the walls. This had the peculiar benefit of creating an insulated basement that was never very warm even during the hot summer months, but neither was it very cold during the coldest days of winter.

By 1861 the ground floor of the new building was a few feet higher than street level. This required that steps again be installed. The land was now effectively on a level with the surrounding lots and, in its new brick incarnation, the Niantic Hotel came to be known as a good hostelry with a reputation for cleanliness and fresh water. This last was hers by a strange twist of luck: a stream had accidentally been tapped when workmen removed one of the old *Niantic*'s pump logs and drove it into the ground as a pile for the new hotel. The stream was to be the main source of water for all hotel inhabitants for decades to come.

A few guests became more or less permanent members of the Niantic household. They paid by the week or month and received appropriate discounts. Two meals a day and a weekly change of linen were included in the price of a room. The dining hall was on the ground floor and served its meals family style, everyone seated at long benches, each taking a portion of meat or potatoes from common bowls and platters.

These guests included a luckless miner returned flat broke; he would have to sell his gear to meet the price of the room. There was a former sailor, recently jumped ship, seeking a source of income in order to buy the miner's used shovel and pan. Half a dozen Chinese immigrants also resided in the hotel. With their seemingly unlimited willingness to work long and hard, Asians were an important factor in the labor market although it was rare to find Chinese residents in such an occidental environment as the Hotel Niantic.

This particular group, however, had been driven to take temporary residence there because Niantic was located only a block from Dupont Gai, later known as Grant Avenue. They were forced out of their cramped quarters in a Chinatown flop house through a harassing piece of local legislation known as the "Cubic Air Ordinance." Patently racist, the law was a thinly disguised pretext to force Asians out of their communal living conditions, which they could afford, into more expensive establishments such as the Niantic. Here they were allowed to sleep six to the room instead of twenty.

A clerk in the bank that opened next door to the hotel, who earned nearly nothing compared to the wages paid day laborers but whose constitution was ill-suited to holding anything much heavier than a pen, rented and lived in a large area of the dirt floor cellar of the hotel.

There were not yet any tourist hotels in the city that was growing up by the bay. Most guests were customers by necessity, not desire. As transients, they were gone almost as soon as they arrived, few hung around long, certainly none stayed long enough to learn from the just-returned miner exactly how difficult the yellow metal was to extract from the hills.

Mr. Loon acquired the Niantic Hotel. He visited only on business and left day-to-day operations to a resident manager and a small staff. Loon lived in rather splendid conditions in another hotel half a mile up Market Street.

Captain Cleaveland and his three sons did not join the ranks of their gold-hungry crew when they fled to the hills. Having already earned more than most grub stake miners would ever see, they were somehow not afflicted by the terrible fever that drove other men mad and their Hawaiian and Irish crew to desertion.

Of course, the Cleavelands could not return to the eastern seaboard because they sold the *Niantic* at great loss to her owners. Nor did any of the money from the sale or from the transport of passengers ever reach these owners. The Cleavelands were last heard of in the Pacific Northwest, plying their trade as seamen amid the logging and fishing boats at the mouth of the Columbia River. Henry Cleaveland never returned to his West Tisbury home and now worn out, barren wife. But he did purchase his own vessel again.

Meanwhile, two dogs slept peacefully in the midday sun under the wood lattice sidewalk that fronted the Hotel Niantic.

§

"I tell you I am not the master of those mongrels who inhabit your stoop no matter what the popular press prints!" Emperor Norton exclaimed.

The most notable nearly permanent tenant of the hotel was a former financier named Joshua A. Norton. Born in England in 1819, Norton emigrated first to New York, then to San Francisco where he went mad. In 1859 following a failed business venture, the man proclaimed himself Emperor Norton the First, Emperor of the United States and Protector of Mexico. Befitting his royal stature, he wore imperial garb including a uniform with gold epaulets and a peacock feather to plume his beaver hat, and went about town issuing proclamations. He taxed businesses a few pennies a month which they sometimes paid and he ate free in many restaurants. The Emperor attended City Council meetings as if he were an elected member of that august body and generally gained the renown of being the city's first true eccentric.

It was said the man lost his fortune attempting to corner the rice market. But if the Good Lord saw fit to leave Norton his wits, the man was fast in the process of squandering those as well.

"It is true we have dined together in the same establishments, but that is mere happenstance. They are not mine to order about. And I take umbrage, sirrah, with your suggestion that I am in any way associated with these common curs."

Norton wore his full regalia and attempted to act in as dignified and imperious a manner as the moment allowed. That, however, proved difficult given the circumstances. The Emperor and the two waif canines were recent subjects of a newspaper cartoon which depicted them at a free lunch counter in a local saloon. Walking the boardwalk the previous evening, Norton came upon a storefront with its newspaper advertisement hanging on display. Next to the advertisement for notions and dry goods, the editors saw fit to run the cartoon. Enraged at being depicted as destitute, this most colorful former New Yorker raised his cane and smashed the innocent but offending window into a thousand pieces.

Now two men held him tightly in their grip on the steps that led to the hotel lobby which they forcibly prevented him from entering. A third man, the manager of the Niantic, stood his distance studying the scene intently.

"It ain't got nuttin' t'do wid who you calls yer pals an' who y'don't," one of the men responded evenly and almost patiently as he restrained

Norton and compelled him to stand still. "What it has got t'do wid is a winder yer was seed to put a stick through last night. We is the repre-sents of that air storekeeper and we is here to collect for repairs."

Each of the men, one silent the other voluble, held Norton's arms none too gently.

"I have the wherewithal to repay the shopkeeper," protested the rotund sovereign. He appeared desperate to be left alone, but was in no way able to free himself.

"Attel be the day. Won't it, Arthur? You spect us to b'leve you got the scratch to buy yerself a fifty-dollar plate glass winder?"

"That is an outrageous sum for such a cheap bit of pane," Norton replied indignantly. "It was worth no more than two dollars. But I shall make a grand gesture and recompense you five," he offered with what little dignity he could muster.

The two listened intently and seemed swayed by the argument.

"Empowered as oi am ter take yer cash, ten dollars an' yer free to go 'bout yer business," said the up to that moment silent Arthur. He confirmed this with a glance toward his cohort who winked in reply.

The two were actually only supposed to collect four dollars, but business was business and anything extra they could shake loose from their victim they could keep. Norton shrugged to gain release from his captors. In as noble a manner as possible, he led them to the top of the stairs and into the hotel. He stopped to stand very still in the lobby, reached deeply into one pantaloon pocket. There was general silence. At last he withdrew his fist and opened it to reveal a shiny gold coin as small as an insect resting in his palm.

Arthur snatched the token from the Emperor's hand before it could disappear. He bit it between his teeth, inspected the indentation his incisors left on it and smiled. Then both shook their heads in wonder and amazement and walked out the door.

"That was quite a trick, Emp," said the manager who watched silently as the drama unfolded. He had returned to take his place behind the front desk. "You a real magician, you are."

"And you, sirrah, certainly could have assisted me," Norton replied with rising indignation in his voice. "You might then have your week's wages paid and my bill cleared. As it is, that was the last coin I possessed."

There was a laconic ease about the other man's speech. "If that's true, you really will be in trouble," the Manager said as he closed an eye and leaned forward on the countertop. "Y'see, we got plenty of call to rent the room you think of as home to somebody who pays regular."

Norton harrumphed in contempt and fled through the open front door. A few steps behind, the Manager ambled slowly around from his position behind the counter to lean forward against a banister at the hotel porch. His gaze continued to follow Norton.

The quiet morning air was shattered by a muffled bark. Two dogs, one a faded yellow, the other a blend of black and white, immediately leaped from beneath the wood slats of the sidewalk and yelped at Norton's heels. They tagged along behind him down the street as he attempted to shoo them away.

Their frantic noise aroused no complaint from passersby who mostly smiled to see these mangy animals. Dogs were as common a scourge as rats in the city. These two, however, were celebrities. They were known to all the merchants because they were such fast friends, one was never seen without the other, and these were the same two which had recently been linked in the papers to the fallen entrepreneur by their common feeding habits.

The Emperor tried to act lordly in the face of their offensive behavior as he trundled down the street. The dogs yipped as the Emperor held his admiralty style two-cornered hat close to the sides of his head. Its lone feather bobbed wildly as he performed a parody of a person running.

At the intersection of Sansome and Sacramento streets, Norton was forced to an abrupt halt. A group of pedestrians blocked his way and made no sign of clearing a path. They stood as one, all leaning slightly forward as if pressed by a subtle breeze into bowing toward the center of the street.

Norton was in such haste to avoid the dogs he cleared most of the distance between himself and the north facing crowd without realizing he was being forced to bump and push his way through. Two bowler hats blocked his vision but parted at that moment. Norton saw why no one ventured off the wood sidewalk into the street.

A driverless carriage raced past him, its two frenzied horses nearly knocked him down. Dust blossomed in the air as they roared within inches of his out-thrust stomach. Norton understood the peril immediately but reacted after the danger was past. He fell back into the crowd, arms spread, and took half a dozen people with him onto the boardwalk. It was like watching a farm hand fall backward onto a pile of hay.

"Can't you take care what you're doing, you idiot!" one angry voice complained.

The Emperor stood and dusted himself off. But before anyone had time to become antagonistic toward him, the carriage made another run at them. The two horses were so spooked they ran up one side of the street, within a block came to an intersection and the cross traffic there, turned around and started their run down the other side of the street.

"Yep," shouted one of the men who had been flung straw-like to the ground when the Emperor flounced, "that shore is a young'un bouncing in the back o' that air carriage! Do b'lieve the little feller's like to have the livin' daylights shook out o' him. That is, o' course, if'n he lives through the ride that is."

Several other bystanders confirmed the sighting of a child gripping the back of the driver's seat from inside the black coach. The infant might be a boy or a girl for all the Emperor could determine, but whichever it was, it could be no more than five or six years old. All that could be seen were its huge frightened eyes which demonstrated it was hanging on for dear life.

"My baby, my baby!" came the plaintive cry of a woman running toward them from across the street. She was nearly knocked to the ground on the coach's next pass as she struggled vainly to grasp the reins. Not a man in the crowd would have attempted such a dangerous maneuver as the woman made.

The horses reached the end of the street and were set for another turn. The carriage was in its third charge at the Emperor and he became certain he would be trampled. It looked to him as if the huge foreheads of the beasts were lowered and aimed precisely at his middle.

A shout came from the other side of the street and he heard the excited voices of people in the crowd gathered near where he stood. Jubilant cheers and words of encouragement were yelled. Norton looked over his shoulder. His glance was just in time to catch sight of the dirty yellow dog and his inseparable black and white companion. Norton was relieved to see they no longer followed him; they had instead turned their attention to the hard pounding hooves of the runaway horses. The two dogs ran alongside the harness and snapped incisors threatening to bite, barking with perhaps a little more vigor than the ferocity they recently vented on the Emperor's heels. To Norton's way of thinking, they were dealing with the carriage in much the same manner they dealt with him. However, instead of being vilified, the creatures were being encouraged and applauded.

"Good dog! Smart dog!" came from the lips of one man who obviously had no personal knowledge of the animals to which he made reference.

The Emperor took heart when he saw how dangerous their situation was. He became convinced the dogs would lose their lives beneath the charging ungulates. The longer he watched, the more he dared hope for such an outcome. One shod hoof actually struck the skinny yellow animal as he came within nipping distance.

The crowd on both sides of the street screamed in anguish as the dog took the hoof in its side, did a double tumble and landed running on its feet. The pained cry changed into a surging cheer as the creature recovered immediately, doubled its speed and attempted to catch up with its partner and the racing rig.

The black and white dog took the lead when its yellow friend fell behind. It barked louder and with more ferocity as it closed the distance between the runaways and itself. Never before had the Emperor or any of those watching heard this usually placid animal make as much noise or act with such rage.

The black and white managed to outdistance the carriage and placed itself in front of the crazed horses before they once again reached the intersection and the cross traffic that had twice made them turn. The dog about-faced and raised its bristly wire head with bared fangs, its canine teeth snapped a flash of white as it dared the horses to continue straight into it.

The huge animals were completely unaware that if they struck the dog on its back even a glancing blow, it would have broken like a twig. As it was, the horses were more scared of the small brazen creature positioned angrily just inches in front of them than whatever frightened them in the first place. They stopped in the middle of the street, reared their front legs in the air in unison and pretended to defend themselves. But it was clear their spirits were broken and they would be manageable again.

The black and white dog glared at the horses as if to tell them they had no hope of salvation should they be bold enough and foolish enough to bolt again. The yellow dog trotted up to his partner, an ugly open wound on his back where he had taken the force of the blow. In his mouth he held the reins of the carriage which drooped loosely in the dust.

From the pedestrian lined streets a loud shout of rejoicing rose as the yellow dog waited patiently for someone to take the leather straps from him. From the looks of him, sitting quietly on his haunches, completely oblivious to his bleeding back, he appeared as though he thought himself solely responsible for the performance of the good deed.

The black and white dog continued to stare at the horses, turned to bite at a flea on his leg. Then he lay down in front of them, placed one paw over another, and appeared to go to sleep. He fooled no one, however, because one eye remained open.

A tall man with the look of a wrangler at last stepped off the opposite sidewalk and took the reins from between the yellow dog's teeth. The man bent to pat the animal gently on top of its head and the crowd began to cheer. Both dogs remained unmoved, soaking up the languid afternoon sun, tongues lolling out of open mouths, rib-cages rapidly pumping with the intake of breath and an hundred people applauding. The woman who shouted that her child was inside the runaway carriage reached into the dark recess and withdrew a sobbing but otherwise unharmed little girl.

A sharp elbow poked the Emperor in his ribs.

"Them's mighty fine animals ya got there, Emp," said the skinniest man Norton had ever seen. "Y'a kin be proud of them today, by gott-cha." The man's elbows had a natural wide swing, not menacing but dangerous from the standpoint of his neighbor. He poked his right elbow into Norton sharply several times even as his upraised hands applauded the animals resting in the middle of the street.

"They's the Emperor Norton's dogs," another person said loud enough for everyone to hear.

Another cry rose from the throats of the audience as they began to chant, "Norton, Norton." This turned into a sing-song refrain similar to a theatre audience calling for the author of the play they just witnessed.

Since there was no longer any point in denying his association with the creatures, the Emperor decided it was time to take credit and stepped into the street where he swept the admiralty hat from his head, placed it over his cummerbund and bowed deeply.

A man claiming to be a veterinarian yelled out he volunteered to sew up the wounds of the yellow hero dog. Another shouted, "They kin both eat free and so can you for a year at my saloon."

Norton was quick to ask who that man was.

The event was duly noted by the newspapers and another appropriate cartoon was commissioned and published. The story of the famous dogs named Bummer and Lazarus and their heroic action appeared in the next edition of both the "Alta" and "Bulletin" newspapers.

Afterwards, the two were seen sleeping curled up one inside the other for warmth, the yellow animal having the more comfortable spot on the inside.

CHAPTER NINE

A RUDE AWAKENING

Monday dawned with Don Worthy asleep in his bedroll at the bottom of the pit. The construction crew arrived promptly at eight. They noticed the sunken land mover before they observed the sleeping Worthy.

Project Manager Henry Simpson was first to investigate. He used a boot on the stretched out form and issued an ultimatum. "Okay, asshole. You're in trouble now. You bums think you can fuck up our equipment like that and get away with it? You're going straight to jail."

Worthy sat up and yawned. He reached for a cigarette.

"Cut the crap, buddy. I have a hole to dig." Simpson kicked the cigarettes out of Worthy's hand which sent them flying way beyond reach. That was too much for Don Worthy, especially at this early hour of the morning. He turned wildly angry and a side of him that could truly be intimidating confronted the foreman.

"Back off, mother fucker!" Worthy shouted. Simpson held his ground. The local riff-raff was usually peaceable. This guy could be a psycho. Better cautious than clobbered.

Worthy snatched up a handful of papers from the ground beside him and brandished a very legal looking piece at Simpson. He said, "Read it and weep, shit for brains. This says I live here. There's a judge won't allow you to touch me. If you do, I'll have YOU arrested."

Simpson took the paper and studied it carefully.

"In case you didn't get that far in school, let me translate for you," Worthy said bitingly as he sat up fully clothed and began to climb out of the mummy bag. "It clearly states that whereas the property in question is under international law and whereas the rightful owners abandoned it and whereas there is a salvage operation already under-way then, whereas the court has issued a cease and desist order that whereas provides for the rightful determination of ownership within one-hundred and twenty hours -- that's five days to you, dick-head -- from eleven o'clock p.m. last night. Whereas. Asshole."

This was a new approach to squatting and Simpson was suitably impressed. He retreated to the upper level of the construction site and reached for his phone. Which is precisely what Don Worthy did. He heard the receptionist answer "law offices" and asked for Rossen. Re-markably, Rossen was available and picked up.

"Benny. Yah, this is Don. Yah, I just met with the construction boss and we had a little discussion. No. He didn't say much, just went back up the hill to pow-wow with his buddies I guess. So the reason I'm calling is to let you know I'm still here and you can put Plan B into action. Whaddya mean, what's that mean? In case I don't call you every hour, you know something's wrong and you call the police, that's what Plan B is. Don't you remember what we talked about last night?"

Benny Rossen sat in his office at the other end of the conversation. He held the phone away from his head and rubbed his brow with tense fingers. "Don, if you want to know the truth, I really don't recall much about last night, let alone how I got talked into helping you with this crazy stunt. I vaguely remember driving over to Judge Tarera's house late with an affidavit and a request for an injunction. And I remember I had a convincing argument for a temporary restraining order to stop construction, but for the life of me, I don't know what I said. And I do not recall precisely what it is we are injuncting. I have a feeling I'm going to hear the argument from Tarera and I won't recognize it."

"Not to worry, Benny," Don consoled him. "We're safe as long as you have a judge who likes you. That Tarera wants this job put on hold as much as we do."

"How you figure that?"

"If she didn't, would she of given you five minutes, let alone five days, to convince her or some other judge we have a valid right to sal-vage something in the heart of downtown San Francisco? Think about it, Benny. She wants to be convinced there's a valid reason to stop the excavation. It's ecology at work. It's preservation of history. It's like the judge is glad you showed up when you did so she could have a hand in stopping another giant high rise project from blotting out another section of skyline."

"Well, I have to admit, Don, I wouldn't have believed you had such a humanitarian streak in you either." There was grudging admiration in his voice. "I mean, giving up everything to sit on that egg is really nice of you. You're performing a public service by keeping them from destroying that boat. I'm actually proud to be associated with you."

Worthy thought he heard his attorney choking up with gratitude for his altruism. He did his best to cut the guy off before a tear fest began.

"Careful, Benny. You don't want to get your silk tie wet."

"Yah, well I lost one to fire last night as I remember." Benny cleared his throat before he continued. "Okay, I'll tell my secretary to take your calls all day if I have to. But we won't be able to continue like this indefinitely, you understand?"

"You won't have to, Benny, believe me. I'll be out of here by tomorrow, you watch."

"Ah, hah! I knew you weren't all that selfless!" Rossen had that I-caught-you-now tone in his voice which Worthy's mother frequently used. "You're not really in it for eleemosynary reasons are you?"

Worthy did what he always did with his mother when she called from Minneapolis. He said goodbye and hung up without admitting he did not know what eleemosynary meant. He felt smug after he snapped the handset closed.

Don anticipated the Boesk Corporation would send someone out for a meeting right away. After all, they were not about to let construction just stop like that without finding out why. So he checked his watch and resigned himself to his early reveille by lighting the cook stove for coffee. Later, if he was still here, he would put up the tent. His plan was simple. Sit and wait and let them come to him.

He was within his rights and thought he still had a few strings to pull if he ran into trouble. If everything fell to pieces, well, Don knew how to bow out gracefully if he could not reach a settlement.

He had no illusions about the value of the hulk on which he spent the night. It was worthless. There was nothing of interest even from an historical perspective. But the people who were developing the site placed a high value on the land. They were interested in completing their project on time. The sooner the job got done, the better. Delays were costly.

Of course, he never breathed a word of his true intentions to his lawyer or Christine. That would have made Benny culpable and Christine, well she would simply have dropped him like a hot potato if she saw his extortion scheme for what it was: an extortion scheme. Worthy was convinced he would be able to negotiate with the Boesk Corporation and mentally practiced phrasing the words: "You are looking at someone who is willing to sell out. Are you buying?"

The ten thousand he quoted Christine was peanuts compared to what the Boesk Corporation should be willing to pay to have him vacate the premises immediately.

§

The view from the 49th floor of the Pyramid building was spectacular. This was the Boesk Corporation's executive lounge. H. J. created it for himself and furnished it to his own taste. He chose the carpet, the curtains and even the wall color and window tint. He equipped the spacious room in a style that was pleasant when first occupied, but which had become somewhat dated.

In idle moments H. J. considered re-decorating, usually reconsidered when he contemplated the comfort of familiarity that would be sacrificed.

H. J. was the sole occupant of this space; all 2,000 open-air square feet of it were devoted to his needs. He spent many hours above the city admiring in silence and solitude all that he had created below. The Pyramid building was not the only significant high rise project he owned. Sometimes, like today, he took the afternoon off and kept his whereabouts hidden from all but a few. He liked to watch the world at his feet as darkness fell.

In moments of lassitude such as this, H. J. compared himself to a Pharaoh. H. J., however, had gone one step beyond these powerful precursors and actually assisted in the building of his Pyramid. He forced the architect to remove obstructions, both literally and figuratively. In order to create a 360 degree view, a special glass-steel was developed by a Boesk subsidiary. Although still somewhat experimental, the product met and even exceeded local building code structural specifications with the result that the walls of this entire top floor were fabricated from the material.

There appeared to be no support for the walls because the glass-steel was invisible to the naked eye from inside the room. Yet it filtered out the ultraviolet rays of the sun. Otherwise, anyone in the room would cook like a tomato in a hothouse.

It was a marvelous invention. H. J. could see out, but nobody could see in. Even a helicopter hovering at that level would observe nothing but a firm opaque windowless metal face. H. J. kept the material off the market for the time being. He wanted to savor being the only person on the planet benefiting from it.

Theoretically this floor, this room, did not exist. It was not advertised in any brochure or talked about in any trade publication. No one on the street ever bothered to count and few knew there were supposed to be only 48 flights in the building. If they completed the entire litany, they would discover there were actually 49.

The city's planning department originally frowned on a 212 foot spire rising without supporting steel girders from the 48th floor. But H. J. successfully out-maneuvered all his critics. When the Board of Supervisors balked at creating the tallest building in town, he twice arranged for special city-wide elections to oust offending board members. Making generous and highly publicized donations to the "correct" charities swung more votes his way. H. J. also engineered the last general election to throw out an anti-high rise initiative which would have hampered his company and his plans for years into the future.

H. J. Boesk was a very powerful and rich man. He knew this and reveled in the knowledge.

The penthouse was the hollow point of a needle that stuck straight up from the financial center of America. New York might claim that status, but the truth was the east had been eclipsed by the West Coast as a source of funds from Asian investment and by the world wide interest in Silicon Valley fifty miles south. H. J. Boesk had already torn off a large piece of the combined technological and financial glacier moving ponderously down hill toward everyone else and shoved it in his pocket.

H. J. really did feel the master of all he surveyed. His latest construction project was beginning to take shape at his feet right next door. He tore down an old hotel and began to develop the land before the anti-high rise initiative could be voted on again. He would probably receive a commendation from the Mayor's Committee when they learned he actually downsized the new project. In the early planning stage, H. J. saw to it that the new neighboring building's topmost floor would be precisely five feet below his lounge. If he chose, he could have built above the Pyramid, but that would have ruined the view he so carefully created for the penthouse.

The early evening sky was the most brilliant time of day to appreciate this perspective, especially when the sun fell on a clear bay and blue ocean horizon. H. J. ambled around the room from any point on the compass and picked out patches of the city he had cultivated. He liked the dark of night as well. Things seemed bigger at night. H. J. Boesk often invited his upper echelon staff to meet at this time, early night and in this place. It inconvenienced them to tell their family they had to work late, but wives and children knew they were in the employ of a man who did not take kindly to excuses.

Winton Chirup tapped his private code into the elevator keypad and the doors opened onto the breathtaking view. He walked over to his boss whose back was turned to him and took a seat. After extracting a single folder from his briefcase, he waited patiently until H. J. revolved in his chair and admitted Chirup into his presence.

"We seem to have a problem with the project, H. J." It was not the sort of opening line he liked, but it was direct.

Chirup had no hips. He wore suspenders to keep stovepipe straight slacks on a level with his belly. This had the peculiar effect of making the pants ride some few inches above his natural waistband. Chirup could not see himself as others saw him. He lacked such objectivity both philosophically and literally for he had no full length mirror in his condo. Chirup thought his ensemble created a distinguished appearance. He fancied his apparel to be that of a Southern gentleman, genteel and unpretentious.

The effect on most people was just the opposite. The secretaries in the Boesk Corporation's finance department thought Chirup dressed like a pimp. New employees often remarked that his pants were halfway to his neck. One of the ruder remarks, one that would not die, was the suggestion that if Chirup shaved his head he'd look like a hard-on in Gucci.

Boesk ignored his highest ranked employee's penchant to dress like a dandy. What mattered was financial acumen. Chirup had that in spades even if he had no sartorial sense or social life.

"Which project, Chirup? Not the Dallas refinery, I hope?"

"Next door, sir. I thought you should learn about it before the press starts asking to speak with you."

H. J. Boesk enjoyed his position of power. He liked going to Board of Supervisors or City Council meetings in different cities around the globe. He did not limit himself to business jaunts, however. His greatest moment was to learn he had been invited to something. A benefit with dinner seats costing $10,000 each, a gallery opening, a fashion show, it did not matter what the occasion, he would go to the opening of a letter.

One thing he did not attend, however, were press conferences.

With the exception of the society pages, H. J. avoided publicity. He was a very private person when not at a public function. He placed a battery of assistants in front of him in order to distance himself from inquiry. A confrontation with the news media was always fronted by someone like Martin Hardin or Mrs. Jacobs.

"Hardin can't handle it?" he asked.

"I'm sure we can intercept any end runs at you, but I don't think this is going to blow over very fast." Chirup waited for a nod from his boss before he continued. "It seems we were unable to resume construction this morning."

Boesk's eyes lit up with that statement. "Tell me about it, Chirup." His voice was cold, stern.

"Well, the way I got it was that a fellow named Don Worthy has claimed certain rights to the property. And he has a lawyer with a court order signed last night to enjoin us from proceeding with the development. Temporarily, at least."

Chirup paused. From a folder he withdrew a copy of the injunction which he proffered. It lay on the desk untouched by H. J. whose steel gray eyes remained fixed on Winton.

"They got Judge Tarera out of bed last night and she signed the writ. If you recall, Tarera put up a hellova fight in that high-rise initiative last spring. Signed her name to every group endorsing height limits."

"I'm sure you have more on the subject. Continue."

"Basically, the man claims he has the right to salvage the boat we abandoned Friday."

"What boat are you talking about, Chirup?" A certain amount of incredulity crept into Boesk's voice.

"The boat that was buried under the hotel we tore down last month. Worthy found it Friday night and, because ostensibly we didn't have any idea it was there, he says it was abandoned. He claimed the right of salvage."

There was a moment of thoughtful silence. Finally Boesk spoke. "Do you know how absurd that claim sounds, Winton?"

"I certainly do, sir, believe me. And we have legal counsel who would agree. But the plain truth is, the man has a court order that prevents us from continuing operations for a week."

"At which time?"

"The best guess is he will not be allowed to pursue his claim. The worst case theory has it he may be able to stretch this out for an additional 72 hours. Perhaps longer. No one believes he will prevail."

The sun had set during this conversation and Boesk sighed at the loss of light. The bay was now a black gap between the blaze arising from the surrounding city of San Francisco, the glow of Oakland to the east and sparkles from the hills of Sausalito in the north. In the middle, one lighthouse torch blinked on, off, blinked on, off, which marked Alcatraz Island. The interior lights of the executive lounge automatically turned brighter as the outside light faded.

"Winton, can you tell me why it took almost ten hours for me to find out about this?"

Chirup could tell this information did not put Boesk in a good mood.

"Nobody knew where you were." Winton flapped his arms at his sides like chicken wings. He was obviously uncomfortable under this scrutiny. "Combine that with a breakdown in communications from pit boss to squatter and we have a classic case of the machine grinding to a halt. The first guy to get wind of this was Simpson, the foreman. He kicked it upstairs to his manager who sat on it for over an hour while he waited for the papers to be brought over from where they had been filed by the court. After conferring with two other guys in his office, they called over here but relayed everything to Davidson. Apparently he went apoplectic when he heard the news and that delayed things another few hours. Figured he could handle things by himself, y'know."

Winton stopped his overview at that point to determine whether or not H. J. had any questions, perhaps to inquire after the current state of health of Davidson, his lead architect. There seemed to be no interest.

"I got a call about three this afternoon. By that time all work was halted. Seems everything slowed down when they proceeded to email memos back and forth, making duplicates of everything and CC'ing everyone they could think of in order to cover their asses. I tried to reach you at that time, but was told you were unavailable by cell and out of town. Apparently you asked Mrs. Jacobs to hold all incoming calls until you countered that order. She did exactly as you requested. I practically had to tell her it was a matter of life and death before she allowed me to get through to you. Which is why I am here now."

There was a moment of silence while H. J. sat unmoving, hands folded quietly in his lap. "How much is it costing us each day of delay?" he finally asked.

Chirup withdrew another sheet of paper.

"I was sure you would ask for that information. Consider first that we are in the early development stage here. When I ran the projections I looked at the figures as of today rather than down the road a month or what it would have been like, say two weeks ago. Interest on the bank loan is only about $15,000 a day. But that's due to the fact that we don't have any large deliveries scheduled for another week. Things change fast after the pit is complete and our window for accepting steel is, uh," Chirup glanced at a sheet of paper on a clipboard, then back to the architectural renderings, "in eight working days. At that point the critical path has several dependent variables. It gets more expensive as that node is reached and passed. Performance and delivery costs shoot up to about a hundred thousand a day this time next month."

That was the bad news in a nutshell. It had been easier than Winton expected. Now the proverbial ball was in H. J.'s court.

"Sounds to me like we could weather this storm just by waiting the man out. Is that right, Chirup?" Boesk was not happy with what he had been told. He did not accept setbacks gracefully.

"No, not really. You see, if this Worthy fellow inspires a news story it is possible we would not be allowed to resume construction any time in the near future. There really is a ship buried there and public sentiment runs to preservation rather than destruction of historic artifacts even if they have no value."

H. J. Boesk expelled a long breath of air. Here he was, a philanthropic businessman who gave generously to the Opera each year. He invested heavily in his community by redeveloping a substantial portion of downtown. His contribution to the arts was well known and certainly not inconsequential. When one considered that his only daughter was the force behind the renovation of the largest legitimate theatre west of the Rockies, what more could he offer?

But none of that seemed to matter much to people intent on frustrating his good intentions, his good deeds, his almost selfless acts. His projects benefited stockholders, not he. It was the rabble of have-nots who hurt Boesk's feelings and hampered his style. Looking out of his forty-ninth floor penthouse suite, within yards of its pointy top, he could feel himself the king of all he surveyed. Not exactly Randolph Hearst viewing the coastline from San Simeon, able to say he owned all the land he could see, but certainly one of the important architects of his age.

Why was he so unappreciated? How could someone as small as this Worthy fellow possibly thwart a man as important as H. J. Boesk?

Winton joined Boesk at the window. "If you look down over there," he pointed at the huge open hole almost directly below them, "you can just make out this guy's camp ground sort of off to the left. That's his lamp glowing."

Boesk turned toward Chirup: "Can you tell me why we did not know there was a boat buried there?" H. J. asked as if addressing a child.

Chirup was unable to shift the responsibility on that one. He had tried, oh how he had tried, to find someone else to point a finger at for that mistake.

"We were well aware of the existence of the boat, sir. But Davidson had a convincing argument against any attempt to raise it. He pointed out, correctly I might add, that there was not much of it left after a mid-nineteenth century fire. Our own crews took core samples down to twenty feet, found nothing. We came up with charcoal and ash, if you remember the soil engineer's report. But nothing solid, and certainly no boat. I believe we will find it rests almost at or a few feet below the lowest planned excavation point, that it is completely rotten and totally worthless.

"Is that why we were caught off balance, Chirup?"

"More to the point, sir, you deemed it expedient not to have an EIR, sir," Chirup concluded. It did not feel good having to tell your boss how he had blown it. Perhaps behind his back one could say that, but not in person when there is only you and him and the Big Thunderer to hear it.

The value and importance of the Environmental Impact Report could not be understated in the context of what had happened without it. Boesk remembered considering the need for a full blown EIR, then dismissing the costly concept as more red tape. He successfully guided the report to describe the existing improvements as not worthy of historical interest and scraped the surface clean before anyone could complain. He also recalled Davidson bringing in the actual bronze plaque which had been hung by the Historical Society on the old brick hotel that stood on the sight since 1907. He made it known the description of the Gold Rush ship would again hang on the new high rise.

"I assure you the old hotel building is not an historic landmark," Davidson said at the time as he propped the metal plate up on Boesk's desk for him to view. "All the society does is run around town and hang signs like this on places of interest to tourists. There's one on Bush Street where Isadora Duncan was born and even a fake one above the

Stockton Tunnel where Miles Archer is supposed to have been shot by Brigid O'Shaughnessy in The Maltese Falcon."

At the time, Boesk liked what he was told. He had a cost estimate on the EIR sitting right in front of him when Davidson began his explanation of why a full report was not necessary. Boesk listened to the history of the building as told by someone with a vested interest. That's where the mistake lay, he realized far too late. The architect did not want anything to stand in the way of what was the project of a lifetime, so he down played the need to have an extensive EIR.

"This whole downtown area is land fill, you know," the architect argued. "It was built up over the years after the Gold Rush. Ships that were hauled up on shore were nothing more than piles of wood ready to catch fire and this one burned down in 1851. The fire was actually a good thing. The city rebuilt to more exacting standards making permanent structures with brick and mortar. A few of them still exist up the street on Pacific Avenue. About then they built the first hotel on this site. It got knocked down in the earthquake of 1906 and another hotel was built. That's the one we're tearing down next week. That's the one this sign came off. And there is nothing buried down there now because it got burned to the ground more than a hundred and fifty years ago."

H. J. accepted Davidson's explanation, considered the even more expensive alternative of an EIR locating some hidden artifact in the ground. Nothing struck fear into the heart of architect and builder alike as the possibility of discovering an Indian burial ground precisely where you plan to put a cement foundation.

The Boesk Corporation filed the correct papers with the state of California. The state was given historical evidence of the fire, it was demonstrated the new building would be no more than ten times taller than the existing structure, which was well within established height guidelines. The happy result was a negative CEQA returned from Sacramento. A negative CEQA meant no EIR required. At the time, H. J. was spending a fortune to get building height limits raised and a favorable planning commission into office. Anything that saved money was viewed with favor.

The next person he would call on the carpet would be Davidson. But before that, H. J. had to clear up the matter of the squatter on his doorstep.

"Chirup, you will do one thing for me."

The man nodded. H. J. Boesk was known for was his ability to make a quick decision on a course of action. Chirup wanted nothing more than to have a plan mapped out for him.

"Walk directly out of here and go to this man's encampment. You will offer him the equivalent of one day of our current loss if he agrees to clear out by tomorrow morning." Chirup nodded again. "That's at today's cost estimate of $15,000. And you have the power to double that figure if he balks. Triple it if he looks like that will do the trick. Call me before going any higher."

Guards in the lobby of the Pyramid smiled and waved at Chirup as he exited the elevator. He went up to one of the uniformed men and asked if he could borrow a lantern or flashlight. The guard reached to his belt and produced a high tech torch which fit the palm of his hand.

"Bright as a car headlight," he said as he handed it over.

Chirup felt like he was crossing no man's land in a war zone as he went from the concrete and steel security of one building to the brown dirt edge of the excavation. There was a chain link fence around the perimeter, but an entry gate lay wide open. He glanced at his watch. Then he pulled the lapels of his coat tighter around his neck and began the walk that was to open negotiations between the two camps.

Upstairs, on the topmost floor of the pyramid building, H. J. pressed an intercom button.

"Yessir," came an almost immediate female voice in response.

"Mrs. Jacobs. Have we leaked anything to Chirup? Has he any idea we've considered inviting him to have a seat on the board?"

"Not that I am aware."

"Good. Instead, I have decided to end his employ. Allow him to complete the current assignment. Then give him his severance notice. Do not bother asking for his resignation. That is all for now."

H. J. Boesk did not like the idea that Chirup had pinpointed the precise source of the problem and laid it squarely on H. J.'s shoulders. Chirup should have had the decency to point at someone else, Davidson, or Hardin or even himself. Not H. J.

Therefore, Chirup had to go. The man would no longer believe wholly and completely in an infallible H. J. Boesk and that could not be tolerated.

§

Don kept a hand on the cellular phone in his jacket pocket. He did not want to miss a call or be unable to make one. As far as he was concerned, he could expect the enemy to try anything at any time.

MacArthur was comfortable on the black 'dozer seat, his bowl full of crunchy food on the ground nearby. The cat raised his head, alerted by footsteps. This signaled Don to look over his shoulder at the pinprick of light coming down the trail.

Chirup hiked the distance to the bottom of the construction project in easy strides. It was dark and he was unsure of his footsteps outside the circle of light thrown by his flash, but inside the halo he set an easy, comfortable pace. He became cautious as he approached the man squatting at a camp stove, stirring a pot with a wooden spoon. The fellow looked up as Chirup neared, broke into what appeared to be a wide grin.

"Hello, hello. Come on over, make yourself comfortable. My name's Don, Don Worthy. And am I glad to see you. What kept you? I been waiting all day. Let's get down to business."

Chirup was taken aback by the warm attitude. Worthy held a cup of coffee out, apologized about not having any dairy cream but here's some powder if Chirup wanted it. Taking the cup, the emissary decided this fellow had his head on straight after all, but wanted the air clear of any possible confusion.

"Listen, buddy, do you know who I am?"

"I'm willing to bet you're from the Boesk Corporation. Right?" He sipped from his own cup. "And my name's Don, not buddy."

"Chirup. Winton Chirup." He extended his right hand. Worthy shook it warmly. "Yes, as a matter of fact I am a direct representative of Mr. Boesk."

"How is ol' multi-megabucks Boesk?" Don asked jovially.

"We do not refer to him in that manner," came the cool reply. Worthy had just lost any points he might have gained in his opening gambit. "You, I assume, are the fellow with the outrageous claim and court order to salvage a boat you found on our property?"

"Not so outrageous," Don responded. "Just the facts, man. Just the facts." He motioned toward a camp cot and two collapsible chairs. "Care to set a while? Rest yer dogs?" Don assumed his best cowpoke drawl. It was not very good so he rarely used it. However, it seemed apt at the moment.

Each took a chair. Chirup waited for more banter but the trespasser merely smiled his wide grin and sipped coffee.

"Let me get to the point, Mr. Worthy. I would like to make you an offer. And to be frank, we want this to end without publicity. Therefore, we are willing to make a sizable contribution to your bank account, assuming you have one. Of course, you must agree to vacate the construction project immediately if you accept our generous offer."

"I'm all ears," Worthy continued to grin.

Chirup had his instructions, knew how much he could start with, but there was no point in being overly generous. He began low in order to test the waters.

"I am prepared to offer you five thousand dollars, Mr. Worthy. Tonight. The money will be at your bank when it opens tomorrow." He paused to see how this offer was taken by the affable character. "And if you have no bank where you are known, we can have an account established in your name with no difficulty. What do you say?"

"Hey Mac, you hear that?" Worthy called into the distance. There was no response.

"Someone else is here with you?"

"Kind of. Yeah. An old friend." Worthy stood and walked over to the bulldozer. He lifted the cat into his arms and walked back to where Chirup remained seated. He scratched the cat under the chin, muttered to it the while. "This is MacArthur. He found the boat, y'see, and I have to take into consideration his share when I negotiate for him." He nuzzled up to the cat in a manner Chirup found disgusting, then looked across at him. "Mac says no. But thank you anyway."

Chirup was silent. He fumed but made no outward indication he was upset. "This is absurd. You tell me your cat guides you in your business deals?"

"In this case, you might say so." Worthy lifted a paw from beneath Mac's chest and made it wave at Chirup. The cat offered no resistance and made no attempt to quit the lap.

"Mr. Worthy. My offer is genuine. You stand to benefit simply by walking away from this untenable position you've taken. I think you ought seriously to consider what I have just said and accept the offer." Chirup fell silent.

"A bird," Worthy finally replied.

Chirup did not know what was expected from him with such a comment. "A bird? What do you mean?" he asked. He was afraid he was being maneuvered into Worthy's court and might not be getting anywhere on his own.

"Everyone's either a bird, a pig or a cow. You're a bird."

"I'm afraid I don't follow you and I'm not sure I wish to."

"It just makes things simple. Everyone is one or the other and you, you're a bird. That means you think like one. You act like one. You even dress like one. And that's what you offered me: crumbs. From a bird, crumbs." Worthy continued to stroke the feline without taking his eyes off his guest.

"That sounds to me like you refuse to accept our offer," said Chirup in an attempt to direct the conversation to the subject at hand.

"You got it. Care for more coffee?"

"Thank you, no." They remained silent. After a moment passed, Chirup decided to increase the price. "I don't suppose that raising our offer would be of any interest to you?"

Worthy smiled sweetly. He was beginning to enjoy himself. Even though five grand was an insult, it was their first offer and the lowest. He would just have to give them a chance to tell him how high they were willing to go. Years of haggling and dealing at the flea market taught him several sales techniques. First, the cardinal rule was: Never accept the first price thrown out on the table.

"How much you thinking of raising it?" He held out for more with no idea how high the bidding might go.

"I'm sure we could double that figure if necessary." Chirup was not in his element. He was used to dealing with people who had already set their price. Here was someone who forced him to raise the ante without paying for any of his cards.

"'Fraid not. Right, MacArthur?" Silence.

"Mr. Worthy, would you please tell me what it is you want from us?" Chirup was impatient and it began to show.

"Why do you think I want anything from you? The object for me is to raise this ship. It's that simple. Admiralty Law says an abandoned vessel can be salvaged by the person or persons who lay claim to the operation. That's what I'm doing. Let me show you."

He stood and the cat fell out of his lap, leaped to the ground. It sat there cleaning its fur while Worthy rooted about in his collection of camp gear. He pulled a long rod and folded shovel from the pile.

"I've already begun the operation. See, I have all I need to complete the salvage in, oh, say six months or so." He held up the tools and looked quite pleased with himself. "Way I got it figured, this ought to be worth a lot to the Maritime Museum or the Museum of Science and Industry or plenty of historical societies. Not to mention the valuable items that might surface when I really get to sifting the earth around here."

As he spoke, Don dug a shovel full of dirt from the outside of one strip of imbedded wood. He dropped the shovel and picked up the ten foot piece of re-bar which he plunged into the earth next to the curved wood bow. The rod went all the way up to its handle before he drew it back out.

"That's a good soft spot to dig." He picked up the shovel and began removing more soil in earnest.

Chirup was dismayed to see the man actually believed what he was saying. Worthy seemed convinced he could dig up something precious. If the man thought he had a valuable project he would place a high price on his so-called salvage operation.

"Don't be ridiculous, Mr. Worthy. None of those foundations or societies you mention have any money for something like this. At best, the hulk is a minor curiosity. At worst, a pile of rotten wood." Chirup finished his part of the conversation and saw no point in continuing. His offer had been flatly rejected and he intended to distance himself from this madman.

Chirup stood and tossed the now cold coffee from its cup. One last time, he was determined to learn if the man had any price which would get him to leave.

"Will you tell me a price you would accept? I would like to hear your terms."

The second cardinal rule of negotiating was not to give away your asking price. Let the buyer choose that, then decide if it is acceptable or not. Or you can name an absurdly high price and gauge the buyer's reaction. "MacArthur seems to think a million dollars would be about right." Worthy looked at his cat as if for confirmation. "That what you said, Mac? A million?" Worthy wore an idiotic smile as he looked at Chirup. "That's what he said, Mr. Chirp. A cool million and we would probably, I say maybe that would be enough to get us to leave. Tell that to your boss."

"That is preposterous, Mr. Worthy. A ridiculously high sum, you knew that from the start." Chirup decided it was time he made a truly substantial offer. He wanted to find just how valuable the squatter thought the hulk.

"I'll up our offer to thirty thousand dollars," he said abruptly.

Worthy broke into an even wider grin. Now that was something he wanted to hear. But he shook his head no.

"Lemme tell you something, it is Chirp, right?" Winton corrected the pronunciation of his name. "Right. Well, Chirup, life is a shit sandwich, as me ol' pappy used to say. And the more bread you got the less shit you have to eat. So out of memory of me ol' dad, I'm gonna have to decline your offer and ask you to go back to the boss and get him to up the price."

Winton cringed at the thought of meeting with H. J. again tonight.

"But don't get me wrong-o. 'Cause I am ready to deal with you guys. Only please give me a break!" He lapsed into a lisp with this last line, lay the back of his arm across his forehead and struck a pose for his visitor. "I really want some real bucks. Okay?"

That was enough for Winton. He turned and began his return climb out. He was careful not to soil his shoes as he found his way to the top. There he turned to look back. The light of Worthy's butane lamp was feeble but sufficient to illuminate the camp at the bottom of the pit.

"Good night," he heard Worthy shout. "Come back and visit anytime. And did anybody ever tell you your mother dresses you funny?"

Alone with his cat, Don Worthy swallowed hard and lit a smoke. He had completely forgotten to reach for one during the entire visit. His hands shook. The adrenalin rush made him tremble and he had a need to feel the smoke go deep in his lungs.

In retrospect, he was proud of how he handled the negotiations. When he felt he had calmed down some, he began to re-think the offer, worried he should have taken it. But all he was doing was haggling, just like he did at the flea market. When someone offered you ten dollars for an old Depression glass bottle, you asked twenty. Normally, that would have been the end of it, but this is a rarified atmosphere where dollars are big. No one had ever offered him five or ten thousand for anything. He did not know how to deal with such sums. Any amount over $500 was more than he had seen at one time in years. Then to hear he was sitting on $30,000! He just could not say yes to such a pile without thinking he should hold out for more. Everything started to look like a million at that point. Asking for it had seemed the natural thing to do.

"Control the negotiation, MacArthur. That's the first rule of salesmanship. The second rule is 'keep 'em off guard.'" Actually, those would be rules three and four.

Mac had been to so many flea markets with Don that he heard these rules repeated frequently. He merely yawned and spread his claws.

Worthy still had the ten foot rod in his hands. He began to idly poke it into the earth here and there as a nervous reaction, to have something to do. The handle welded to the end made plunging it into the ground as far as it would go relatively easy.

"Did you see how that guy paid attention to me? I had him from the moment he arrived." The rod passed into the earth up to its handle.

He walked in a circle just outside the perimeter marked by the bands of burned wood which he had begun to think of as the hull. He took care to note where he began and where he had already tested. He did this in a seemingly nonchalant manner but with the practice of many similar searches. He muttered out loud as he poked the dirt.

"I got the feeling he wanted me to ask for more. Really. After all, he knows that I know that they know it's costing them a whole lot more than a measly thirty thousand dollars to hold up this project. I bet it costs fifty thousand a day. And I know they want to get back to work. So you can count on a gold plated flea collar, ol' buddy, just as soon as we come to terms."

Worthy plunged the rod into the soil up to its handle, withdrew, plunged it in again, withdrew. He walked a few feet and stuck it in again. He was bored. Sticking pins into something took his mind off the negotiations, even if the pincushion was only the earth. He poked the rod into the soil for an hour until he was too far from the lamp to see well. Then he went to bed.

CHAPTER TEN

A GOLDEN TALENT

"A room, sir."

The voice belonged to an older man with shoulder length blond hair and crooked yellow teeth punctuated with gaps. He positioned himself at the front desk, entering quietly while the Manager stood at the rail outside. The Manager returned and took his place behind the counter.

"Got one on the fourth floor with a nice sunny morning no extra charge." He grinned widely at his new guest. This was the only time day or night when the Manager's facial muscles pulled back lips in the rictus of a smile. It made him feel good to quote such absurdly high room rates. "Be fifty cents a day unless you figure on being a week or more in which case we charge three dollars even per week."

He caused the guest book to spin around and aimed the quill pen dipped in ink at the man's hand where it rested on the counter. The hand disappeared below the desktop without touching the pen.

"How 'bout down stairs? You got a basement here?" the man asked in response to the offer. He tossed two two-bit pieces of silver on the counter and spun the register back. "You fill it in for me, sonny. The name's Gregg with two gees. Mister Gregg."

The coins were dropped into a waistcoat pocket. It was the first time in memory any new guest requested the basement and it caused the Manager to adopt a cagey attitude. The least expensive rooms, admittedly, would be found in the least desirable areas of a building. Perhaps that was what the stranger wanted, bargain price for his lodgings.

"A basement we have, yessir. But no rooms down there really. Not one as we would put a guest in, anyway," the Manager replied. "I mean ter say, we've yet to put a short-term guest down there. However, I could for a lesser amount let ye have something on the first floor nearest the kitchen. Say, forty cents a day. Two dollars fiddy the week."

The old man nudged a bag at his feet. He appeared nervous, but in control. His skin had an unnatural cast to it, the color of pale paper. He fished out another two-bit coin and laid it gently on the desk.

He was seventy-five cents to the good without having so much as handed out a key and by this juncture the Manager was willing to consider almost any proposal.

"I like basements," the stranger said politely but pointedly. "So if you have one, maybe you'd see your way to lettin' me stay in it for a little less than that noisy kitchen you was talkin''bout."

"We got a cot in one corner o' the cellar," the Manager admitted. It just occurred to him he could rent out an area of the lower floor not occupied by the bank clerk, Smith, and save the real rooms upstairs for future arrivals. The Manager was no longer in a mood to argue; the silver had done its work. The second coin joined its mates. "Thirty-five cents a day, let you have it for two forty the week in advance. Savings of five cents. Which'll it be? Day or week rate?"

"The week," said the sallow-skinned old man as he passed a two-dollar legal tender note over the counter. The Manager handed back one of the two-bits and a dime. The Manager rang for help to show the new guest his lodgings.

A shrunken Indian woman, her face as wrinkled as a sun-dried plum, shuffled to the side of the long haired stranger.

"Take him down to the fireman's room. And come back for a lamp and extra blankets," he directed.

She nodded assent, her face so contorted by time it was impossible to tell whether or not she displayed surprise when directed to the subterranean part of the building. She bent and picked up the bag at the man's feet, began to walk away. He attempted to wrest it from her. She clung tightly, stubbornly to it. At last he gave up after looking intently into the expressionless face.

The Manager called out from behind the old man's back: "That includes two meals a day, one in the morning, one at night. The cook's kind of fussy if you miss either you may not get t'other. Want a wake-up knock on the door? I'll mark the time down."

"No thanks," the stranger said turning in mid-stride. "I have my own wind-up clock. I'd just as soon you mark down you won't have no one ta disturb me a-tall."

The man stopped at the top of the stairs leading to the basement. He turned and gazed around the foyer with a puzzled expression on his face. Before he took the first step down escorted by the tiny woman, the Manager heard him mumble and shake his head: "This place sure don't look like I thought," the stranger said to no one in particular.

The Manager took it to mean his new guest was remarking on the way the city had grown. It never entered his mind to think in terms of the hotel itself. That certainly had not changed in the two years since he'd been behind the desk and probably had not altered much during the ten years since the building had been built.

Twice that day the stranger left the hotel under the watchful eye of the Manager. Both times he returned with items associated with the gold country. It was normal for a prospector to pick up gear before heading up the Sacramento River. A shovel and strong boots were common and recommended. Two good sized wood stave buckets, now that was something new. Most new men listened to the shopkeeper who outfitted them, purchasing light weight canvas saddle bags and other minor but necessary items. Buckets? That was an unusual purchase, the Manager thought. He said nothing, however, as he sat chewing on a match stick in his chair behind the counter. He watched as the old man carried his supplies down into the dark cellar, returned to his newspaper which was spread on the counter top. He thought nothing more of the new tenant.

§

Nathan Smith was not used to guests sharing the basement with him. There was easily 5,000 square feet of floor space down there, but much of it was given over to cold storage and housekeeping supplies. One storage room contained the sparse furnishings which went with the rental of the rooms. Another area held the leavings of hundreds of guests, the forgotten Bibles, threadbare coats and worn boots left behind in their haste to get to the gold fields.

Thin whitewashed walls separated Nathan from these storage areas. Made of cheap slat boards, the powdered chalk surfaces were a constant threat to his dark wool bank uniform.

Smith's accommodations were Spartan enough. The bed was his most prized possession, comfortable but old. Sitting upright on a small table was an oil lamp, a clock, and three books. A rickety wash basin next to an armoire were his only other pieces of furniture. Each night, six days of the week, he carefully hung the wool suit in the armoire and donned canvas pants, an old work shirt and boots. Then he lay on his bed and luxuriated in the only softness in his life.

Most nights Smith wrote long tedious letters to his mother and sisters or re-read his copy of "Pilgrim's Progress" until his eyelids grew heavy. There were other menial chores which sometimes occupied his time but, for the most part, he led a sober stay-at-home life.

Smith woke to the flickering light of his kerosene lamp about to expire. He had fallen asleep while sewing worn stockings that had been repaired many times in the past. A needle and thread lay amid a pile of material on his chest. At first he was not sure what had brought him back to reality.

He realized it was a new sound that had awakened him, a soft noise, a scratching that might be coming from one of the storage areas. No one else was supposed to be down there and he could think of no reason for the noise. He considered that the sounds had been in the background of his dreams along with the soothing tick of the windup clock on his nightstand.

No one had informed him he had a new neighbor. At first he attributed the subtle scratching to rats, the scourge of the city, scurrying in the black underground. A glance at the clock face told him it was an hour past midnight. The noise persisted and developed a certain rhythm.

Smith raised his lamp, adjusted its wick higher as he got up from the bed and followed the glow into the darkness. It was always dark in the basement, even during the day. Another lamp's light shown from beneath the door of a little used room which was where lost and left items were stored. The door had no lock. He lifted a wood peg handle and the door opened easily. A lamp lighted the room as Nathan poked his head around the corner, saw a man standing deep in a hole in the ground. A mound of earth lay to one side.

Nathan's presence was given away by his own lamp. The man in the hole looked up from his work, startled. There was a moment of silence as each scrutinized the other.

"Didn't know anyone else lived down here," the man said. He rested with his hands atop a shovel handle.

"Neither did I," said the bank clerk tersely.

"Fact, I was tol' there wasn't no hotel guests stayin' this part of the hotel."

"That's 'cause I ain't like the other folks. I live here permanent."

Nathan began to feel foolish explaining himself to a man standing in a hole knee deep in the basement, his basement. He was pretty certain the man had no business doing what he was doing and was prepared to say so. "Mind letting me in on what it is you're digging that hole for?"

"I have been pondering how I would answer that question for the last several hours," the man replied with restrained dignity.

"Did you come up with anything?" More curious than concerned, Nathan waited out the answer.

"As a matter of fact, I believe I have. Young man, would you like to be rich?" the fellow asked as he flipped his long hair back with a shake of the head and lifted himself out of the hole with a thrust of his arms. He clambered to his feet, slapped his palms together, nodded at Nathan and proceeded without waiting for an answer. "I thought you might. Are you a drinking man or tea totally?"

Again before Nathan could answer, the other fellow, who appeared in the twin wick lights to be considerably older than Nathan, grabbed Nathan's elbow with one hand, his own lamp with the other, and ushered the clerk down the wide hallway which partitioned the basement into rooms. They entered what was just another storage room, the one commonly referred to by the staff as the fireman's room for no good reason the clerk had ever learned, where a cot was set up on which a leather bag rested.

"Sit," the older man said as he shifted the bag to the floor near his feet. "My name is Gregg. Walter Gregg. Perhaps you've heard of me." Was it disappointment or relief that washed across his face when Nathan shook his head no? "Well, it's been nearly twelve years, so I suppose not many would. Drink?"

With his teeth Gregg pulled a cork stopper from a brown bottle and poured a large splash into a tin cup. He offered this to the still silent bank clerk who held it in his hands without tasting.

Gregg poured another for himself which he quickly drank in one gulp.

"You still haven't told me why you're digging in the basement of the hotel. You a miner?" inquired Nathan naively.

"Not by a long shot. What's your name?" Nathan told him. "Well, truth to say, Nathan Smith, I was a practicing attorney hereabouts some dozen years ago. San Francisco was a bit wilder, a lot more open, and only had one thing on its mind then. Still does near as I can tell. Gold."

Gregg joined him on the opposite end of the cot taking care not to sit down too fast for fear the legs might give way.

"Allow me to tell you a story," he began. Gregg proceeded to explain that he had been a successful attorney in San Francisco in 1850. He and a partner had a practice directly across the street from the Hotel Niantic. California would enter the union in September, but until that time, Territorial status was granted the infant state. Civil law was under the jurisdiction of the community while capital crimes were the province of the Federal Marshal. Gregg said he practiced civil law and divorce law, the latter a controversial issue at the time.

One of Gregg's clients was a prospector named Hale who came to him with the desire to buy half a section of land outside town. Hale had succeeded in making his fortune in the gold country and wanted to build a mansion on the property. Though well versed in the ways of prospecting, Hale was not particularly savvy when it came to grant deeds. He hired Gregg to hold the purchase money, research the title and prepare the documents which would conclude the transaction.

The price was not an insubstantial sum, and Hale led Gregg to believe he had plenty more gold salted away that he had allocated to the building of his castle.

"He would a whole lot rather trust a shyster lawyer than a thieving banker any day," Gregg told Nathan as he drained his cup a second time. Nathan winced at the reference to his own profession but said nothing.

"The night before the transaction was to be completed, I come back to the office late. I had just had dinner with Hale at Tadich where we discussed some of the finer points of the transaction. I wanted to be sure everything was in order for the early morning meeting with the seller. I went to my second floor office and realized someone was in the back room where our safe was. A wick was flickering which might indicate someone had legitimate business in there, but I took care to get my pistol ready just in case. I kept a .44 in my desk drawer."

Gregg stood and poured a third drink for himself. Nathan's metal cup remained untouched, but it received an additional dram from the generous storyteller.

"I was relieved to see it was just my partner, not a thief. Then I saw the open safe. It was empty and his satchel lay on the floor. I'd caught him in the act of absconding with Hale's money. He didn't see my gun, but he knew I wasn't going to allow him to run out like that. He rushed me and I raised my hand to protect myself. The pistol fired. Just like that, he fell away, dead at my feet."

Gregg took a sip and sighed. He seemed genuinely affected by the telling of his own macabre tale and when he sat down again he looked incredibly tired.

"I was going to report the accident immediately when I remembered the gold on the floor. I realized it was a perfect opportunity to take advantage of what looked like a robbery. There was an out building being rebuilt which workmen had removed next to the hotel. The fill was soft and tools were lying around so I threw the gun into the satchel, ran across the street and buried everything."

"That's what you're looking for," Nathan nodded sagely. "An old shit house."

"I don't think of it quite like that, sonny," the man said indignantly. He took a sip before he continued. "I went to my office as usual the next morning, discovered the crime and called the Sheriff. It worked out just as I'd planned. I told them I'd been to dinner with Hale and expected him to back up my alibi. Funny thing was, they bought that part of the story completely, never did associate me with my partner's murder."

Nathan grew uncomfortable with what, to him, had become a complex yarn of murder and deceit. However, his curiosity kept him perched on the cot, hands wrapped around the cup full of whiskey.

"But why now? Why didn't you get the gold a long time ago and skedaddle?"

"Because I've been in a Federal prison for more than ten years," was the matter-of-fact reply. "I was convicted of murdering Hale," the man said. He paused in his narrative to allow this fact to fully sink in on his listener.

The bank clerk remained silent. What he heard suddenly made no sense. Gregg correctly took the silence to mean he should clarify his statement.

"Hale was robbed and killed right after I left him that night. Since I was the last one seen with him they naturally come after me. The fool bragged to everyone about how much gold he'd found. Anybody could of robbed and killed him. When they hit him, his skull cracked. Just my luck."

The clerk had a sickening feeling this man with the long hair and strange story might be dangerous. How had it happened that he, a simple bank clerk, was awake at midnight drinking distilled spirits and sitting on the side of a bed in idle conversation with a convicted murderer? Nathan began to worry his fear might be obvious and translate itself into something that would anger the ex-convict. He almost dropped his drink as the man continued.

"They asked me where I went after dinner with Hale that night and I couldn't very well explain I was at that moment shooting my business partner, could I?"

"Why you telling me this?"

"I'm telling you all this so's you'll help me. I'm not up to this kind o' work, boy. That prison took a lot more out of me than I thought. Hell, I'm only forty-three and I feel like I'm ninety." It was certainly true Gregg looked much older than he said he was. His face was drawn and thin in the cool light. A shiver shook him like a leaf and he began to cough.

"I been in there shoveling and piling dirt around me for hours and I feel all wore out. I almost hoped someone would catch me at it just like you done. I wanted a partner, y'see." He assumed a conspiratorial air and winked at the frightened bank clerk. "I'll share the whole thing with you. Split half and half. What do you say?"

Nathan considered the question. "Why me?" he finally asked.

"Just lucky, I guess. Besides, you can take it. You're young. You look fit." Nathan found his hand turned palm up in the coarse grasp of the other man. "I admit your hands could do with a bit of strengthenin', but there won't be much work to it. I know exactly where to dig. Trust me."

"I have a job. I gotta work in the morning," Nathan responded. Yet even he thought the excuse sounded weak in light of the promise of finding a fortune in gold coins. "Besides, they come down here all the time, the maids and the others, who'll find us out. How do we cover our work?"

He felt himself being drawn into the scheme against his better judgment. The conflict was between his secure position with monthly pay and a desire to get what so many of the bank's customers had found in the hills.

Nathan Smith had grown certain that any gold in the mountains was an unapproachable dream for him. Unless he undertook to dramatically change his fortunes, he was doomed to remain behind a counter taking the precious metal in but crediting it to other people's accounts, never his own.

"You rent a room down here, don't you?" The clerk nodded. "With a lock on the door? Then listen to me."

Walter Gregg guaranteed Nathan that the exact area to dig in was the room where he had been discovered. Fortunately, that was a little-used storage area with small possibility of being caught if they worked only at night.

"I paced it off myself a thousand times in my cell. Couldn't be off by more'n a couple of feet. The office I had was right across the street in that brick building as is now used for a warehouse. It's still standing today. Now you mark my words, young Nathan Smith. Work with me and you'll be a rich man tomorrow."

Nathan could not let the lure of sharing a pile of gold slip away. He agreed to assist in the search after close of business that day. Back in his room as he fell asleep, Nathan was soothed by the thought that at last he would be a wealthy man.

§

"You sure you counted exactly how many feet from the street we should be digging?"

Nathan was worn out. He leaned on his shovel and looked up at the man with long yellow hair who promised riches in the next few inches of digging.

"Paced it myself. No doubt about it. But you set a while and I'll think it through again in my mind." Gregg sat back on his haunches and assumed a thoughtful position. Presently he opened his eyes. "Yep. Right here. Or just about right here exactly. No way I could be wrong about this. Thought it over so much I walked it hundreds of times in that prison. The gold's in this room."

Nathan crawled out of his hole and hefted a rope with two buckets, one on each end, over his shoulders. Laboriously, he carried this weight to his room at the end of the hallway. He opened the door with his foot, carried the harness in and dropped to his knees.

The room was filled with dirt. His bed was nearly covered and the armoire was sealed by the weight of earth in front of it. He dumped his load and lumbered back into the storage area where Gregg hunkered over the dig. Nathan fell rather than jumped back into the hole.

"So that's your game," a familiar voice said from the dark behind them.

The Manager stood arms folded across his chest, framed in the light of the doorway. There was no way of knowing how long he had stood hidden there before announcing his presence.

Nathan gulped in a deep breath and slowly sank to his knees. Discovered, he had no strength to continue. In a way, he was pleased with the revelation. Now he could sleep again. His cohort, however, looked up with a smile at the newcomer.

"Well, sir. How are you this wonderful evening?" Gregg asked jovially. "Glad you could join us. Mind if I tell you a story?"

The Manager listened intently while Nathan dozed on the cot in Gregg's small room. When the story was complete, the Manager asked a question Nathan had failed to ask.

"How much is buried here?"

"Near ten thousand. In small eagles," the ex-convict responded. "Hale kept a heavy sack, believe me. In a gingham satchel with a leather handle. Real neat an' tidy."

"I'm not so sure I believe you. But that fool boy on the bed sure does." There was silence except for Nathan's snoring. "Prove it to me."

"Gladly." The convict rummaged around in the bag he brought with him to the hotel. He produced a piece of paper which he handed to the Manager. It was a pardon from the U. S. penitentiary at Wichita signed two months previous.

"That says you were in prison. It don't exactly say you know where there's gold buried," the Manager said after he read for a moment.

"How about this, then?" Gregg placed a newspaper clipping in the manager's hands. The clipping was dated in the upper corner in pen, ten years previous. Again there was silence as the Manager read to himself.

"This says you did a killin', and it says some gold is missin', but it don't say you know where that gold is."

"For that you will need to believe. And believe firmly that I do, indeed, know where there is gold. Buried here, in this room or perhaps in the hallway area, but here in this hotel basement no doubt."

The Manager was silent long enough to come to a decision. He looked at the stranger with the cold eye of a calculating business man.

"Let's say I help you find this treasure." He studied the exhausted form lying on the cot. "You already got one partner. And I'd make a third."

"There's enough for all of us," the long-haired sallow-skin man replied. "Ten thousand's a lot of money. Why, it'll buy each of us a lifetime of pleasure. No need for him to work in a bank or you behind a desk. Believe me, there's plenty to go around and I can speak for the boy because he's just a boy and I cut him in so I can cut his share down to fit you in."

The Manager thought carefully before he replied. "Tell you what we can do." He proceeded to outline his own plan of excavation.

Nathan no longer carried the dirt to his room. There was no space left to put any more. Instead, the earth was shoveled onto a hand cart with a large front wheel and levered up the basement steps while one man pushed from behind and two stood on each side to balance.

The dirt was carried outside and spread on the back lot with care being taken to apply it evenly on the surrounding topsoil. Its color, however, was lighter in comparison and did not blend well at all. For this and other reasons, they feared discovery every day and continued to work only at night, as silently as possible so they would not disturb tenants sleeping on the floors above. They rested when the sun rose.

After the first night of toil, with the Manager looking on, the old man and Nathan both complained about being the only ones doing any work. The Manager agreed to pay for two laborer's wages until such time as the gold was actually found and then he would be reimbursed out of the proceeds. Nathan agreed to cut the Manager in as a partner. Although this resulted in a smaller share of the pie all around, Nathan soon considered it a bargain and well worth his while, to give up part of his future fortune for freedom from digging in the present.

Two Chinese laborers were hired to fill the cart and trundle it upstairs while the Manager supervised. The Chinese were hired only after the Manager was satisfied they did not speak English beyond "yes" and "no." This insured they would not talk about the clandestine project except among themselves and they were never told why the dig was taking place. Nathan and the old man shared the work in the hole and assisted in pushing the wheelbarrow up the stairs.

At first the Chinese were not allowed to work in the hole for fear the sack of gold would be struck by one of their shovels. None of the three partners felt much like sharing the payoff with anyone else. As time went on, the two Chinese took on more of the digging as the area of excavation expanded to other parts of the basement.

By the fifth night, the entire area inside the fireman's room was dug out right up to its thin walls. Fortunately, they were not load bearing. Completely undermined, the wood partitions hung by square nails from the ceiling without support from below.

Come the morning and the brickwork foundation leaked sunlight. Work was called off for the day. The Chinese laborers exited under the watchful eye of the Manager. He checked the upstairs foyer and signaled when it was clear for them to depart unobserved. Nathan gave them each a ten cent piece of silver and a shove to make them break for the door.

The three men now ate all their meals together because they feared allowing one another out of sight. They were afraid one or both of the "partners" might sneak back into the cellar and miraculously find the satchel without them.

"Why those three thick as thieves all of a sudden, I wonder?" asked Miss Betty to herself as she ladled grits into their bowls for breakfast. "That manager, he don't like nobody no-way. And that Nathan, he ain't had a friend since he got here. Why you 'spect they cotton to that grizzly ol' man anyhow?" She scooped mounds of white mush into the common bowl for each table and walked on. The substance was eagerly grabbed up by rows of men who fought each other for a share. Pitchers of milk and tubs of butter were emptied into the hot white cereal.

The rest of the meal consisted of toast and coffee, one egg and one rasher of bacon per guest. Out of the corner of her eye the fat woman kept as careful a watch on the three at a table by themselves as she usually kept on how much anyone was served. In order to have an excuse to overhear their discussion, she wandered in their direction carrying a plate of sourdough bread.

"Yah, I could be wrong, but I know I'm not. At least not by the length of a stride," the newest guest said through his crooked, loose teeth. She thought how the mush was probably all he could eat anyway. The rest of his teeth were ready to fall out of his head or stick to the bread if he took a bite.

"Maybe we gotta dig deeper, that's all." said the clerk as he wolfed down his egg and bacon. He saw Miss Betty with the plate of sourdough and beckoned her over. The men helped themselves to several pieces which, surprisingly, the cook did not prevent them from taking. Ordinarily, she thwacked the back of your hand with a wood spoon if you took more than one piece.

"Deeper don't make no sense," the Manager responded. Then he noticed the bulky woman within earshot and made a motion which all three heeded immediately. She got no more information for her painful generosity that day.

Reluctantly and with considerable force of will power, the clerk went to his day job at the bank. In his absence, the Manager and the ex-convict remained above ground. All three agreed it was too suspicious to work during the day. The old man slept on the couch in the front lobby, his hat pulled over his eyes which did cause some gossip and much curiosity among the rest of the staff. The Manager made no attempt to shoo him away as had been his policy with others in the past. Instead, it appeared almost as if the Manager himself dozed at his seat behind the desk, although he sat up smartly every time someone appeared at the counter.

The Manager made sure no one but the three partners and two Chinese workers entered the basement. Night or day, the area was closed as far as the rest of the world was concerned. He posted himself at the top of the stairs during off hours and redirected the kitchen help and maids when they started down. If there was something they absolutely had to have, he went to fetch it himself. If they could be sent to the vegetable market or another merchant instead of the basement, he made that an option they could not refuse.

Once, when the Manager's back was turned, the old Indian woman began to wander down the steps. She was headed off by a frantic Gregg who must have been sleeping with one eye open. He leaped from the couch and ran past her on the stairwell where he waved his arms like a windmill and generally threw a fit in front of her. She became convinced he was crazy and made the sign of the cross as she backed up the stairs, then turned around and went to attend some other task.

§

The area of search widened. Nearly half the space below grade from the front of the building to the rear on the side bordering Clay Street was converted to a giant hole in the ground. Yet nothing had been found and everyone, with the exception of the paid help, was growing impatient. Nathan had not been to work at the bank for two days; he was simply too worn out. He slept on the cot while the others excavated, took his turn when the Manager or the ex-convict wanted to lie down. When he closed his eyes, sleep overwhelmed Nathan quickly. The Manager was the only one who never picked up a shovel but he, too, suffered from the long hours in the dim light. During the night, his duty included guarding the top of the stairs from errant travelers.

The eighth day dawned with no gold found.

The Manager abandoned his watch and went to assist in closing down operations for the day. Miss Betty, who was usually the first at work in the morning, had been waiting patiently in the kitchen, the door cracked an inch and her eye glued to the reflection in the mirror she had carefully hung the day before at a specific angle to catch the action. When the Manager disappeared, she took that opportunity to creak down the stairs behind him and investigate.

Gregg and the two Chinese were at the far end of the building, too engrossed in hauling up the last barrow full of dirt to realize anything was amiss. The Manager was walking toward them to explain that the sun had risen, had just mentioned this to a weary Nathan whom he passed along the way, when Nathan looked up and was startled to see Miss Betty standing like a fat angel on the edge of his grave.

Her meaty hands rested on even meatier hips above the sweating, soul weary bank teller. He nearly fainted with exhaustion and fright when he recognized her. Her glance had been known to wilt strong men and he turned sheepish under her stern gaze. He put his shovel down and reached up for a helping hand. She hauled him out of the pit as if he were a Raggedy Andy doll.

"You want to hear a story, Miss Betty?" he asked in a hoarse voice. The labor had taken its toll and he barely clung to consciousness as he asked this question.

"It better be a good one, boy," she said with arms folded. "And make it quick. I got food to prepare."

Ultimately, Miss Betty became a fourth partner. In exchange, she allowed them to be served large quantities of food at both meals and supplied them with additional nourishment while they worked nights. Furthermore, she agreed to tell no one about the excavation in the basement and stopped sending her crew down there which freed up more time for the men to rest during the day.

§

"I have to go back to work," an exhausted Nathan said as he dropped into the cot in Gregg's room.

"Then on yer feet, boy," responded the old man. "We only have another yard to dig 'til we find the gold."

"I didn't mean back to digging. I have to earn a living." He was losing faith the satchel was within a city block, let alone a few feet. "They haven't seen me at the bank all week. I'll lose my job if I don't show up tomorrow." He was growing despondent.

Gregg studied a piece of paper. Nathan had enough strength to lift himself on one elbow and look over the old man's shoulder. It was a pencil diagram of a street labeled Sansome and clearly drawn was the intersection where the Niantic Hotel stood.

However, the drawing was hopelessly out of date. It showed empty lots where buildings now stood and clearly sketched at the inside corner where the streets met was the crude drawing of a boat. Next to that were the words "The Schooner *Niantic*."

The bank clerk's suspicions were aroused.

"You tol' me you knew exactly where the gold was buried, like the back of your hand. Walked it in your cell so you knew it perfect," Nathan said with an accusatory tone in his voice. "Why you need a map to find it anyhow?"

Gregg quickly folded the paper. He'd been sure Nathan was asleep or too tired to be inquisitive enough to look beyond the cot. He cursed himself for being so presumptuous.

"Give me that!" Nathan shouted as he reached for the scrap of paper. He wrested it from the old man who could hardly have kept it from him if he tried. Even in Nathan's weakened condition he was stronger than the ex-convict on a good day.

"It's just a description to where the gold is buried, I swear."

True, it appeared to be nothing more, Nathan realized. But his life was being measured out based on the scratches he found here, on this paper, and if there was anything to be gleaned from it, now was the time.

"What I don't understand, old man, is how you can be so sure how far from this damn boat you was when you buried that sack! The hull ain't marked here in the ground and you just be guessing you're within the area where it used to be. I mean, you don't even know where the boat was originally! You can't know where the outhouse was if you don't know where the boat was."

"Boat?" the ex-convict asked sheepishly. "What boat you talkin' 'bout boy?"

Nathan became incensed. He rose from his bed and picked up the nearest heavy object which happened to be the old man's nearly empty whiskey bottle. He held it by the neck in his cocked arm and aimed it directly at Gregg's head. With his free hand he grabbed the old man around the throat and began to squeeze. His muscles had, indeed, hardened to his work and the neck seemed quite frail.

"You mean to tell me you don't know this here hotel used to be a boat? A three-masted schooner?" He waved the bottle menacingly near the frail skull.

"Hotel," choked the old man. "It was a goddam hotel. All I ever hear tell of was it's a goddam hotel."

The younger man loosed his grasp on the throat. "There's a sign on the door out front tells the tale of how this place was once a boat came round the Horn and was burned to the ground in the fire of '51. Didn't you read that the first day you was here and every day since?"

There was no response. Nathan waved the map under the other's eyes and directed the head by its chin. "Read that," Nathan said with pinched lips. "Read that line right there and read it to me out loud."

The old man made a stab at it. "It says 'The Hotel Niantic.' And it counts out some numbers, how many paces to where the gold is buried."

Astonished, the clerk dropped his arms to his sides, hands holding the paper and the bottle. "You ain't no damn lawyer," he said in utter amazement. "You can't even read." He let go the paper and the bottle as both hands went to the neck of his erstwhile partner. "There is no gold, is there old man!" he shouted. Nathan was exploding with rare anger. "Tell me there is no gold! I want you to tell the truth old man. Because I am ready to kill you!"

The thin man shook in Nathan's grasp like a flag in the wind. He was very nearly being choked to death, but was able to respond to Nathan's words.

"There is gold, son, I swear it," he whispered through his nearly closed windpipe. "'Cept I lied cuz I ain't the one what buried it here."

Nathan was incredulous. He let go the throat and stared at his own hands. The fact he was capable of throttling someone was just sinking into his mind. "There is gold but you didn't bury it?" he asked stunned.

"Well, there probably is gold, lad. But I don't exactly know where, that I'll admit to ye."

"Then who are you? You ain't a lawyer, that's for sure. Are you Walter Gregg? Or are you an imposter there too?"

"Not perzackly Walter Gregg, no," the old man said looking down at his feet. "I admit that too. But close enough. Close enough so's I know there's gold buried here and I aim to find it," the ex-convict replied as he waved an arm toward the environs. Nathan was dumbfounded. For a moment he was at a loss for words and stood stunned.

"Then just who are you if you're not Walter Gregg?" the young man asked.

"I was his cellmate," the convict responded with dignity returning to his voice. "In the prison at Wichita. For seven years. It's his story right enough I tol' you. 'Bout how he and his partner parted company and he went to jail for the killin' of Hale. And he tol' me about the gold many and many a time as he walked back and forth in our cell for all them years."

Nathan could do nothing but stand there exhausted.

"He told me exactly where he buried the gold. I'm sure he did. And he drew up this map for me just before the end came and said I should go to California and get it when he was gone. Over and over as he walked in the cell he talked about the hotel, the Niantic Hotel. Right up to the time he died of pneumonia, he kept telling me he'd buried ten thousand dollars in gold here and I come to claim it."

Nathan said nothing. Finally the old man broke the silence. "We still partners? Even if I ain't who I said I was, hit's still there like I tol' you. An' hit's still worth digging up, ain't it? We still partners?"

Nathan slumped where he stood. It was too much for him to bear, too much heartbreak to learn he was dirt poor again. He wanted to cry.

The old man tugged at Nathan's sleeve, insistent. "I cain't do it all by myself, y'know. I needs you, Nathan." He looked despairingly into the younger man's eyes. "We still partners?"

Nathan lay back and would have gone right to sleep if tears had not begun to stream down his cheek. The canvas cot felt luxuriant compared to the bed he had buried in his haste to become wealthy.

The last thing he remembered thinking was that he had to get up early in the morning to be at work on time. Monday morning would be the start of a long week.

CHAPTER ELEVEN

THE MORNING MEETING

H.J. Boesk did not take the news well. "A MILLION dollars! That asshole asked for a MILLION to get off the site?" He was incredulous. He was incensed.

Winton was no happier than his boss. He realized he was caught up in someone else's pipe dream and it looked as if he were being used as tobacco.

Rather than take the bad news back to Boesk immediately, Chirup took the problem home and slept on it. To cover his ass, before turning out the lights, he called H. J.'s voice mail and left a verbal description of the meeting with Worthy. The failed negotiations continued to nag Winton even in his sleep. The entire night his dreams were filled with carnival-like street hawkers offering to sell everything from broken records to shredded pieces of paper all for the same price: a cool million.

At 5:30 a.m. he received an angry wake-up call from the boss himself. "Chirup, you were authorized to go as high as forty-five thousand. What happened?"

"I did my best to feel him out," he said defensively. "I started lower than that," he did not want to tell Boesk exactly how much lower, "but I raised it to 30k right away. He refused to even discuss our offer. That's when he told me what it would take to get him off the site." As an after thought, he mentioned the bird analogy. "Said we were offering him crumbs like a bird."

Boesk said nothing, hung up without a polite goodbye. He decided he had a major problem on his hands. He began making phone calls, arranging to meet with everyone involved in the project. He called for a meeting in his penthouse office at nine with representatives of the bank, the anchor tenant, the contractor and the architectural firm.

The room held six men, each with a strong interest in seeing a successful conclusion to the impasse. Beside Boesk and notable by his absence should have stood the architect, Sean Davidson, who had been hospitalized. His surrogate was Tom Arno, a junior member of the firm. Two other men represented corporations created by Boesk for the project. These were holding companies which owed their existence to his attempt at circumventing federal government anti-trust laws.

The fifth man was Martin Hardin. His was a dual position as a member of the Board of Directors for the Boesk Corporation and as Vice President of Development for a large West Coast bank. Hardin sat as a member of the BOD at Boesk's behest. It was also Hardin's duty to see that favorable loans were available to the limited partnerships created to build the project. However, Hardin could do nothing once the funds were in place. They began to draw interest from the moment they were called upon to pay the bills and a substantial amount had already been committed to the next portion of the project.

Winton Chirup was privy to this meeting although his position with the firm had been terminated at 5:35 a.m., immediately after speaking with Boesk. He had not been informed of this, would, in fact, be the last to learn of the decision. Boesk thought Chirup might at least be useful for part of the day.

"Forty-five thousand is not crumbs, Winton," the financier began. "You and I may not see it as much, but crumbs it is not. I may have dropped that much at the Yacht Club in lunches last year, but it was money well spent. And I didn't have ingrates like that shithead telling me it was peanuts!" Boesk fell silent. No one wanted to disturb his thoughts. He stood pensively at the window, staring into the cavernous hole at his feet. Barely visible at this distance was a human figure, moving with the deliberate pace of a tortoise relatively in the center of the excavation.

"Anybody seen my thirty-ought lyin'round?" Boesk said at last.

"Wait a minute, Aitch-Jay," said Hardin. "You can't just pluck him off like a pigeon on a fence. Not here, anyway."

"Whyzat?" H. J. asked, one eye squinted, his left index finger crooked as if on a trigger, his right hand holding the stock of an imaginary rifle.

His aim was almost straight down, directly into the construction project below them.

"Because it's within the city goddam limits, for one thing! And for another, this steel glass wall won't goddam open. Third place, we're too high up. You'd have to be at ground level because none of the windows open from the fourth floor through the forty-ninth floor. You'd have to stand outside or blow a hole in your own goddam executive suites!"

"Stand outside the building, you say?" and H. J.'s gaze turned toward Hardin. It dawned on Hardin just what that look in Boesk's eye might imply.

"Now wait a minute, boss. I am NOT going out on the HVAC system of the 48th floor and hang like a bat. Especially not to shoot someone just because he's a pain in your backside."

"Not you, then maybe we can find someone else to do the job for us." When Hardin's eyes widened to the size of dinner plates and the others gasped audibly at the suggestion, Boesk backed down. "Just kidding." He was not the type to joke about business, however, and there was doubt among those gathered in the room it had been a lighthearted comment.

"If I may offer an observation." It was Hardin.

"We're interested in anything anyone has to say," Boesk replied. "Let's hear it."

"After today, this guy only has three more days he can delay us, right? The injunction expires, then we can evict, right? So I say wait and see."

"That was my initial reaction, too," Boesk said. "Chirup here disagreed." Boesk frowned in Winton's direction. "It would still be a good position to take in light of the fact that this Worthy fellow does not seem real interested in calling in the media. Which we first feared. Else he would have done so by now. Too, we must still consider the possibility that Tarera will extend the injunction indefinitely. That is why I come full circle on the issue and say we need to pay this fellow to leave. Frankly, I think he's counting on us to buy him out. All of which is in keeping with the profile we worked up for his dossier."

Boesk held a folder in the air with an 8 x 10 glossy photo of Don Worthy on its cover. The face was contorted in a wink.

"Hardin's people were able to come up with this. Martin, you can take over from here," Boesk said passing him the folder.

"Thank you, sir." Hardin held the 8 x 10 up for everyone to see. He turned to a summary page in the folder. "My people were able to gather this information overnight, so it's really kind of incomplete." He sounded as if he was excusing himself and his staff. Actually, he was fishing for compliments. "I got the call about six last night, y'know." He waited as if anticipating applause or a pat on the back. Neither came and he continued. "Anyway, the picture that emerges is not pretty. It seems we are dealing with a low-life, very nearly a petty thief, who lives by selling almost anything he can get his hands on at local flea markets. Name is Donald X. Worthy. No one we talked with knew what his middle name is, what the X stands for."

A pause in this speech allowed Boesk to interject, "Maybe it's like the G in Maynard G. Krebs."

Silence as everyone except Arno said, "You mean the character in the fifties tee vee series Dobie Gillis?"

"Well," asked Hardin. "What did the G stand for?"

"Walter."

No one knew how to react to this. There was a beat as the answer was mulled over. Hardin took up the slack and continued his recitation.

"This guy Worthy is always late on his rent, at least a week, sometimes more, has not filed income taxes since his discharge from the Navy nearly twenty years ago and he did not distinguish himself there either. Because he has not filed a 1040 since his discharge, the IRS was interested in learning why we were asking about him. They thought he was dead. He shares a four bedroom flat on Waller in the Haight with three roommates and because he's the master tenant, he pays nothing. He charges the others enough to cover the rent, his groceries and fund his lifestyle. He's a pot head, who thinks he's an artist. We located his dealer. And we talked with his landlord. Worthy lives in a rent controlled apartment which his landlord would love to see him vacate. He has no steady girlfriend, but we have located a former live-in lover who still does him favors. That's how he got his equipment into the pit over the weekend: she drove him. This guy Worthy has no bank account we could find. He has few assets, certainly nothing you or I would consider valuable. He's no intellectual giant though he has been known to describe himself as a part-time deep thinker. In short, we have a societal misfit on our hands. He fits the psychographic morphology of a 'Survivor,' though he is not as old as many in that group and attends first run movies rather than wait for the video. He smokes heavily."

Hardin ended his speech.

"You've proven to me he's greedy," Tom Arno representing Davidson's architectural firm spoke for the first time. "We knew that yesterday. And we were pretty sure he was the type to break the law with impunity. But can you tell us what it's going to take to get him out of there? Besides a million bucks?"

Hardin rotated his body in order to look into the eyes of each man before speaking again. He lay the folder on the table with the picture of Worthy on it face up. "Raise our price," he said calmly. "Obviously the man has one. It is merely a matter of finding it."

"And what's wrong with waiting him out?" asked Arno.

"That should be obvious," said Chirup. "Judge Tarera. I got a chance to discuss her with our legal people late yesterday afternoon. She does not and I mean NOT like the project and will do anything to stop it. She also blames the Boesk Corporation for the recent reversal of the public's attitude toward commercial projects. She's about as no-growth as they come. She will certainly accept any argument from Worthy's attorney to put a hold on construction. If you wanted my bet, I'd lay odds that on Friday that Hearing to Show Cause is going to go against us. The injunction will be extended."

Boesk almost said, "What do you mean us?" but thought better about making the wise crack. Instead, he backed Winton's judgment. "And I must grudgingly concur," said H. J. "Therefore I recommend we extend an offer through this man's attorney to ninety thousand. The source of these funds shall be split equally between the four corporations represented here today. Can I have your agreement on that? Mr. Arno you may have to confer with Davidson, I understand. You have two hours to secure his approval. Otherwise, anyone disagree?"

Chirup swallowed silently. He cringed at the thought that he had only offered a few thousand to the squatter, then thirty, but now the return bid was going to be nearly a hundred. None argued with Boesk's request.

"Good. Meeting adjourned. Arno, I want you to stay here and we can work out how you will make the offer. Gentlemen, good day."

With that, H. J. Boesk turned his back to watch the fog burn off the early morning air of San Francisco.

Winton Chirup knew he had not been shown in a favorable light by this morning's proceedings, but he was totally unprepared to be handed his walking papers by Mrs. Jacobs as soon as he left the conference room. He was not allowed to return to his office to pick up any personal items.

"You will not clear your desk," she told him. "Everything will be sent to you. And I need your card key," she held out her hand to receive the plastic entry card.

§

MacArthur mewled and licked Worthy's face. Don awoke, much against his better judgment.

Tuesday morning. It was as bad as his first full day in the pit. Worthy was not sleeping well on the cot even though conditions were at least as good as the last time he hiked Yosemite.

"I wasn't comfortable then either, if I recall," he grumbled to the cat and reached for a cigarette. He was not going to climb out of the sack until noon if he could help it.

The cat was acting strangely. MacArthur padded over to the dirt path that was the only way in or out and sat almost as if he were a dog on point. The cat made a small crying sound again and ran back to the relative comfort of Worthy's camping gear. He scampered underneath the tent flap.

"What's got into you, boy?" Worthy asked as he inhaled his first drag. He glanced at his watch. 10:30. Still early. He refused to exit the bag. He felt relatively safe in his bedroll, secure in the knowledge that his new landlord could not evict him until Friday. He must remember to call Benny and ask how the extension on the injunction was going.

The gate was open at the top of the excavation site. No one from The Boesk Corporation had bothered him since the late evening visit from the guy in the business suit. The construction crew did not even poke its hard hats over the edge this morning.

Worthy reflected upon the last night's proceedings. He expected another and a better offer within the day. He probably ought to get up and get dressed if he was going to have guests.

He was only half propped up in his mummy bag, not yet consciously arrived at the decision to climb out, when the entrance at the top of the excavation site was breasted by a large vehicle followed by a group of marching people. Two or three more SUV size trucks launched themselves over the rise following the cluster of marchers.

From his position deep in the hole it was difficult to tell if the small army was really in synchronized step, but they appeared so uniformly purposeful they might as well have been. Don's Navy training snapped into focus. He saw heavy equipment on the shoulders of several of the uninvited guests, immediately took it for weaponry. It looked to him from where he lay as if some of the invaders were wearing helmets and carrying anti-tank weapons.

"Jesus Christ, MacArthur," Worthy shouted in dismay. "They sent a company of soldiers with halftracks to haul us away!" He tossed his cigarette and tried to get out of the sack, but could not extricate his legs. In his excitement he had forgotten how nearly impossible it is to move quickly out of a mummy bag.

He was still scurrying to get free when the leading vehicle ground to a halt at the base of the roadway. On its roof was a radar dish aimed directly at him. Gradually, the dish rotated until it was pointed at the sky. Then the people in back of the vehicle came around to within ear-shot. Worthy overheard the clipped conversation.

"Shit. The guy's not out of bed yet. See if you can find the boat. Can't show him in his underwear."

Don stood wearing only boxer shorts. He had never felt so naked. Even getting locked out of Christine's house in his bathrobe had been less embarrassing. A hand holding a microphone was thrust in his face and a familiar voice introduced the speaker.

"Willie Van Amburg, Mr. Worthy, Channel 3 News. How are you today? I see you haven't had time to freshen up. However, we're on a tight schedule so if you could get your drawers on, we can get on with the interview."

The face was so familiar Worthy at first thought the guy was his next door neighbor or a best friend he had not seen in years. And the voice. It sounded like someone he talked to all the time.

Worthy focused on the lapel of Willie's blazer. There was a small red circle with a number in the center. Right. Don snapped his fingers. This was a local newscaster. From one of the national affiliate television stations.

It dawned on Don he might at that very moment be staring knock-kneed into the homes of millions of people. He froze. Then he crossed his hands in front of his groin in a ridiculous attempt to cover himself.

A woman's voice stifled a laugh. Several of the intruders gathered around him. Others, the men wearing cameras on their shoulders, wandered about in Worthy's parlor, kitchen and the dining room of his new home.

MacArthur disappeared completely.

"Don't worry, Mr. Worthy," a beautiful young Asian woman with round almond eyes and a pleasant smile chuckled and stuck another microphone in his face. It was a reflex action on her part. "We have enough sense of responsibility to show your best profile," she quipped. "But do hurry and get dressed, please."

At least fifteen people gathered in the small area Don had come to think of as his bedroom. Three among them were women. An over-whelming sense of super modesty came upon him. Turning his back, he stuck one leg into his pants, then the other, zipped his fly and buckled his belt with his back turned. They gave him a chance to arrange his hair. He found a tee shirt in a sack and pulled it over his head. Then he took a tube of toothpaste from his Dopp kit and rubbed a finger-full over his teeth washing it out with water from his canteen. He stuck a cigarette between his lips, lighted it and took a long pull.

"Where did you all come from," he finally had the temerity to ask. The audience of news people stared at him like he was the dumbest question since Groucho asked a contestant, "Who is buried in Grant's tomb?"

"From our places of employment, Mr. Worthy," said a less than affable fat guy with button eyes and a graying Hitler moustache.

"I guess what I meant," Worthy tried again lamely, "is why are you here and what do you want?"

"Mister Worthy," a microphone was nearly pushed down his throat and a blond woman with swimmingly beautiful blue eyes loomed into his vision. "We are here because of your find. The boat you uncovered over the weekend is of interest to our viewers. Can you tell us what you discovered in the hulk?"

It was a direct question and he answered without thinking. "An old boot and a box of square nails."

"You must be joking," said a black woman with a perfect figure. She also used her microphone like a weapon held up close under his nose. Worthy found time to marvel at the fact he was surrounded by so many beautiful ladies and some rather unctuous men.

"What's wrong with this guy?" asked a beefy fellow whose head was stuck behind a shoulder camera. Bundled in a flack jacket, a belt of batteries around his waist like rifle cartridges, wires dangling from ears and mouth, he looked more like an extra terrestrial creature than a cameraman. No wonder Don's first reaction was to fear an armed invasion.

"Mister Worthy," questioned a peremptory voice that must have belonged to the dean of announcing it was so crisp and clean. "Are we to believe you have brought us down here to learn you discovered nothing in the hold of the Gold Rush ship you are excavating?"

"Now just a damn minute!" Worthy was suddenly in charge of his own interview, thank you very much. "I didn't invite any of you down here and I don't know who did."

"Cut that, Elmo," said a stern voice. "Willie, you aren't going to use that are you?"

The news people were suddenly individually checking their equipment, talking the interview over between themselves, each concerned with some small aspect of their job, none looking at or talking directly to Worthy. With the exception of a silver haired fellow who kept staring directly at him, Don could have been a flea on Mac's belly, he was that important.

"Listen, Worthy," the white haired man turned to him and said patiently. "We are not going to trudge back up that steep incline without a story. Now, you arranged this little palaver and you ought to consider the consequences of not giving us what we want. A little information is all we are asking. Something which we can show our viewers." Icily, he concluded: "You can co-operate on that, can't you?"

"Yah, well I have a couple of questions for you. The biggest question I have is how you all got here? Today. All at the same time. I didn't call you. So who did? Can you answer that?"

There were mumbled jibes from a few of the news people. "What's he talking about?" asked one interviewer. "Can you beat that?" another complained. "Calls us in and then won't talk. I hope the next guy — What's he got? Roller skate brakes? — Hope he's worth a few feet of tape. Compared to this joker we ought to be doing parachute jumps."

Don was getting angry. "I had nothing to do with calling you here. Why do you keep saying I called you?"

One man fumbled a piece of paper from his breast pocket. He opened it and read the assignment. "Tip says there's a guy named Worthy who found a sunken treasure ship on a construction site in town and we ought to visit him. Press conference called for ten thirty. Unsigned." He nodded toward a man carrying more gear than the guy with the camera. "Hamilton, call City Desk and find out who made the call to us. Thanks."

There was a moment's delay during which two people with hand held pad and paper tried to nudge their way into the area where Worthy stood. They were rebuffed in their attempts by all the electronic media people. Eventually, they settled for positions outside the throng but within hearing distance if Worthy spoke loudly.

"Stayton was on duty last night," Hamilton finally responded. "Call came in at about eleven. His notes say the caller was a woman. She phoned our station, the competition, then the guys across the bay, four radio stations, three daily newspapers, a weekly, a monthly and two tabloids. She tried to get a New York and a Chicago paper to return her calls. I'd say she made the rounds. Reason we're here at all, George, is our people called their people," he pointed at one of the news crews, "to verify and they said yes, they were coming over to cover it." The big man became silent. "You think there's really a story here?" he finally asked.

"I know there's a story. I just don't know where," said the silver haired newsman. "We can't find any boat around here. Care to talk about it Worthy? Off the record, you could say."

"Well," he said reluctantly, "truth is there is a ship buried here. But it burned down during the Gold Rush and all that's left is these two arced ribs in the dirt," he replied. "I intend to dig the rest of the hull out by hand."

The microphone dropped from in front of Don's face and an incredulous voice accused him of grandstanding. "What? You don't have anything to show us? This is Tee Vee, mister, and viewers demand to see things. You mean to tell us you have nothing down here but two charred lines in the dirt? Where's this boat? The masts and the rigging? What kind of a stunt is this anyway, Mister?"

"Well, the deck did give way under the weight of that bull dozer over there," Worthy pointed out the half sunken earth mover. "That's where I found the box of nails."

Again, a woman tried to force back a giggle and control her obvious mirth with the situation. Worthy felt he gained nothing by talking with these people. He was fairly certain who made the phone calls to the media and now he wanted to make a few calls of his own. Was Christine really responsible? Had she called these vultures down from the sky? If she had, he was not pleased. And why would she have gone and done something like that in the first place? What also bothered him was how much they knew about her calls. Each news station seemed to know everything about the others. They had a complete record of whoever was responsible for contacting their editors as well as the competition. It was as if they each knew who was doing the spying and who was being spied upon.

"Do your people know every move the others make?" Worthy asked innocently.

The woman controlling her laughter suddenly snickered. This was the worst thing that could have happened at that moment. Don reacted by blowing up entirely. "That's it! Get the fuck out of here! I don't need your goddam help." He raised his shovel, realized it was folded with the blade tucked away making an ineffectual and rather silly looking weapon. He twisted the base loose and plopped the blade into position as a hacking tool which he menaced at his tormentors. They broke form and began to back away.

An announcer's voice wafted from the edge of the crowd: "We are leaving the site after having visited with the man who found the Gold Rush ship," the short fat fellow said into his microphone. "We will talk to him again after he has successfully excavated his find. Thank you, Mister Worthy."

The news teams backed up until they were at the foot of the dirt ramp. Then they began an orderly retreat, their trucks in reverse backing up the slope with care. They left evidence of their presence behind: spent battery packs, film wrappers and empty canisters, the waste product of the news industry littered the ground where they walked.

Worthy immediately ran to his phone. He tapped out a number and stood pensively. The ringing in his ears was interminable. At last someone answered.

"Hello?" said a male voice.

Worthy hit the end button, closed the phone in disgust. "Damn bitch," he said as he tossed it into the open briefcase. Then he picked up the instrument and phoned Rossen. He recognized the voice of his attorney's secretary. "Pat, this is Don. Worthy. You gotta let me talk with Benny. Is he there?"

"Terribly sorry, Mr. Worthy, but Mr. Rossen's in court this morning. He said I was to take your calls. He said I was to expect to hear from you every hour. But this is the first time you've called today, is that correct? I mean, the service didn't miss any calls before now, did they?"

"No. Yes. I mean, I want Benny to call me as soon as he gets in. I'll be here until he does, believe me."

He said goodbye and closed the clamshell. It rang almost immediately. He opened it, said, "Hello. Benny?"

"Don, I'm so glad I caught you" It was Christine's voice. "Did you just call?"

"Yah, that was me. A man answered so I hung up." He realized how foolish this sounded and wished he had not admitted the jealous truth.

"That was Roger. I thought by now you'd recognize his voice."

Worthy could feel the anger rise in his throat and wanted to stifle the urge to respond, but found himself asking, "Yah, well what was he doing answering your cell phone?"

Christine obviously did not want to explain herself. "It sounds like you're in a tunnel. Must be that hole you're in."

"I'm in a hole in more ways than one. And I want you to tell me the truth. Did you call the newspapers and television people and send them here?" Silence on the other end gave him his answer. "Just tell me why, Christine after I told you to keep it a secret."

"I was so worried about you. I thought you could do with some help. I didn't want you down there all alone. And I got a strange call from a man late last night who asked all kinds of questions about you. I just knew it was the developer checking up on you. So I thought maybe publicity would be a good thing. That way they couldn't just take you out of there without the world finding out. Isn't that the best way?" She was quiet a moment. She added, "And besides, you weren't supposed to find out it was me. How'd you guess anyway?"

"Never mind. The damage is done. I just wanted to clear it up. I gotta go. Got some digging to do. Catch you later."

He hung up. There was an empty feeling, a loneliness in the center of his stomach that was unfamiliar and not very pleasant. He felt suddenly very unsure of himself, insecure about his future. This was not the way Don Worthy liked to feel. He lit a cigarette, picked up his metal prod and walked to what he had come to think of as the stern of the boat. He stuffed the rod into the earth outside the outline of the hull, pretending first that he was stabbing a Voodoo doll of Benny Rossen, then a doll of his landlord, then a doll of Christine.

He conjured up older acquaintances, like the guy who had him thrown in jail. Then he imagined it was the flea market manager who charged ten bucks a stall he stabbed; then the representative of the Boesk Corporation who visited with him last night. In this manner Don worked his way in a pattern around the outline of the boat.

§

Boesk's second offer was made directly to Benny Rossen as he exited the Superior Court during a recess. The case he was in court about was an auto accident with a heavily insured commercial driver. He was certain to get a substantial settlement, unlike the Worthy case which was a pig-in-a-poke as far as Rossen was concerned. He still did not know exactly what motivated Worthy nor why he had agreed to charge the man by the hour at substantially less than his usual rate.

It dawned on Rossen somewhat ruefully that he liked Don Worthy. He was certainly his most interesting client and the most personable, even if he was a character right out of Mama Rossen's worst nightmares. Don Worthy was exactly the kind of boy Benny Rossen was never allowed to be friends with when he was growing up. Worthy was the kid who was always in trouble, who never did his homework, always had a leg in the tree and was about to fall out, who never really got over being an adolescent even in middle age. He was also taking up far too much of Benny's time. Between Sunday and Tuesday morning, he accomplished nearly nothing constructive and had to wing it during this and another court appearance. His clients would suffer unless he put Worthy safely out of his mind.

"Mr. Rossen. May I have a word with you?" The man stood outside the courtroom, partially hidden in the shadow of a marble bust in an alcove. He was leaning against the polished surface, arms folded across the breast of a three piece Brooks Brothers suit. Something odd about the cut or how it was worn nagged at Rossen as he responded to the inquiry.

There was a background din of walking feet and booming voices caused by the reverberations of sound on the walls of the Hall of Justice. For Rossen, it was a reassuring dissonance that always made him feel comfortable. He rested his briefcase on the visitor's bench without releasing the handle. He speculated that the guy could be from the insurance company.

"Is it about the matter under consideration in the court?" he asked reasonably.

"No. Not today's proceedings, that is. My name is Tom Arno and I represent the H. J. Boesk Corporation. I am here on behalf of Mister Boesk himself."

Rossen slapped his brow with his free hand in mock surprise. "Worthy again!" he said aloud. "I swear he's gonna be the death of me. Or my practice." The other man did not appear to be amused. "All right. I have a minute. But I gotta get back inside in ten to talk with my client. What is it?" he asked with evident exasperation.

"We would like to prevent any further inconvenience to you or Mr. Worthy. Frankly, we do not wish to meet him in court. Therefore, we are prepared to offer him a substantial sum of money to quit the property and any claim he may have to the buried boat. Will you listen to our offer and do your best to convey the fact that this is our final proposal to your client?"

"Have you spoken to Worthy about this?" Rossen thought he detected annoyance in the man's demeanor, as if the mention of Worthy's name was a slap in the face.

"I have not. But one of our representatives held a meeting with him last night. Has he not told you?"

"I haven't heard anything from him since he called early yesterday. What has my client discussed with you since then?"

"We offered him a sum of money to vacate the premises. He refused."

"I see," Rossen nodded agreeably. "Well, my client doesn't get up as early as all that, so I expect you haven't talked with him yet today. I intend to discuss this and other matters with him in the near future and will be pleased to take your new offer to him. Care to tell me what that is?"

Arno opened his briefcase and extracted two typed pages. "We shall see to it that ninety thousand dollars is placed in escrow with Worthy named as the beneficiary in exchange for his immediate removal from the job site."

Rossen's heart stopped. Ninety thousand! Holy shit, Worthy really stumbled onto a gold mine after all! In two days they were already being offered a settlement larger than he expected to get from four month's of back and forth with an insurance company.

"And privately, Mr. Rossen, I am in a position to see to it that an additional twenty-five thousand is deposited directly into your bank account if your client is off the property by midnight tonight. We can call that a bonus between you and us."

Benny was in a state of shock. He had the presence of mind to ask for Arno's business card and a number where he might be reached before midnight. "They know how to contact me at this number. If I don't answer, simply give your name and a return phone number. I will get back with you in moments."

Rossen took the card and lifted his briefcase. Dollars were floating before his eyes like a school of fish flopping around in a net. He was elated. All his bad faith in Worthy was erased in an instant, replaced with the burning desire to dig out his cell and call his client.

The auto accident was forgotten as Rossen dialed his office and learned from Pat that Worthy had, indeed, telephoned an hour ago. He got the number from her and punched it into his phone.

The ringing in his ears persisted. It continued ten times. On the eleventh, the phone was picked up by an out of breath Don Worthy whose voice was muffled by the deadening effect the deep hole of the excavation had on sound.

"Don, you must listen to me. I have just learned that Boesk is willing to pay you to leave. By midnight tonight. How does that sound?"

"You met a guy who dresses funny? Wears his pants up around his neck with both a belt and suspenders?" Don asked, describing the highlights of Chirup's attire.

"Different guy," Rossen replied. "Didn't look like that at all. He was named," Rossen glanced at the card in his hand, "Arno. He just left me. I have a number to get back to him with your answer. And let me tell you, Don, it's a great offer. I recommend you take it, no questions asked. Really."

"So what is it this time, Benny? Did they come up to a hundred yet?"

Rossen held the phone away from his face and stared at it with a dumbfounded expression on his face. "How'd you guess? That's almost exactly what they offered. I mean, they offered ninety, but this guy Arno said it was their final final. And you must be off the property by midnight tonight."

"I know they're getting desperate, Benny. That's how come I knew they'd come back with real money."

"What do you say, then? You'll take it, right?"

"Nope."

The phone went dead in Benny's hands.

§

Throughout the day Don drifted from shovel to rod, putting on a show for himself as much as for anyone who might be watching from above. He was careful not to work too hard out of concern that he might break a sweat.

He wished he had enough water for more than a face and hand wash. He had only the ten gallons filled from the tap on Sunday night and he took care not to waste it. Late in the afternoon he knocked off and settled into his bunk to read.

He prepared himself a final meal for the day by re-hydrating a steak and potatoes over his camp stove. He finished clean up just as the sun was going down. He lit the Coleman lamp, pumped the butane valve as hard as he could. It hissed with the release of gas as he fell back onto his sleeping bag with a glass of wine in his hand.

MacArthur lay at the foot of the bedroll completely acclimated to their new living conditions and surroundings. The cat's ears moved suddenly. They were Worthy's first sign of an intruder in the darkness. The animal tensed. Don heard footsteps and reached around behind his head until he had hold of his hunting knife. He could see nothing outside the halo of his glowing lamp.

A face swam into view, lighted with the white glow of the flame.

"Christine!" he said with genuine surprise.

The girl was cloaked by the night, but he could see she wore a light camping parka and carried a large paper bag in her right hand.

"Hello, Don. How are you?" she asked.

He rose from his reclining position and went over to her. He was barefoot, wearing only his pants. His upper torso glistened in the lamp light.

"I can't complain. 'Cept maybe for the lack of indoor plumbing. Running water. That sort of thing."

"So this is your new place." She scuttled around him and moved toward the card table on which the lamp rested. Glancing at the night sky, she remarked, "Roomy. I like it."

"Yah. Glad you could drop by. But," he chose his words carefully, "care to tell me what's up? I mean, why you're here? Don't get me wrong, it's good to see you," he hastened to add.

Christine put her bundle on the table and her purse on the chair. She turned to face him, the expression on her face blocked by her having her back to the lantern. He could hear in her voice, however, genuine concern.

"Don, I miss you so. I really do. And I want you to know how bad I feel about calling the press on you. But I thought it would be good for you to get the exposure. So I called them and I really didn't want to cause you any harm. Honestly, I didn't."

She was on the verge of bursting into tears, so he opened his arms to envelope her. She put her brow against his shoulder and keened a high pitched wail. After the whine died down she lifted her face to him and added one more piece of information. "Plus I kicked Roger out of the house today."

"What'd you do that for?" he asked.

"Because he made insinuating remarks about you and me after I called you back this morning."

Don's dander rose when he heard this. The hair on the back of his neck bristled and he gripped her by her elbows, holding her away from his body where he could see her face.

"What'd the little creep say?"

"He just said I hadn't been faithful to him. And with you calling like you did, he thought there was something between us. That's all. So I got angry and threw him out."

Don mulled this over for a moment, then suggested they both sit rather than stand around in the lamplight. From her shopping bag she extracted a bottle of white wine.

"I already have one opened," he smiled and reached for another white plastic cup. "Allow me," he said as he poured a liberal amount into both. "Room temperature. Sorry it isn't any colder."

After a moment spent sipping, she asked him, "Don, would you mind telling me what you're really doing down here? I mean, you don't expect to dig this boat or whatever it is up, do you?"

He mulled that for another moment before answering. "I honestly don't know. I kind of like this place. Quiet. Off the beaten path. Natural surroundings. Why? What do you think I'm doing here?"

She sipped quietly while he spoke. Finally she said: "I'm not sure you know, Don. Do you? I mean, you never were big on planning, especially big things like this. You just go and do stuff without realizing what the consequences might be."

He knew she was right. He had not really thought through the potential results of his actions. He merely pressed ahead each day, minute by minute, in the hope that everything would become clear to him some time, somehow, some way.

"You're making me think too hard on this, Christine. I mean, I may be in a hole but things are okay right now. Nobody is pestering me, I got a lawyer to keep them off my back and all."

She pulled her chair closer to where he sat on the edge of his folding chair and placed a hand on his thigh. "I know it's late, and it's awfully dark out there, Don. And I brought something that could be useful, if you'd like." She again reached into the bag and produced a cloth bundle. He realized it was an additional sleeping roll tucked tightly into a stuff bag. He was suddenly charmed by the idea of making love under the stars in the center of a pit that would someday be another skyscraper on the city skyline. He pulled her closer in order to steal a kiss. When they parted, he suggested she shake the bag out of its carrying case. As she did so, she talked: "I thought I'd ask you if you have some idea what you really want, Don. I mean, maybe you intend to dig this thing out of the ground, or maybe you just want the owner of the property to come along and pay you to leave. Is that it? You looking to sell out? 'Cause if you are, I don't know what you're expecting to get from these people. Like, f'rinstance, how much do you want to be paid to leave this place?"

He stopped her suddenly by placing a hand on her arm. She was in the midst of tossing the compressed sleeping gear in the air when he grabbed her and turned her toward him.

"Wait a minute. Who you been talking to?" His eyes squinted into hers like a fierce wind forcing his brow to bend ominously. His features were clear in the dim light. "You been in touch with the Boesk Corporation? Is that why you're asking these questions? Did they get to you with an offer of some kind? Is that it?" He could see fear leap into her eyes. He knew the answer was yes without hearing it from her.

"You didn't have a fight with Roger. And you don't really give a shit about me, either, do you? Answer me. Do you?!" His hand twisted her arm behind her back and she yelped in pain.

"Ooow. Don. You're hurting me." She cringed with the accusation as much as with the pressure he brought to bear. She went down on one knee yelling for him to stop, "Please stop it. Let me go," she cried.

He loosed his grasp and gave her a shove. She staggered away. He was disgusted and wanted her to know how he felt. He picked up the now open bedroll and threw it at her. "You'd have fucked me for them, too. Wouldn't you?" His voice reflected the hurt as well as the contempt he felt for her. "You must of got paid plenty. Or was it next to nothing? Know how much they offered me and I still wouldn't turn into a whore? Well, I bet they didn't offer you a fraction of what they were willing to pay me. What, you got maybe a thousand dollars to come out here and get me to tell you what my price is? I'll tell you what it is, goddamit! You can go back and say it's doubled. No, tripled! You got that? Tell them it's three times what they offered me today. Make that an even three hundred thousand and I'm outta here."

She receded from the lamplight. He heard her sob, but it did not mean anything to him any more. "You got here alone, find your own way home!"

He only wished he had a door to slam behind her. Instead, he blew out the light.

CHAPTER TWELVE

BUMMER & LAZARUS

"I'm hoppin' mad, Oi am. An' it cost me near forty dollars to correct wha' they ruint!"

The angry gentleman held a rounded top hat in his hands and waved it in the air to emphasize his point. He was standing in front of a dozen men seated at a long black table which occupied the far end of a spacious room. It was late afternoon during an unusually hot summer which required that all the windows be left open for the comfort of the hundred or so people in the audience who sat facing the table as well as those seated behind it.

Everyone listened intently to the fellow's complaint.

"So I comes to you wot made them bowsers citizens of this 'ere city. And this here's my bill. Laid at your feet."

The man then boldly walked the ten paces forward and closed the gap separating him from those to whom he sought redress. He placed a slip of paper on the surface of the table which elicited a gentle murmur from the audience. It was impossible to tell whether they approved or disapproved of the gesture.

Mayor Henry Frederick Teschemacher let the sheet rest untouched where the little man with the bowler hat placed it. No other council member made an effort to pick it up.

"If I may speak," Steve Ragsdale finally broke the silence and rose from his seat in the audience. He bowed toward the mayor adding: "As a friend of the city's council."

"Mr. Ragsdale, a legal consultant, may address this assembly," Teschemacher said with a nod in Ragsdale's direction.

"It appears there does exist a responsibility on behalf of this body to accept liability for those honorary citizens it has allowed to roam freely, as it were. In the instance of Mister Bummer and Mister Lazarus, however ill advised that may have been, the City Council did create a special decree exempting them from the curfew and making them wards of the city. That being the case, it is incumbent upon this same body to make restitution should these same citizens cause any property damage. I would recommend that recompense be paid out of the General Fund. I see little alternative."

A petition had been presented to the Board of Supervisors requesting that two dogs, known as Bummer and Lazarus, be specifically exempted from recently enacted leash laws. Several points were cited in their favor, not the least of which was their notoriety, some might say infamy, as rat catchers which weighed heavily in their favor.

"By general decree, the two animals known individually as Bummer and Lazarus, are henceforth and forever after to be recognized as solid citizens of San Francisco," read the decree posted on the courthouse steps. "All the benefits of such citizenship excluding the right to vote shall be theirs."

Signatories included the Mayor and fifteen members of the council with no abstention. Thus, all felt culpable when it was shown the dogs had damaged this citizen to the tune of $40.

"Before we expend from any fund," Teschemacher said, "may I ask how the two were able to cause such extensive and, I may add, inordinately expensive damage?" Teschemacher pinned his gaze squarely on the man who had just presented his bill.

The fellow with the bowler stepped forward to address the council members and mayor.

"I c'n only c'njecture, yer honor, but I believe they was asleep together behind one of my news stands when I closed up for the night. That would be Satiday. And when I come back on Monday, early to open up, Oi finds the place a terribo mess. They must a waked and been 'ungry 'cause they chewed the shelves and ransacked the entire front o' my store. It was a 'orrible mess it was. And they shit all over the papers what had just arrived from the East."

Until this revelation the audience had contained itself and remained outside the discussion. But with the admission how papers had been fouled, many began to howl with laughter. It was an apt desecration of the New York newspapers and their contents. The constituency apparently heartily approved of the dogs' behavior.

"I believe that shall be sufficient," Teschemacher said sternly, his gavel striking several times before its noise was heard above the loud guffaws. When there was silence, he said: "Council members, you have heard this man's request. And here is an itemized bill for damages. Shall we vote to pay the price in question?"

"For the record, I move we vote as stated," spoke one member.

"I shall second that," chimed in another

"Good. Let us put it to a vote then. Resolved: to pay the bill for damages to Towne News caused by Citizen Bummer and Citizen Lazarus. All in favor, raise your right hand."

There was a quick count of the show of hands.

"All opposed." There was one lone dissenter. "The ayes have it. Bailiff, see that a chit is issued as credit and we now take up the next matter on the agenda."

Before that discussion could begin, however, there was a round of applause. Teschemacher was only able to restore decorum after pounding has gavel several more times.

"By the way," he said as if in afterthought, "where are the two malefactors at present?"

No one knew for certain although several guesses were thrown from the spectator section. "Digging up the streets, likely!"

"Breaking the backs 'o rats under the sidewalks," suggested someone.

"Saving a runaway carriage!" yelled another.

But at that very moment, the two friends were fast asleep beneath the steps in front of the Niantic Hotel.

§

No one knew from whence Bummer hailed. The *San Francisco Bulletin* carried one of the first reports of his existence describing a noble past. It was more fiction than fact, concocted by a bored reporter on a slow news night.

"He made the journey to California across the plains, fought with the Indians, lost his master, became demoralized, and arrived in Sacramento a disappointed and disgusted dog. The disgust was not lessened by a residence in that one-horse town, and after a brief sojourn there he made his way to San Francisco," the anonymous journalist wrote.

A perhaps more accurate and true-to-life description of the animal was published by another paper: "Bull in his fighting quarters and

Newfoundland in his vital parts. His color was pure white and pure black, spotted."

Bummer had no other name than the one he picked up by visiting restaurants and free lunch tables. He made the east side of Montgomery Street his special territory, working the food tables between Sacramento and Washington Streets with clock-like regularity.

Hundreds of dogs roamed the streets of San Francisco in the summer of 1863. Many were domesticated pets left thoughtlessly behind when their owners took off for the gold country. Many more were the offspring of bitches without pedigree caught in hapless childbirth on the streets, alone and friendless, victims of their body functions. Bummer could have been a whelp of one of these, although he seems to have always been grown, like Minerva springing whole from the head of Jove.

There were so many of these animals loose on the streets, dogs were soon considered a public nuisance. More than merely a nuisance, they were a public health hazard as their excrement fouled every sidewalk. And when they ran in packs they terrorized both child and adult equally.

Often diseased and sickly, their plight was compounded by the lack of food. One reporter described them all as being "creatures without hair and with skeletal tails -- living anatomies."

Hungry dogs will attack each other over the smallest particle of bone or morsel of fat and vicious fights were common. Humans would stop in their tracks to stand idly by and make book on the outcome.

The street offered an insecure life for even the toughest mongrel. Bummer would have gone unnoticed by any except those who threw him a handout if he had not distinguished himself one sunny dusty morning on Montgomery Street.

Two equally mangy curs were growling over a piece of bacon rind tossed from a butcher's stall. One dog was much larger than the other and was certain to win the contest. He was known in the neighborhood as a tough customer.

His opponent for the rind was a thin yellow canine with patchy fur who was obviously not in the best of health, having a lean and hungry look. Too small an amount of skin was stretched over too great a quantity of ribs. Obviously he was not a fighter by street standards, but he was starved and would not back down. The larger dog was not satisfied simply with scaring the other away. He lunged, teeth bared, snapping fiercely. He took a leg in his jaws and began to shake his whole body from side to side. This had the effect of wagging the trapped pup like a tree branch. The yellow mutt was helpless and began to whine. A crowd of pedestrians gathered to watch.

"When at a dog fight," remarked one man in a white suit to a woman companion, "root for the underdog."

"But bet on the winner," observed another sanctimonious gentleman who sported an absurd moustache.

"I don't think I can watch," said a woman in gingham whose eyes, nonetheless, remained glued on the gladiators. The piercing scream of the smaller animal became a siren in the air.

"That little feller's 'bout to have his leg near chewed off," observed the first man. "Looks mighty painful to me."

"Yep. Bet that smarts," opined a third.

At this moment Bummer leaped into the contest. He had been standing placidly on the sidelines, his own eyes fixed more on the speck of food than the battle, when he determined to change the odds. Leaping from between two men lounging against a hitching post, he attacked the larger dog with such savage vigor he made the animal drop its prey. The angered attacker turned his attention to Bummer with bared fangs. Bummer held his ground and responded in kind. Within seconds, the large animal turned and ran.

"Would you believe that? Why idn't that ol' Bummer to the rescue?" asked the man with the moustache. There was a general murmur of assent. "An' he kind of raised that yellow dog from the dead, wouldn't you say?" More agreement. "Sort of the way you might say Lazarus come back from the dead almost."

This heroic deed would not pass quietly into obscurity, but was instead widely publicized by competing newspapers. The *Alta California* reported the incident in detail. Their reporter claimed to have come upon the dual near its conclusion and his description of the surprise end of the battle was exciting news to read. Overhearing the spectators' conversation, he dubbed the skinny yellow mutt Lazarus and the name stuck.

The *Bulletin*, not having a reporter on the scene, published an even longer, more detailed description of the incident which told how the underdog had been saved from almost certain death. The article stated as unabashed truth that Bummer had gone on to fight two other battles that day and won these as well.

As far away as Nevada, the *Territorial Enterprise* picked up and embellished the story by inventing two dozen more protagonists, adjusting the number Bummer routed accordingly, and claimed to have eyewitness accounts of the mongrel massacre.

The *Californian* reprinted a synthesized version of the dogfight which incorporated all the preceding accounts and ended by suggesting they would offer a substantial purse if another bout could be orchestrated between the offensive large dog, his army of mongrels and the diminutive (by comparison) Bummer. They stridently called for a rematch.

What actually occurred after the single incident with the one large dog was unusual by any canine or human standards. Limping and attempting to lick his wounds at the same time, the dust-colored dog that Bummer had literally saved from the jaws of death wandered over to his savior and leaned up against the street-wise animal. Bummer took his new friend under tutelage. He stayed close to Lazarus, finding food from the saloons for both of them until the festering wounds healed and Lazarus was again able to forage on his own.

The frontier names of the two had been forged. Their exploits made popular and imaginative reading for years to come. They were described sleeping together in doorways or under wood sidewalks, in back alleys and in the warm trash heaps with which Bummer was familiar. He shared his friends and his handouts, his haunts and his fleas with the yellow dog. They were remarked upon by candidates running for office and talked about by parents who wanted their children to learn from their example.

The parable of the undying friendship between Damon and Pythias was often invoked to describe the four-legged creatures. They were frequently seen stretched out together on the sidewalks of Washington Street, one head resting on the other's hindquarters.

But they also earned their living by serving as public servants. For a time, Bummer and Lazarus became the best known rat exterminators of the city. In one instance, the Gould & Martin fruit stand was cleared of its counters and cupboards and a rat hunt begun. With the help of Bummer and his pal, the men with clubs were reputed to have broken the backs of some 400 vermin!

Lazarus was not, however, quite as magnanimous as his benefactor. It was reported, with good repute, that whenever Lazarus could snatch a fat bone unobserved, "He was ingenious about getting it in possession. On such occasions he seemed suddenly fond of solitude. And when half an hour later he returned, fetching the bone to share it with his partner, there was not any marrow in the place where the marrow ought to be."

Bummer pretended to overlook his friend's failings.

§

Clarence Gladding took his job seriously. His duty to the citizens of San Francisco was to rid the streets of pests and from this he would not shirk.

He was the city's first dogcatcher.

This was an onerous job by many standards and considered by all except Gladding to be quite unglamorous. It was true he wore no suit, hat, or spats while addressing the courts on behalf of its citizenry. Still, Clarence considered himself to be no less a luminary than any judge seated on the bench. And to a certain criminal element, the strays, the ugly dogs who obeyed no one, Gladding was certainly both judge and jury as well as executioner of those unfortunate miscreants he managed to capture.

The dogcatcher actually performed a benevolent, even humane act for many of the strays. If not for him, they would have died of poisoned food which was often left in the streets to get rid of these animals. It was a slow and painful death that killed indiscriminately.

Clarence was good at what he did. One of his favorite techniques involved luring the creatures to his wagon with bits of ground horse meat. They followed unerringly the trail he dropped, almost waltzing into the open paddock of his converted hayrack, usually stopping just short of it, probably at the insistence of the other recently captured hounds caged behind a wall of boards nailed midway up the flatbed and sides of the cart, hounds that yelped unseen but very much heard.

Clarence was prepared for the most recently lured animal's hesitancy, prepared to swoop down upon the creature with a large hoop net as the animal stopped in its tracks or foolishly bent its head to gorge itself on a final fistful of red meat.

The net was Clarence's own design, an improvement over the standard butterfly-type, which he hoped some day to sell to the city fathers or to neighboring San Mateo county's dogcatcher. It was made of the strongest weave he could find and had a draw string as long as the handle which allowed him to snap the opening closed, to quickly sling an animal sack-like into the air and onto the bed of his cart.

Lazarus was in hot pursuit of the trail of horse meat. The beast had left his best friend alone to fend for himself when he caught the scent of sweet raw flesh landing nearly at his feet.

Clarence drew the animal on toward the trap with a few more well-placed pieces of ground meat. Then the skinny yellow cur paused just as the others had when within earshot of the tumbrel that was parked around the corner on Stockton Street. Another lump of horse meat fell just inches away from Lazarus' nose. He was torn with conflicting desires. Either swallow it whole or heed the yelps he heard and abandon it and run with his no longer empty but certainly not full belly back to the relative comfort of the familiar sleeping area beneath the sidewalk in front of the hotel which was now some blocks distant. He whimpered as these anxieties tore at him. The result was that he stood stock still, neither taking the ball of food in his mouth nor running from it.

At that instant the net dropped over him and he leaped, jerked frantically into the air. It was a futile and belated attempt to bolt for safety. Clarence clubbed him with a heavy stick he kept for that purpose.

It was a quiescent Lazarus who awoke and found himself in the back of the vehicle with four other strays. Meanwhile, Bummer was already searching for his friend.

"Want a bit o' bone, there Bummer?" asked a shop owner who knew the animal. Bummer refused the offering. Instead, he scurried off, nose to ground, following the trail of a unique odor in the dusty streets left behind by his lost pal.

"Wonder what's got into him. Not like him to pass up food." The shop owner looked around at one of his helpers. "You didn't see his buddy loungin' about, did you? Now where can that Lazarus have got hisself off to I wonder."

An old chicken coop had been given over to Clarence for his kennel. The yelp and bark of thirty dogs greeted his rumbling, squeaking cart as he brought in the morning's haul. Lazarus was awake and aware by the time he was deposited in the yard of the coop.

"Don't s'pose you'd want another bite of breakfast, would you, you ugly brute?" Clarence enjoyed teasing those in his care. He had another trick to play on the animals. "Here you go, you yellow bastard. Try this on for size." He tossed a particularly large piece of meat into the kennel near where Lazarus stood with his head lowered. Before Lazarus could grab it, however, another smaller and more agile dog, a terrier, leaped in front and scooped it up. The meat was gone in an instant. Clarence cursed. He searched through the butcher bag in his lap for another mound of meat to toss, realized that was the last. He cursed again, and rose to his feet. He intended to get another pound from the room that doubled as his office. He paused when the smaller dog that had taken the offering began to whine.

The little terrier was alone in a corner, whimpering. Its small body was shivering as its lungs tried to take in enough air to keep the heart beating. It was a failed attempt. All the blood in its body was being drained out of several holes in its stomach and intestines, puncture wounds inflicted by the pieces of broken glass Clarence had concealed in the horse meat tidbit. The whimper never rose above a low moan although the stomach wounds were extremely painful. Death for the terrier came within minutes, but it was not merciful and it was not swift. Finally, the animal rolled over and closed its eyes.

Clarence did not have a long attention span. He grew tired of the sport well before the terrier quit breathing and completely forgot he had originally intended to treat the yellow dog to this agonizing death as well. Now he went in search of food for himself; he returned to the shack he called home.

There he kept a large piece of jerked beef in his pantry. From this he cut a chunk. As Clarence slowly chewed and swallowed, the act of eating distracted him so completely he forgot he had intended to return to the kennel for the sheer pleasure of watching the yellow dog die. Fortunately for Lazarus.

§

Bummer passed up so many offers and nuzzled so many doorways looking for his friend that it became obvious to everyone the other animal was missing. Eventually the neighborhood took up the cry and Lazarus became the object of a search party.

News boys stopped hawking their papers in hopes of earning a one dollar reward rumored to be available for the person or persons finding the animal alive. Fifty-cents would be paid anyone who happened upon its carcass.

There was not enough time to get an edition of the paper out proclaiming this offer before the street was alerted to the lost member of the community. The reward doubled. Then trebled.

"Oi seed 'im," cried one of the more inebriated patrons of O'Malley's when one boy began his search in that venerable establishment.

The boy's hopes brightened. He was getting ready to claim the reward and asked excitedly precisely when and where.

"Rye here, I seed 'im," replied the astonished drunk. "As live as you an' me, boy. Rye 'ere. Why, it was las' week I think it wuz an' I 'anded 'im a piece o' cheese, Oi did." The child knew he'd been fooled and ran back out the swinging doors in hot pursuit of other, more reliable information.

It was late afternoon before anyone thought to ask if the newest member on the city payroll might be responsible for the dognapping.

As pound keeper, Clarence was completely within his rights to pick up the un-owned Lazarus. The City Council had no desire to allow packs of wild dogs to roam freely in what was supposed to be a civilized town and the curfew they enacted was imposed on all dogs: if they were not locked up at night, they were subject to arrest. Clarence was merely following the Council's bidding, the members of said organization being well aware of the political correctness and social benefits of enforcing this law.

The Council also created a ten-cent bounty for all strays brought to the pound. This gave the legislation teeth. Aware that a citizen might knock at his door at any time to deliver another mutt and collect his bounty, Clarence was not prepared for an army of vigilantes pounding at his chicken coop. When he saw the approaching sally of men he thought another fire had broken out and he was being drafted into a bucket brigade. In less than a minute he had his boots on and suspenders in place and was reaching for a shovel when the first of the search party banged on his door.

"You in there," a voice shouted from the yard. "You dog catcher. You come out and let us have a talking." Several more men joined the first in calling for his appearance. Clarence stood ready to assist as a volunteer fireman, but he did not like the tone he heard in the voices of the men out front. He could tell it was an unfriendly group that had gathered and he delayed as long as possible responding to them.

An angry mob greeted him when he at last opened his door. Dogs in the kennel began to bark as some of the men ran around to the side where the makeshift stockade stood. Clarence stood dumbfounded as he watched three of the men rattling the wood gate. It began to splinter in their hands.

"Here, you can't do that," he began but was cut off by a giant of a man wearing leather breeches and carrying a nine pound hammer in one hand. The blacksmith was drawn straight from his forge to Clarence's dog impound. Standing in front of Clarence, the man looked like he could beat back the gates of hell if the Lord only asked.

"You got one of our own in there and we wants him back," said the blacksmith with a straight forward eloquence that surprised the dogcatcher. "If you don't mind," he added with chilling politeness.

Clarence's eyes widened and he backed away from the crowd. "Take whatever you want. 'S all right with me." He was looking around for the back door, remembered there was none, and opened his palms in front of him. "One of your own what?" Clarence managed to ask with a shaky voice.

"One of our own mutts is been picked up is what."

The stockade shivered and fell apart. The collected rabble behind its fallen wall yelped as they realized they had suddenly been freed. Their barking was not, however, louder than the thump of Clarence's heart as he stood in the doorway facing the mob. Dogs leaped the pile of boards and wire that had been their pen and collided with each other in their hasty break for freedom. Clarence realized there must be a few more strays in the kennel than he had thought. The number was certainly greater than the small prison was able to accommodate comfortably. That fact became abundantly clear as the flood of escapees continued.

At the last, a lone figure remained standing in the center of the pen. It was Lazarus.

"C'mere, boy," the smithy coaxed. "C'mon out of there, boy. You can go home now."

Lazarus began to move not toward the gathered men but in the direction of a lump of fur off to one side of the stockade. He walked to the fallen terrier and nudged, then began to gently lick the body, but was unable to bring it back to life.

"Mebbe he likes it in there," observed one of the men in the crowd.

Clarence realized he was no longer the subject of the posse's anger and quietly retreated into the relative safety of his one-room shanty. He slammed the door and dropped a board across it to keep his attackers out. Then he crept into a corner where he stayed for the rest of the night.

CHAPTER THIRTEEN

THE RIGHT PRICE

Tom Arno stood behind a wheelchair, his hands resting on its handles. A pasty-faced Davidson lolled in the vehicle.

Hardin held up a newspaper and stabbed at a front page headline. "He had his press conference. I saw it on the ten o'clock news last night. The papers got it this morning." His tone was threatening and demanding at the same time. He turned toward Boesk whose face betrayed nothing of the anger that frothed inside him since their meeting yesterday.

"Look, H. J. If you want to keep making offers to this guy, that's fine. But you might consider the fact he's refused two and there's no reason to believe he'll accept a third." Arno's voice turned deferential in the midst of his speech as if he suddenly remembered his position in the firm's hierarchy

Boesk sat with fingers tented on the desktop. He sighed. "I saw it too," he said referring to the newscast. He was frustrated. Friday's hearing in front of Tarera cast a pall on the meeting. No one thought it was going to doom the project, but the probability of more delays and more expense loomed.

Last night's television features discussed Worthy's hole and contained references to the anthropological and historical importance of an authentic Gold Rush ship. One story suggested scholars could now learn exactly what kinds of food the miners ate. Another speculated on what artifacts might lie close to the surface around the vessel. A third announcer concluded by asking how much deeper archeologists might want to dig in order to uncover Indian remains.

"Jesus, that's all we need," Hardin complained. "An Indian burial ground on top of everything." No one commented on the pun except Davidson who moaned. "Or should I say 'below' everything?"

Arno bent at the waist to listen to Davidson and the room was filled with a respectful silence. Eventually he stood up and announced a translation of the architect's whispers. "He said shoot the fucker."

"Well, that remains an option," Boesk remarked.

"Frankly," said Hardin, "It does not. If that son of a bitch dies on us while presenting his case, his attorney could hold up the entire proceeding in probate and then carry on for the heirs. I'm already worried an estate has been created here. Our legal department was quick to point out he had better not die intestate without having completed a deal with us."

"The news crews didn't waste any time, did they?" said Arno. "So when is Chirup going to take another offer?"

"Winton is no longer with us," replied H. J. in a voice that sent a chill up the spines of all present. Even Davidson felt it, straightening in his chair momentarily. After an appropriate few seconds of silence, Hardin returned to the extortion suggestion.

"It does appear the fellow has a foot on our necks. If you do negotiate a settlement on this third try, it's imperative you include a total buyout of his position. No archaeological digs, no sand sifting, none of that. He leaves and that's the end of it. All rights to any excavation become ours, now and in the future."

H. J. exhaled deeply and the room was silent. His very breathing was imperious. "I have read the life history of this man," Boesk began, "and I am positive he is for sale. That's why he's down there. To be bought out. We simply must find his price."

"Well we can't just increase without end, can we?" asked Hardin.

"Without end?" Boesk repeated. He separated his hands and flattened them on his desk. It was a classic pose for him. It meant he had arrived at a decision. "Without ending perhaps, but not without end."

No one spoke. A gurgle came from the throat of the architect in his wheelchair.

"We will not increase our bid. We will force him to come to us and he will tell us what he will accept."

"That don't make a lot o' sense, H. J., if you know what I mean." It was Hardin who stuck his neck out. Everyone waited for his head to be cut off. No one voiced another opinion or contradicted the boss.

H. J. was silent. He returned the remark with a wry smile but said nothing more.

§

Don was up early. It was not even nine-thirty and all he could think about was the comfort of his apartment. Last night after Christine left, the night turned unseasonably chill. His tent remained drafty no matter how tightly he tucked in the edges, cinched the webbing or re-staked the ground pins.

He missed little things he used to take for granted. Like electricity, running water, indoor plumbing and a wall heater. A refrigerator, even an empty one, would have been welcome. He was not enjoying his self-imposed exile and wanted desperately to take a shower. He thought longingly about a luxuriating bath and a book.

Don was in the midst of a general cleanup. During his three day stay, the campground had become as cluttered as his dwelling. He was amused by the thought that he did not need to go anywhere in order to be in general disarray. He picked up his metal earth-pick and studied it. He suddenly lost interest in cleaning house and walked over to the area where he knocked off probing the ground yesterday.

In the late 1960's and early 70's, the City was on a residential housing building spree spurred, in part, by federal grants. Entire blocks of Victorians in the Western Addition were knocked down. Hundreds of buildings were smashed and cleared of land they occupied for a century or more.

In an earlier time, in a period when "disposable" referred to being worn out and no longer useful rather than referring to extra income, nothing valuable was wasted. Buildings were well built and rarely wore out. Typically, if an existing structure had to be removed, it was not thrown away, destroyed and discarded. Instead, it was moved to another vacant lot and set on a new foundation to endure another hundred years.

However, this changed in the last half of the 20th century. Instead of preserving a Victorian, the old building was torn down and replaced with a new "modern" structure. Redevelopment meant you first cleared the land eliminating anything already on it. Displaced persons were created without war, unless you thought of the urbanization process as a clash between nations and their own citizens.

The stately Victorian was replaced with lesser quality multiple-unit structures. These new buildings would not last as long as their depreciation schedules. In an ironic twist, the bureaucracy that tore down the old was told that federal funding guidelines prohibited using the funds to build new structures for at least a year after the date of demolition. Sometimes two years. This left many weed grown lots behind wire mesh fences.

During this period, Don Worthy and hundreds of other scavengers became weekend treasure hunters. They discovered valuable artifacts buried in the soil of these newly vacant plots by opening the outhouses of the last century.

In order to find an outhouse, the hunter plunged a long metal rod into the earth until it hit an obstruction. Careful not to press too hard lest something were to break, once a potential site had been located the diggers set to work.

Absinthe bottles and porcelain doll heads, all having come around Cape Horn, metal buttons from the first forges of the City, China plates and pewter mugs, this was the trash of the Nineteenth Century thrown out as fill on top of a waste hole. There were no public garbage dumps in that age. When the outhouse became too full, the hole was covered, a new hole dug and the small wood room on top moved to that nearby location.

Don and his cronies uncovered black beer bottles which were opaque and had a unique design feature: A seam ran their entire length showing where the twin halves were melded together. They found glass ginger containers, colored a green opalescence that was the result of poor cooling techniques during manufacture. They discovered lead glass that had turned dark purple with the passage of time. Animal bones carved into dominoes from a miner's last game were discovered. They discovered metal belt buckles used by both horse and man, usually corroded beyond use, almost beyond recognition. Remarkably, a Gold Rush oyster tin stamped with the embossed portrait of the seller, Isaac Beckhow, his New York address prominent and readable, was found in almost perfect condition.

Don became adept at identifying rare artifacts. After several hundred passed through his hands, he was easily able to spot an unusual glass specimen. He learned how to price them and rarely sold too low, even to other dealers. A complete doll was the best, most valuable find. The cloth body was usually long disintegrated by the time it was disinterred. All that remained were head, hands and feet, but they brought a high fee from collectors. Rumor had it that one porcelain-faced toy actually sold for $450. Don later heard it had been resold for twice that.

Olive bottles and pewter spoons, spent rifle cartridges and square metal nails, Asian porcelain platters and lead weights all materialized. Worthy could have gone on digging and selling indefinitely, but the supply eventually went dry. The City issued all its residential building permits and paved parking eventually covered any uninvestigated ground. After that, there was a five year moratorium on bulldozing to build in San Francisco. A recent election changed that and the pendulum appeared to have swung back toward development and growth as environmental concern gave way to big money. Construction in the heart of the heart of the city began again in earnest. Once more, the dense downtown sprouted the City's unofficial bird, the crane.

Worthy worked the rod while he walked. He called it an earth-pick because it had no other name. This one was his own fabrication, made from a length of rebar to which he wound a piece of tape for grip on the bent end. Force of habit rather than a belief he would discover anything guided his hands. He pressed the rod down until the handle prevented it from going in any further, pulled it back up, judged a little less than a foot of distance from the last sounding, and plunged it in up to its handle again. This was not a job that required much concentration or intelligence. It offered him a chance to think about the last offer from Boesk as he did something moderately constructive. In hundreds of plunges like this since his arrival late Sunday, he found nothing. He did not expect today to be an exception.

Half an hour passed before the rod clicked and stopped in mid air. It was sunk at about the three foot level.

"That's interesting," Don remarked to himself. He withdrew the metal and this time moved it only an inch or so rather than twelve. It went down to the handle and struck nothing. He tried again, feeling around with his probe until he hit another obstruction close to the first. Both were at the same depth, about two-and-a-half to three feet. He prodded gingerly and gently, not wanting to damage something delicate and valuable.

He withdrew, plunged again, withdrew, plunged. He mapped out an area no larger than two feet square where he knew he would find something. In all, he made ten insertions before he was satisfied he was not striking a rock. He could not be absolutely certain, of course, but reasonably so. Rocks have a tendency to come in clusters; he found no other objects within a few feet and no rocks had turned up to deflect his other probes. In the 1800's this would have been a clean fill operation. He decided there was one single thing within a small area at about the three foot level and, since he had nothing better to do, he decided to retrieve it.

Before beginning, however, he glanced at the upper ridge of the construction site. No one was immediately visible, although that did not mean no one was watching. He was so confident there were spies that he continued to poke the ground long after he decided precisely where he would dig. He made it look to any observer as if he still had not decided to do anything in particular except poke the ground. And he had been doing that for the last three days.

The area was clearly defined in his mind's eye, however, and at last he made a big show of giving up and returned to the task of setting his camp in order.

He picked up the cot and chair, replaced them in an orderly fashion a few feet from where he intended to dig. He struck his tent, folded it and snapped shut the flexible metal poles that held it upright. This made a neat bundle which he moved directly onto the spot he intended to excavate. There he re-pitched and, with the back of a small axe, positioned the tent pegs and drove them into the soil at an angle.

Merely the act of picking up and putting down his belongings in a new place straightened out the campground. The area no longer looked disheveled and it actually bolstered his self-esteem when he moved the cooking stove and his few utensils to a new spot. It had the same effect on him as having just cleaned up his kitchen at home: ah, the dishes are done.

Finally he gathered a few articles of clothing, his bedroll and, as unobtrusively as possible, his shovel. With these in his arms, he yawned unashamedly and entered the tent. He hoped it looked like he was going to rest after a long day of hard work even if it was still early afternoon.

Inside the tent he unzipped the ground cloth which was a square sheet of plastic, and pulled it away to reveal the dirt floor. He took care not to bump the sides, afraid to shake the walls of his shelter more than necessary or it would look to an outsider like he was up to something. He was unable to stand to his full height, was forced instead to stoop as he set to work.

"How about that, Mac?" The cat was inquiring at the mouth of the shelter. "I'm digging a hole inside a twenty or thirty foot deep hole. Whaddya think of that?" Worthy talked and muttered all the while he spaded.

The earth was soft. His collapsible shovel turned the dirt easily. He found his stride within minutes and worked like a ditch digger, mounding what he removed far enough away to prevent it from falling back into the hole. But he would soon have to begin taking the dirt out and spreading it around, or else there would be no room inside the small tent to work.

The sun this time of day and this deep in the earth cast an eerie cold light that quickly turned to long shadow as the afternoon wore. It was not dark inside where he worked, but more like perpetual dusk. The new pit he dug was not well lighted even after he opened all the vent flaps.

He reached a level he estimated of about two feet and could no longer see the end of his shovel nor the bottom of the hole within a hole. Meanwhile, the mound of dirt had grown large enough to threaten collapsing back. It became nearly more than the tent could hold. He vaguely formed an alternate plan to remove the dirt on the pretext that he was clearing a comfortable place to sleep. He was not sure he could pull that off, act out the charade with any sincerity should the time come.

Worthy made his burrow as narrow as possible and continued to dig. At about three feet his shovel caught on something that would not yield. He worked the tool beneath and around the object, eventually prying it out. He was at last able to lift it up for inspection.

He found he had unearthed a piece of leather. It looked like a handle with rusted rivet holes. His next shovel full disinterred a rusty metal object.

"What a mess," was all he could say when he looked at the solid piece of slag. No part of it could ever be made to turn freely as a mechanism again. It was identifiable only by its shape. The butt of the handle must have been made of wood; the grips had long since returned to their elements.

"A pistol. Cap and ball type, from the looks of it." He fingered a portion of the barrel where a metal rod was welded by oxidation into a fixed position.

Worthy was pleased with his find, but was determined he had to have more reason to dig than a hundred-year old piece of scrap metal. He set the point of his tool back in the ground and bent over it. He gave a shove with the inset of his boot.

The shovel would not budge. He wormed it around with his hands and planted his foot again. This time it succeeded in cutting the ground, but a sharp scraping sound made him stop immediately. If it were porcelain or glass he might already have damaged it. He knelt toward the shovel bite, squinting in the poor light.

Worthy realized he should have exercised greater caution after the rotten leather handle came out. No telling what amount of damage he could do with the metal shovel point in his hands. He discarded it in favor of his fingers and lay prone on the surface in order to wedge his upper body into the hole in the ground. He hung over the lip and struggled to grab hold of any object that might be down there.

His fingers tightened on something smooth, something metallic and slippery. And there were a lot of them. He closed his hand around the indistinct shapes and withdrew his arm. Even in the poor light inside the tent, he was astonished to see coins, gold platelets about as large as his fingernails. He heard some of them tumble and spill inside the wound he had made in the earth. They fell from one side of the hole as he reached down to scoop out a handful and more scattered around the bottom. The ones he retrieved reflected dully in the feeble light and clinked as he hefted them, tossed them in his palm.

It dawned on him just what he held in his hands: Gold. The real thing. And lots of it. He would need something, a can or bag to put them in. First, however, Don scooped out as many as he could and shoved them into his pant pockets. He threw himself into the task of picking every coin out of its former grave. He lay on his stomach scraping the earth with his fingers until fairly certain there were no more to be found.

He thought suddenly he might have brought some up with his shovel. If so, they were probably in the dirt pile where they might now be buried. He would have to search the mound looking for them.

His heart raced as it became too dark to work inside the tent.

He exited to get a better view in the fading light of day. His pockets were full and he was overwhelmed with exhaustion as he sank gratefully into one of his folding patio chairs. He let coins filter between his fingers, dripping them from hand to hand.

"MacArthur, will you look at these!" His excitement finally caught up with him.

He studied one coin closely in the cold early evening light. It glinted an unmistakable yellow. He placed it between his teeth and bit. It was soft and bent slightly.

"What dollar amount you think these are?" he asked his cat who was at his feet and ready to leap into his lap. He examined one coin closely. The head side displayed the bust of a woman with the word "liberty" above a crown of stars. There was a date below her head, 1849. It had a ten dollar denomination, U. S. Treasury clearly visible on the tail side.

"A ten fucking dollar gold piece for crissakes! Hundreds of ten fucking-a dollar gold pieces, MacArthur. We're rich, goddamit, we're rich!"

MacArthur was unmoved and yawned cavernously.

Worthy managed to contain his ecstasy. No point in letting anyone up on the rim hear him. He casually got up from the chair. But he had difficulty making a slow trip to his kitchen supplies, nearly broke into a run aimed at the box which held a roll of sandwich bags. He grabbed a handful of baggies, inserted one inside another to double their strength, then a third. He made a strong triple wrapped sack, then another. He emptied his pockets into these, located baggie twists in the box and tied them shut.

Holding the heavy baggies close to his chest, he made a painfully slow, nonchalant waltz back to his tent picking up his lantern along the way. When he reached the flap he nearly tore it as he scrambled and clawed his way inside.

He was correct: he found coins in the dirt pile, under the shovel and beneath his feet. Carefully he began sifting the earth with his hands. Coins turned up with every fistful and he carefully deposited them in more plastic sacks.

He sorted through the dirt piled inside the tent with his fingers, measuring each lump of earth, mashing it to mush. He was covered with perspiration by the time he gave up, with regret, and climbed out of his tent and the newly dug hole for the last time that day.

His hands were filthy, his clothes covered in light brown earth and he was exhausted. He dropped into one of the folding chairs in front of his card table.

Now he was confronted with a truly terrifying thought: what should he do with what he found? How would he protect it? He could not very well bury it again. Except the pistol. That was nothing compared to the coins, so back into the earth it would go.

He had six and a half triple bagged plastic sacks packed tight with the precious metal. Together they weighed more than ten pounds, maybe twenty. He gathered his loot and crawled back into his tent and spent a half hour re-filling the hole. It reminded him of the pointless jobs the Navy used to force on him. Filling in the treasure mine was like being told to dig a hole and use the dirt to fill in that other hole over there which he had just dug.

He flattened the earth with his spade, pulled the ground cloth cover back in place, zipped it tight. It was a clean surface on which to lay his bedroll.

Nagging in the back of his mind was the continued worry about the safety of his new found wealth. He retrieved his briefcase and extracted his cell phone. Though it was against his principles, he tapped the number for information. Making that call meant an additional charge, but one thing he failed to pack was a telephone directory. And besides, it wasn't his phone bill to pay.

"Directoryassistancewhatcity," said a less than human voice.

"A coin shop please," he responded flatly. He hid his excitement behind the quiet response to the operator's question.

"What city please."

"San Francisco. Sorry. A coin store please."

"I have nothing like that listed."

Don realized this was not a Yellow Pages inquiry. He squeezed his eyes shut and concentrated. The name of any coin shop would do. Had he ever been to one? He fumbled in his Dopp kit for a pencil as he tried to come up with a likely name. "The Coin Exchange! How's that?" he asked. He surprised himself with his instant talent for making up the name.

"I'm sorry, I have nothing like that listed."

"The Coin Box then!" he nearly shouted.

"I'm sorry I have nothing like that listed."

"I have one more chance!" he shouted before she could hang up. "I get three. I've only used two!"

The silence at the other end was so deep he thought he was talking with Lily Tomlin.

"Directory assistance, what city please?" she ultimately asked.

"San Francisco. Please. The Stamp and Coin Shop. Please."

"I have three of them. One is on Ninth. Another on Lincoln. The..."

"I'll take them all," he blurted out before she could cut him off. He wrote the numbers frantically on a piece of scratch paper.

"For an additional fee of one dollar I can connect you to one of these."

Don Worthy had never in his life paid to have an operator connect him to a phone number. Numbed by the reality of fifteen pounds of mint condition gold coins in his possession, however, and with the magnanimity of the newly wealthy, he said, "Please do." In the back of his mind, of course, he knew the phone bill was not coming his way.

When a man answered, Don asked to speak with the owner. "You got him," said the voice at the other end smartly.

"I have a question about a few coins my uncle left me in his will. They're gold. At least I think they're gold."

"Easy enough to tell pal," the voice at the other end responded. "Bite one. Right. Did it taste metallic? Right, it's not supposed to. Okay, now try to bend it. Bent a little, eh? Good chance it's gold."

Worthy hung up the phone when the ringing began in his head. It was the sound of coins clanging as they fell in a heap in his palm. There really were hundreds, perhaps a thousand. He had yet to count them.

The second place he called asked him if the Liberty was standing. He said yes. "It's probably worth $350.00 if in good to excellent condition," the salesman told him. "Bring 'em in. No charge to look 'em over for you. How many of 'em you have?"

By the conclusion of his third phone call, Don learned each coin probably weighed a quarter of an ounce. The ten dollar standing Liberty was common in the west through the Nineteenth Century and they were worth more now for their numismatic value than the current price of gold.

"Get you four hundred easy. Each. Get you more if they got different mint markings. My name's James. Can I have your phone number and call back with a proper price for you?"

Worthy dropped the phone into its holster without saying goodbye. He was lost in a dream that did not have alarm clocks or telephones. He was multiplying by adding zeros. If he found a thousand coins and each had a value of $350 to $500, he had nearly half a million dollars in his hands! He began to gloat as an insistent tone made a noise near him.

The sound was coming from his briefcase. It was the cell phone. Someone was calling him. With a slow, zombie movement, he lifted the phone and flipped it open.

"Hello!" he shouted into the handset. The bag of gold in his hand clanged against the phone and jangled in his ear. He was kneeling beside the briefcase. He thought wryly how this might look as if he were praying to the God of economics. Dignified, with phone to ear, he rose to his feet.

"Jesus, not so loud," said a voice in the crisp cool air. "I been trying to reach you for hours. Your phone's been busy." It was Benny whose tone was conciliatory. "What's a matter? You all right? I thought you'd never pick up when I finally got through."

"Yah, Benny. Hi. I'm fine. Sorry. Didn't hear it ring." Worthy tried to collect his thoughts. Coins clinked as he set the bag down on his table.

"Saw you on the tube last night. Local channel. Don't think the networks picked it up yet, but they might. They take a day or two on anything that isn't hard news. So tell me, Don, why'd you call a press conference? I thought you didn't want any publicity unless they refused to talk to you."

"I didn't call the press. They just sort of showed up." He hid Christine's involvement for no reason other than that he did not want to talk about her. He was still calculating and recalculating the treasure in his head. Having the actual coins in his possession was a powerful distraction. He took a bag out of one pocket and sat on it like it was an egg.

"Listen, pal, bad news. I just put a call in to one of Boesk's attorneys and they say they haven't been authorized to make another offer! Can you believe that?" The silence was palpable. Obviously Rossen expected some response from Don's end. "Have you got a minute?" Benny asked with characteristic equanimity.

"Funny thing, Benny. I really don't." Don was thinking fast. He wanted to find a safe place for his treasure and he did not want to spend time talking on the phone.

Rossen was not going to be put off. "Just listen to me, okay, pal? I mean, give me a minute, okay? I think we can come to a good resolution if you just be patient and listen. They hinted at the old offer still standing, but I don't know. Okay? 'Cause this is just the lawyer I talked to, not Boesk himself or any of his flunkies. So take their offer. That's my advice. But you'll have to agree to be out of there immediately. Whaddya say?"

Worthy was silent.

"You there, Don?"

"I'm here." Silence.

"Well I tell you what," Rossen continued. "I can't believe you got this far. Let me tell you, I didn't think you had a thing going for you when you came to me with this crazy idea the other night, but now I gotta hand it to you. They actually came to me and asked if I would present you with this offer yesterday. I mean, it was a good offer then, but you wouldn't listen. But now, with the court appearance coming right up, things could get kind of iffy. So what do you say, Don? Can you handle having ninety thousand gee's given to you? Does that sound like a good week's work?"

Silence.

"Don, I gotta hear you talk. Say something."

"Sounds interesting," was all he could muster.

"Great. Let me call them, tell 'em what you said, get back to you. You can start packing. Or leave everything. What the hell. You can leave all your junk and just start driving away."

Silence.

"Don, you have to tell me you're leaving. I need to hear that. Otherwise, the deal is off. You don't have that much time, you know. They mean business, they mean it. And the judge only gave you five days. Which time, I might point out, is more than half over with. And I have no idea how the hearing will go day after tomorrow so you're taking your chances if you don't accept this final final, I am certain it is a final, offer."

Worthy fingered a coin and thought of all its brothers that might be buried in similar underground grottos. Could he pass them up? Were these hundreds in his hand as good as the birds still in the ground? He was torn between taking the offer and going back to his apartment contrasted with fear of missing so much more gold that might be buried right at his feet. "I can't decide now. Let me get back to you, Benny."

There was a spluttered sound at the other end as Rossen attempted to hold his client's attention.

Don closed the phone. MacArthur came over and rubbed against his leg. The sack of coins on the bedroll rattled with the cat stepping on them. Mac jumped into Don's lap and stood with two paws on each of his legs. The animal turned its head to accept a hand rub behind the ears.

What do you say, ol' buddy? Do we dig for more? Do we hold out for more?"

§

By late afternoon the next day the chill had returned to the bottom of the pit. It never really left, Worthy thought as he tightened his jacket about his neck and glanced over his shoulder.

There were thousands of pin pricks in the ground out there. He had spent the last eight hours poking and probing, hoping to hit another patch of solid material. None yielded anything but soft earth. He felt as if he'd been pulling a slot machine at Vegas. His shoulders were sore, his right arm falling listlessly at his side.

He sat at his card table, the ground-pick at his feet. Now he really needed a shower but all he could think of was ordering a hamburger from Howard's Diner on Ninth Street.

He made a decision: he decided to call it quits, to leave the construction site. It no longer mattered what amount of money he received from the Boesk Corporation. Anything would be gravy on top of what he found yesterday.

A great relief washed over him once he made this resolution. Don stood and gave the earth probe a good toss, watched it sail through the air away from him. It arced like a javelin, coming to rest point first twenty feet from the tent.

He began packing. He envisioned the shower, hot water steaming as it bounced off his aching back. He began to smile as he worked, realizing he had finally found a fortune. And he had done it without incurring any legal fees to speak of.

Don looked up to see one man, a briefcase dangling from his left hand, standing at the upper rim of the dig. The man began walking down toward Worthy and the sound of footsteps smacking the dirt path rang in the empty air. The distance was too great to get an immediate fix on who it was. Don had a sense of foreboding, anticipating a member of the opposition, perhaps a new bargain, perhaps an ultimatum. Worthy finally recognized his attorney. No doubt Rossen was come to talk him into leaving and accepting the last offer. Take the money and run, Worthy thought — and laughed.

"Donald, Donald, you gotta listen to me. I've come in person to talk with you." Rossen reached the bottom of the roadway and came toward him. "I couldn't believe it. I called them back to tell them you were less than enthusiastic. They switched me to a new guy, one I never talked with before, he said you already have their last offer. So do me a favor and sit and listen to me. Okay? Will you sit for a minute, please?"

Worthy humored the man by taking out a cigarette and leaning his butt on the edge of the kitchen table. Rossen took a folding chair. "Are you ready for this? Can you listen to me without arguing?" Don lit up. He smiled with closed lips. "They won't increase their offer another penny. They say they're willing to take their chances in court and ninety thousand is tops. Do you hear me? Tops."

Don nodded and looked calmly in Rossen's direction.

"You can still make out like a bandit on this, Don. As your attorney, I must make the best recommendation I can, which is take their offer and don't look back. But you havta sign away all riparian and littoral rights. Now and forever. Got that? It means you abandon ship, sort of. I don't know what that does for your sense of high purpose or your ego, but ninety kay ought to sooth your conscience a bit. Make for some smooth sailing for a while, don't you think?"

Don bit the inside of his cheek but said nothing.

"Hey, c'mon." Rossen snapped his fingers in front of Don's face. "Yah, Benny?"

"Is it a deal, Don? Can I call them and set it up?"

"Yah, Benny."

"I heard you right? You said you agree to the price?"

"Yah, Benny."

Rossen became excited. He reached in his pocket, then patted his chest seeking something. "Can't find my cell. Where's your phone?" Rossen became even more excited. Don stepped toward Rossen carelessly holding his instrument by its strap. Rossen looked up, smiled, took the case out of Don's hands. He punched the number pad, stabbing with a vengeance. He waited while it rang. Worthy watched amused.

"Yes, Mrs. Jacobs? Benjamin Rossen here. I represent Don Worthy, and I was given this number to call if my client decided to accept the Boesk Corporation's generous offer. Is Mr. Boesk or his legal counsel available?"

Rossen placed a hand over the mouthpiece and winked at Don. "We'll have this finished in no time."

Someone must have returned to the other end of the call because Rossen became officious.

"Yes, Mr. Hardin. Good to speak with you again. This is Benny Rossen. The attorney representing Don Worthy who occupies the boat found on your construction site on Sansome Street. We spoke yesterday morning, you and I, about an offer which my client could accept if he removed himself from your property and gave up his right to salvage the vessel. Well, I am pleased to inform you that I have convinced Mr. Worthy of the value of your offer and he has accepted. Ninety thousand dollars, I believe the amount was."

Rossen stopped speaking. Only a few seconds passed, hardly time enough for him to hear two sentences, but Benny's face became ashen. He sat back on the chair as if he needed support, said next to nothing. He managed a few words, "but," and "yah, but," and a final "goodbye," before hanging up. All of this mystified Don who had anticipated a jubilant conversation with a pleasant ending.

Rossen returned the phone to Worthy who could not make out the attorney's expression: It was one of stunned confusion. Don waited, saying nothing.

"They withdrew their offer," Rossen said. The news was hardly devastating to Don, but it crushed his attorney. Ben had been taken to the top of the mountain and then had been thrown back to earth. The effect on his emotions was too great. He began to whimper.

"I can't believe it," he said in a weak voice. "They refuse to hear any more on the subject and look forward to seeing us in court Friday.

Jesus, I thought I was going to sleep peacefully tonight. Get to bed early."

Don was surprised, but it was not as if he had been dropped off the same cliff. That might have been true yesterday. He patted his waist where nine hundred and eighty-seven ten dollar gold pieces were wrapped tightly into a dish towel tied like a money belt. He made it late last night before going to bed. Using his Victorinox Swiss Army Knife, he removed a plastic clasp from one flap on his rucksack and sewed each end like a belt buckle and tongue to the towel. His own ingenuity never ceased to amaze Don Worthy.

"This is a catastrophe," the attorney said slack-jawed. "This is the worst thing that could have happened to this case. We don't want to go to court. Not if they're willing to settle. This is horrible, Don, a catastrophe."

"Benny, what say we leave this place? Now."

"Leave?" the man said wide eyed. "You mean just pick up and walk?"

"That's right, Benny. Just pick up and go. I promise I'll pay you for your time so far. I can manage that. We just end it here and now."

"You gotta be kidding, Don. After what you've done here? The newspapers, the tee vee, the radio news. It's not like you get to come back once you go." Rossen looked up at Don with red eyes. He was on the verge of losing more than a court case, but he had an inner resolve which gave him the strength to rebound from emotional disaster.

"Let me give you some more advice. I thought you shoulda taken the offer, now I think you ought to stick it out. See what they do in front of Tarera. It's only through tomorrow and believe me, you have an important issue here. I mean that sincerely, Don. You stick it out. Okay? And I'll be with you the whole time. Got that? Hey, listen, you got enough to eat? Maybe I could have a pizza sent down to you?"

Rossen appeared to have completely recovered from his grief. He was on his feet and active again, already reaching for his briefcase.

"Tell you what. I have a case tomorrow at ten, after that my calendar is open. Why don't I bring down a bite to eat, a couple beers, some deli sandwiches, corned beef or Reuben? Which do you prefer? We'll do lunch together, what do you say?"

Before Don could stop him, the pin-striped suit in which the attorney was wrapped stood on the slope leading to the rim of the sky. Rossen turned and smiled. "Don't worry about my fee," he said as he began to trudge up the hill.

Right, Don thought as he watched his chance to shower and shave depart with Rossen. I won't.

CHAPTER FOURTEEN

THE BET

Nathan's job was still waiting for him. It was not as if there was a lack of qualified young men available to fill the position at the bank, which was one of being a clerk at a window by day, an accountant and transcriber by afternoon and evening. Rather, there were few who would take the long hours for such low pay.

Bone weary from the nearly two weeks of self imposed hard labor, hands blistered and back aching, Nathan sat behind a window on his stool Monday morning. He had been greeted at the door early, before opening, by a surprised bank manager who remarked that he had nearly given up on seeing Nathan again.

"Thought you'd headed for the gold fields sure."

In his bay, a glum expression covered Nathan's face. He kept his head down so that when a customer entered all they saw was the bill of his eye shade which hid Nathan's anguish over losing his share of a fortune.

"I'd like to open an account," a voice roused him from his reverie.

Nathan looked up to see standing before him a well dressed young man with a thin string tie that mimicked his long thin moustache. There was a wad of Federal notes in his hand.

Nathan glanced toward his supervisor's desk, found it empty as usual. It irritated Nathan to think of how much freedom the man had compared to him. Now, in addition to his regular duties, Nathan would have to go through the motions of issuing a passbook, creating the ledger entry that would cause him to generate a statement, post the deposit and get back to his window before a queue developed and customers began to complain of poor service.

He smiled wanly, closed the folding doors to his cloister window and directed the young man with a sweep of his hand.

"I can open an account for you over here, sir." He removed his eye shade. He forced a smile to his lips, brushed his hands across the sides of his head to force his unruly hair into a more presentable position.

Seated opposite one another, Nathan had time to reflect on the new customer's dandy look. The first thing he noticed was that the young man wore an expensive Stetson rabbit-fur hat which he removed and placed on the desk as they began their business. His white shirt was a delicate combed linen with a tight weave that nearly shone like it had been polished. The shirt had a wide collar, ruffles on the sleeve cuffs and down the placket.

Nathan thought it might be a new fashion, one which the East was familiar with but which San Francisco had yet to embrace. His own collar stuck straight up like twin scissor points that caused him grief each time he turned his head quickly. They threatened to poke him in the ears.

"My name is Nathan. Nathan Smith." The teller extended his hand in greeting. It was accepted in a strong grip that shook, then in an uncanny move that suggested awareness and intelligence, Nathan's hand was turned over to reveal a torn palm.

Surprised by the unplanned discovery but remaining nonplussed, Nathan said, "I'm a weekend prospector, Mister. . ."

"Makala. The name's Makala." The young man smiled widely without revealing his teeth. "Greek. My father was from Athens."

Makala had piercing gray eyes that shone like twin torches lighted behind them.

"Well, Mr. Makala," Nathan said as he gathered the proper papers. "I usually offer to fill out the information our bank president requires of all new customers." He plucked from an inkwell and proffered the quill pen. "However, if you prefer to do so yourself, that is of course acceptable."

The young man took the feather pen in his left hand. Nathan moved the ink pot to be more convenient for dipping.

As he began to write Makala spoke. "The President's office is on the mezzanine level, isn't it?" he asked nonchalantly. Nathan nodded. "What's the man's name?"

"Gianini," Nathan replied with equal indifference. "Italian. I think his father was from Rome."

Nathan felt immediately comfortable with the young man and thought how quickly he took in his surroundings. The layout of the bank indicated offices above, true. Nor was it any great intuitive leap to guess the primary business offices were located there, the president and his staff. It was not untoward to inquire who ran the establishment. Many people would not have deposited any amount of money without a complete scrutiny of every employee and a convincing argument from Nathan's supervisor, possibly a face-to-face with the president, before they should feel safe investing with the bank.

The inquiry and the answers passed as idle conversation for this young man while he filled out the forms.

Nathan thought to himself how similar in age the two were and yet how different their circumstances. He read the script upside down as Makala wrote in the appropriate spaces.

On the line that asked for his current address, Makala wrote Hotel Niantic. Where it requested his occupation he wrote "none."

Finally he signed with a bold swirling motion that filled the entire blank autograph space with ink.

"Well," Nathan said with some surprise as he retrieved the documents and the quill. "We seem to live in the same building. However I'm something of a permanent resident there."

Makala said nothing, merely gazed at Nathan with a totally unreadable expression.

Nathan decided it was best to return to the business at hand.

"How much do you have to open the account with, Mr. Makala?"

"Two thousand dollars," he said matter-of-factly.

This was not an unheard of sum. They were, after all, in Gold Country. But it equaled or exceeded the total amount of money transactions the bank might have for any given week. Nathan's face brightened as he counted out the notes, all crisp government paper. They were going to like this upstairs, Nathan was certain.

"You be staying in town long, Mr. Makala?" Nathan asked as he licked a thumb and snapped another bill on the table top.

"Haven't decided." The same unreadable smile on his face.

Nothing more was said between them as Nathan presented a receipt made out to Eero Makala. He handed a passbook with the balance neatly inscribed on the first line.

The day proceeded uneventfully to closing. Nathan balanced the books at his position easily enough, turned in his money and accounts, reconciled everything with his manager. It had been as dreary a day as he had ever spent. With the exception of the rather large opening deposit by his new customer, it had been completely typical. The clock above the front door informed him he had only spent ten hours at work.

He felt a tap on his shoulder and turned to see his manager, a pinch lipped expression on his face.

"Bank examiner needs your statement and you for another hour or two, Smith. He's in the meeting room upstairs."

Nathan could think of no way to refuse. After so long an absence he felt he was already skating on thin ice. He certainly could not plead illness on his first day back.

He watched as the manager picked up a hat and coat and placed a hand on the door handle. "See you in the morning."

Nathan had forgotten how loudly that door could slam shut.

§

"Good afternoon, Nathan," a cheerful voice caught him off guard. He was busily summing and subtracting in an attempt to keep his ledger close to the closing balance he would turn in shortly.

Looking up from his page, feathered quill in hand, Nathan was surprised to see Makala's beaming smile. The man offered his bank book to the clerk.

"Need to make a withdrawal?" Nathan asked prematurely.

"No sir. I'd like to make a deposit, if you please." Another roll of bills came out of a pocket and, with a subdued flourish, subtle yet revealing a quietly proud demeanor, Makala began to count them out. Most were in twenty dollar denominations although a fifty and several hundreds turned up. In all, Makala intended to make an additional three thousand dollar deposit.

Nathan was suitably impressed. As the clerk went through the motions to write up a receipt, Makala indulged in small talk.

"Didn't see you at the dinner table last night, Nathan. That Miss Betty sure is a wonder at setting a table. Heaps of roast beef last night. Cooked tender. Like as I haven't had for many a month." His voice held a mid-western twang that was indistinguishable from most of the country west of the Allegheny River. This was the longest conversation the young man had with Nathan. It provided the first opportunity for the bank clerk to consider the man's background.

Nathan made several piles of bills in ascending denominations, then recounted each forcing himself not to be distracted. He placed his thumb marking the last count, mumbled something about being late to the table last night because of an auditor's report. When he finished the task at hand, he looked up and said ruefully: "I ate in my room. Alone. Late."

"Sorry to hear that, my man."

"My own bad luck, you know." He handed back the book with the new entry recorded and the balance brought forward.

"I don't know about that at all," Makala said as he put the transaction report in an inside coat pocket without even looking at the numbers. "Way I got it figured, you make your own luck," was his last enigmatic statement before walking out the door.

§

Nathan was not surprised he did not see the new lodger in the common parlor or on a hallway stair or even entering or exiting the hotel. There were tenants whom he never saw and some whom he thought moved out long ago he would encounter once or twice with months in between. His usual schedule, which he had returned to, kept him busy from dawn to dusk and he was still not ready to spend time socializing. He had wounds that needed healing, literally and figuratively.

That night, pondering the apparently wealthy young man, Nathan reflected how they might never have met at all. If it were not for Makala having approached his window at the bank instead of another available teller, they could have dwelt in the same building for years without even seeing one another.

Nathan was again late to dine, but still within the appointed hour. Miss Betty was strict about seating her guests, having set herself up as a petty despot whose realm was the kitchen and its environs. She retained a soft spot for the teller, even after the debacle of the dig, and made an allowance for his overtime work. She frequently saved his portion which he could take to his room. She knew what he had just been through and how he was back at a job that sucked the life out of you just as much as working a claim could, but with less reward.

There were few diners still in the room so it was easy for Nathan to look around for Makala. The man was nowhere to be seen. He asked Miss Betty about him.

"We got three new ones this week, Nathan," she said with hands on hips, a soup spoon dangling from one fist. "Which one you askin' after?"

He could never be sure if her chiding attitude was equally distribut-ed to the rest of mankind or if she saved it for him alone. He described the moustache and hat, the wide collar shirt and thin neck tie.

"You mean the fop in the macaroni uniform?" That could be no other than how she would describe Makala, so Nathan said yes. "He only ate here once. Last night was the first time I seen him for sure. He's been checked in for mor'n a week now. Desk clerk tol' me I was to look for a new eater that long ago, but he never showed. You can ask at the front desk o'course. Naw, I ain't see'd him for mor'n that one sittin' and never for morning meals that's for sure."

Nathan thanked her and took a seat. He'd have to eat fast though, she warned him. True to her word, she chased everyone out fifteen minutes later.

§

A familiar face stood in line about mid-day Wednesday. It was Makala waiting patiently behind two ladies, one pushing a perambu-lator. There were several more people in line behind him.

Nathan was busy with a customer, a butcher who wore his blood-covered leather apron like a badge of honor. Nathan's first glance was confirmed with a sidelong look seconds later. Makala had his hands in his pockets and was disinterestedly waiting his turn.

It took considerable time for Nathan to complete the business his customer requested. As the butcher walked away, studiously reading his pass book as if he might gain a few more pennies by the scrutiny, Nathan was surprised to see Makala walking toward his specific win-dow. Surely someone else should have taken him as a customer by now.

Makala came up to the open grill and Nathan realized the man had allowed other customers to pass before him in order that he might go only to Nathan's teller post. He smiled, but was inwardly embarrassed by the tacit compliment. Makala was already an important depositor at the bank and to be singled out by him was something of an honor.

"Hello, Mr. Makala. Good to see you today." Nathan was afraid he was being too loud and looked self-consciously around. No one appeared to have taken notice. "I won't presume to think you wish to withdraw funds this time. What can we do for you?"

"I have another small deposit to make," Makala said with empty palms pressed against the marble counter. Nathan looked at the hands, a silent question in his eyes.

"Oh, yes." Makala patted his breast pockets, came up with nothing. His face wore a light frown as he moved his hands down his body to the pant pockets, then started over again on his coat when nothing turned up. A smile lit his face as he patted the right breast for the second time and he withdrew a different wallet than the one he had the other day. Slowly, painstakingly careful, with a dignity even royalty could not duplicate, Makala began to count out the money. He finished with a hundred dollar note that he crinkled between his hands, pinched between thumb and forefinger with a snap, and laid on the rest of the pile.

"I'll make out a receipt for thirty-seven hundred dollars, Mr. Makala," Nathan said with astonishment written all over his face.

"Eero. You may call me Eero. Greek. It was my father's, now it's my first name."

Nathan updated the passbook, handed over a receipt again written out to Eero Makala. His client took the brim of his hat between two fingers, tipped it toward Nathan by way of farewell and departed the bank.

§

The Niantic's manager sat at the front desk. He was busy reading an issue of the *Daily Evening Bulletin* newspaper, absorbed in the details of the War of Rebellion which was under way in the East.

Nathan had avoided him since returning to work at the bank. Now he had no choice if he wanted to learn anything about the unique customer they had in common. He walked up to the desk with the same wariness he would afford a rattlesnake; he half expected to be presented with a bill for the wages paid the Chinese laborers.

"How do?" Nathan asked after waiting an unresponsive moment to be acknowledged.

"Do." The reply was concise to the point of being rude. The paper had not moved an inch from the tip of the man's nose.

"Mind if I talk to you about that new fellow checked into the hotel 'bout a week ago? Makala, he's called Eero Makala." The paper still had not been brought down, but there came a reply without enmity near as Nathan could tell.

"Fellow who wears real dandified duds? Moustache? He's in room 430. Sleeps late. Real late usually. Comes in real late nights too. That who you want to know 'bout?"

Nathan considered this for a moment, thought he might get a subjective opinion out of this man yet.

"Where you think he gets his money?"

The paper finally dropped to the man's lap. "Don't know. Don't care. Don't care to know. Don't think you ought to be wonderin' neither."

Nathan left feeling he had wasted his time.

§

Perched on his clerk's stool about one-thirty in the afternoon Thursday, Nathan felt nearly as tired as the tiredest he had been during the basement debacle. He had done just about the same thing, too, having spent the night on a couch in the hotel foyer, catching only a few hours of sleep. He attempted to note Makala's return, but finally gave up his vigil and shuffled off to the basement just before dawn. Far as he knew, the man never had returned to the hotel.

Early afternoon sun glinted off the marble top at his window causing enough discomfort for Nathan to turn his head. There in front of him with no other word of introduction was Makala. He fanned more paper money in front of Nathan.

"Deposit this please, my man."

Nathan counted. He made out the fourth receipt in as many days, this time, though, for a mere two thousand four hundred dollars.

As he picked up his piece of paper and account book, Eero looked Nathan squarely in the eye. Perhaps it was a hunter's trick the young man had learned to captivate prey; maybe it was that of a mesmeriser to stare fixedly. Either way, Nathan felt compelled to return the gaze, almost transfixed without a will of his own to move.

"Do me a favor, won't you Nathan?" The voice was calm, soothing, compelling.

The teller nodded assent.

"Say hello to your Bank President for me, won't you? This Gianini fellow. I might even like to meet him if that's possible."

Then he was gone. The sunlight was again bright and the clerk turned quickly away from the front windows of the bank. Nathan's eyes stung with the glare.

He had never even met Mr. Gianini.

§

Nathan drifted off to sleep almost immediately after supper. He had not the will to remain awake and alert a second night in hopes of spying on his neighbor and customer.

Next morning he had breakfast and was well rested by the time he reached the bank. It was almost eight o'clock Friday morning. Greeting him at the door was his supervisor. Over the jangling of keys in the lock, Nathan mentioned Makala's request.

"Hmm. Yes, I have noticed a substantial increase in our balance over the week. Perhaps it would be good to arrange an interview," the supervisor said with uncharacteristic warmth and receptiveness to a suggestion by Nathan. "I shall be pleased to announce this man's munificence at this morning's meeting with Mister Gianini. Thank you, Smith, for calling this to my attention. I shall not forget you in this."

Nathan delivered his message without being reprimanded. He felt some relief. It did not bother him that the supervisor would forget whose idea it was if the meeting between Gianini and Makala proved worthwhile; it did concern Nathan that the supervisor's recall would be markedly improved should the meeting prove to be a reproachful event.

Still, it was a matter of policy that major customers be treated with obsequious deference. Makala certainly qualified for princely treatment.

"Should you see your Mr. Makala today, Nathan," said the supervisor an hour later, "please advise him that Mr. Gianini would welcome a visit to his office. You may call me to escort him there when next you see him."

Nathan did not expect to see Makala until the following week if at all. It remained highly unlikely the young man would return to the bank for a fifth day in a row. After all, it was not as if he had opened a business in town requiring regular deposits and withdrawals or the exchanging of bills for gold or silver coins.

It was with some surprise, then, that Nathan, glancing at the clock, saw Makala enter the front doors. It was nearing noon and the rush had not begun. There were available teller windows, but Makala strode directly up to Nathan's and presented his bank book. It was bulging with folding money which counted out to be another three thousand dollars exactly.

Nathan handed the proof of deposit, made the correct notation in the passbook and in his ledger. Then he mentioned he had conveyed the request to see Mr. Gianini via the supervisor who would be pleased to take Eero upstairs to meet the Bank President right now if he wished.

"Why thank you, Nathan. That would be wonderful. Tell you what, why don't you and I have supper tonight? Not at the hotel. How about Tadich's? Don't worry," he added hastily when he saw the teller wince at the thought of spending money at a restaurant. "You're covered. I'll put it on my account. I could use your banking expertise for a little project I have in mind." Makala assumed Nathan would be agreeable and continued without waiting for an answer. "Meet me in the lobby of the Niantic at seven-thirty and we shall take it from there," he said to the astonished clerk.

Turning toward the supervisor's desk without being directed to it, he stuck out his hand and introduced himself. He was greeted warmly, Nathan saw as the supervisor stood and the two shook hands. The young man was immediately taken upstairs where the supervisor merely nodded at the secretary seated in the anteroom to the president's office.

The secretary knocked twice, received an entry command, and swung open the door to Gianini who was seated behind a large desk. The secretary continued to smile benignly.

Inside, there was a moment of introduction, the obligatory handshakes, and the supervisor took his leave.

Makala let the conversation follow Gianini's lead. The man talked about the direction the city was taking, about expansion and civilization to rival the Eastern and European capitals of New York and London. He was affable enough, and spoke with a slight accent that revealed his foreign ancestry. Gianini asked where the young man was residing.

Eero told him he was at the Niantic and Gianini launched into a remarkable story.

"What a strange coincidence," he said. "You know it was a ship originally?"

Makala admitted there was a sign which told of this out front, but he had not been inquisitive enough to investigate further.

"I was on the final voyage which the whaling ship *Niantic* made into San Francisco harbor in July of '49. She'd become a passenger ship to accommodate hundreds of foolish young men trying to avoid Cape Horn. I took passage in Panama and damn lucky I was I'll have you know. Yessir," he said glancing at a timepiece in his waistcoat pocket. "But it's lunch time, don't you know. What say I stand you for dinner? Maye's Oyster House has a remarkable menu this time of year. I can finish my story there over a mug of porter."

Makala readily agreed.

§

Gianini took his time over the meal. He was a man familiar with gormandizing on an expense account. He ordered a local "steam" beer and offered to supply Makala with any drink he desired. Coffee was available, though dear, said the waiter.

Makala settled for a cup.

The restaurant floor was covered with sawdust.

"Do you mind telling me what sort of business you're in, Mr. Maka-la?" Gianini asked as he swallowed a raw oyster and followed that with a pull on his beer.

"I'm not really in any sort of business at all," was the reply.

"A man of independent means, perhaps?" The president was prying and made no pretense about being shy when it came to trade.

Makala settled comfortably in the booth with his mug of coffee. Idly, he spun the cup by its handle before answering. Then he changed its position again. He looked at Gianini with much the same intense expression he had used on Nathan the day before.

Makala replied: "No, Mr. Gianini, I am not independently wealthy. I earn my income where I lay my head, from towns such as yours. You see, I'm a gambler. But not the sort of gambler with which you may be familiar, Mr. Gianini. I'm a percentage gambler. And what's more, I never lose."

For the uninitiate, a percentage gambler avoids the race track or the gaming tables. Dice and cards are only used by this kind of gambler to develop one play: a single toss of a fair die or the turn of a single card in a correct deck. On that single roll or selection, a percentage gam-bler will bet vast sums of money. It is this which draws him, not the progressive pot with a small ante and regular increases; not the odds of the track or table where sums are won and lost in minor amounts and the table or the track is the favored winner; nor the unendurably long play of the roulette or baccarat tables or even the less effete play at a poker table. As a matter of course, a percentage gambler is willing to bet on anything, even which pile of shit a fly will land on, so long as large sums are wagered and won. Or lost.

"Let me ask you a question," Makala said as he took a sip of his cof-fee. "It is a personal question, but I hope you will humor me."

Gianini appeared willing and nodded his head.

"May I ask if you have any tattoos about your body? Any inked markings on your skin anywhere?"

Gianini thought the question rude and became indignant.

Nonetheless, he replied, "Of course not," with his beer to his lips. "Why on earth would you ask a question like that?"

"Merely a whim of mine. Little more than that. I sometimes make bets with men or even women who have no tattoos."

With that comment, Eero pulled back the sleeve of his right fore-arm and revealed an intricate image. It was a rose in full flower, created by such an artistic hand that the president thought he could smell the perfumed odor of the bloom as he stared at the drawing.

"You see, I am of the opinion that everyone — men and women — will someday have something just as beautiful inked on their skin," Makala said.

The president harrumphed and spattered beer suds on the table top.

"Preposterous idea, that. I know I certainly would not have something like that done to me. And on a woman . . ." he trailed off. "Why the very idea is repugnant." Gianini quaffed half his mug before resting it on the table in front of him.

"Well then, Mr. President, we may have some common ground here after all."

"What do you mean by that?"

"Merely that if you are so certain of that statement, I may be willing to wager you $5,000 on the strength of those words. Right now."

Before Gianini could raise a startled protest and say he was not a gambling man, Makala stated the terms of his play.

"I am willing to bet you $5,000 Mister Gianini that by Monday you will have a tattoo. A red rose tattoo, to be precise, Mister Gianini, not unlike the one I just showed you."

The idea astonished, but that was not the final element of the wager.

"Furthermore, it will be on the inside of your right thigh. High up, near the crotch. What do you say to that, Mr. Gianini?"

"I'd say you're crazy, Mr. Makala, that's what I would say. What could possibly induce me to have such an abomination inscribed on my skin? Let alone do such a thing over the course of this coming weekend?"

The young man with the steel gray eyes was unwavering in his stare.

"That information is not part of our scheme, Mr. Gianini. You know I am quite serious, though, don't you?"

"I believe you are, sir. I also believe you have made a serious mistake." Gianini sat silent as he mulled over the proposition. It was quite against his principles to deal in something that smacked of risking money, his own or the bank's, in any but a business-like venture.

"It is a tidy sum, Mr. Gianini, wouldn't you say? You know I'm good for it. After all, that and more is in your vaults in my name right now."

Gianini came to a decision. "For that sum of money, you have a wager, sirrah."

The waiter brought the bill and, as the bank president attempted to reach for it, Makala snatched it up. He lay two silver coins on the table without looking at the amount due.

"Allow me," he said graciously, and rose to his feet.

When he returned to clear off the dirty plates, the waiter was quite pleased to find the two coins. One would have been sufficient to pay the damages and still allow a reasonable gratuity.

§

The bank president was not without concern for the amount of cash he had just staked against Makala. It was a tremendous sum even for him to consider chancing on what superficially seemed to be a sure thing. He had no intention of participating in any sort of activity which might result in his receiving a rose tattoo. Frankly, he could not conceive of what that activity might be, but rather than take any chances, Gianini returned to the bank immediately after lunch complaining to his secretary of a stomach ailment. He left his supervisor in charge. An overly solicitous but moderately quizzical staff accepted his statement that his luncheon had not agreed with him.

Gianini picked up his carriage intending to drive directly home. The livery man was surprised to see him so early in the day, but brought the buggy around without comment.

Gianini took great care climbing aboard the surrey and ordered the driver to go slow, approach all cable car crossings with great circumspection and each intersection on the notoriously hectic Market Street climb toward Twin Peaks with the utmost respect for his condition.

Upon arrival at home, his wife ran out excitedly to greet him when she heard the buggy's approach. She listened to his complaint, placed a hand on his brow and pronounced him free of fever. Still, she linked arms and walked him through the vestibule, into the hall of their Tudor style home, clutched his elbow as if to support him should he faint.

"I wish to retire to my chamber, madam," he informed her at the base of the stairs. He made his voice sound convincingly pain wracked even to himself. "I should not like to be disturbed except at meal times, please, through Sunday. I am sure I'll be well enough to return to the bank come Monday."

Feigning weakness, shoulders bent as if in support of a great weight, the bank president held the banister tight as he retired to his room. He did not remove himself from bed until the following Monday morning.

§

"Good to see you, Nathan," Makala greeted the teller enthusiastically. He clapped him on the back like a long-lost friend. "You can show me this town in terms of its night-life, what say?"

"Don't you get enough of that during the week, Eero? Uh, you said I may call you Eero?" Nathan asked deferentially.

"Of course you may. As for my activities after dark, I've been working every night since I met you." He looked genuinely surprised at Nathan's evident surprise to learn this. "Oh, you wouldn't know about that. I've not talked with you about how I earn my living, have I? Come with me, then."

On the boardwalk in front, they made their way toward North Beach. This was an area which Nathan had never ventured into by day or night. He knew it to be inhabited primarily by Italian émigrés, many of whom had begun legitimate businesses like Mr. Gianini, but the area was as well known for its gangs of thieves and drunken sailors as it was for its houses of ill repute. Nathan had never been tempted by the latter and had no intention of encountering any of the former if he could avoid them.

He was reluctant to continue when he saw where their footsteps were directed.

"You know, I'm not so sure I want to have dinner in that part of town." Nathan motioned toward the last hill before the City met the Bay.

"Are you kidding? We're not going this way to find a place to eat. We'll be eating at that fine restaurant I found on California Street. First I thought perhaps we would start with a drink or two and attempt a momentary dalliance with the ladies, set something up for later this evening, you know."

Nathan did not know. He was in unknown territory but was not comfortable admitting it to himself or to Makala.

The first establishment they entered was on the corner of Grant and Fresno streets. It was dark and seamy, a smoke filled room with a piano and a stage at the far end. There were several round tables, only one of which was occupied. Three men were dealing a deck of cards, Nathan noticed, as Makala approached the bar and ordered drinks. Nathan was served a small glass of beer and a tumbler of hard liquor which he did not recognize. Makala quickly drank half his beer, poured the shot into the remaining golden liquid and downed this in one long swallow.

Nathan had yet to taste either glass before Eero had both of his drained and empty on the bar in front of him.

This was of no concern to Makala. He motioned the bartender to serve him again. "Just a tall draught this time. Whatever you have in the keg."

He threw a coin on the counter and began walking toward the card players, beer in hand. "You gentlemen interested in a little money game?" he asked politely.

"Depends on how little," said one.

"Also depends on how much," said another.

"Hundred dollar buy-in sound reasonable to you fellows?"

All of them agreed. Makala pulled up a chair and made himself comfortable as he peeled five twenty-dollar notes from what Nathan took to be a relatively thin quantity in his wallet.

"You care to buy in, Nate?" Makala asked congenially. Shaking his head no, the teller resolved himself to a late supper and drew a chair over from another table. He sat backwards on it, leaning over the back with his drinks still untouched in his hands, a respectful distance from any of the players.

"Mind if I watch, though?" No one complained and the cards were dealt.

Two hours later, Nathan's stomach was complaining. All he had done for it so far was drench it in alcohol. He did not feel very clear headed although he had nursed his two drinks the entire time without ordering more.

Makala, on the other hand, was in something of a bad way as far as Nathan could tell. The deal had just been passed to him, but he first had trouble shuffling, then in handing out the cards. He was on his fourth or fifth round of drinks, Nathan had lost count, and was betting heavily. A crowd had formed and with each bet those who watched around the table muttered and seemed to think he ought to exercise more caution.

Makala threw a final card to each player and said, "Antes in. Pot's square. Left of dealer bets."

Everyone received five cards. Betting went around once and it was time to take cards if the player wanted any. Everyone did and one exchanged four, the maximum, indicating none had much of a hand, Nathan thought.

Makala rocked back in his chair in a most precarious position. After discarding and taking a card, he said, "Dealer takes one."

He placed the deck near the pot in the center of the table. Dealing was done, betting began in earnest.

His voice may be clumsy but the eyes were sharp, Nathan noticed as Makala surveyed the players. There were six now, two more having joined in the last half hour. Though he had won a few, Makala had lost several hands. By far his largest investment was in the deal currently in play. In fact, thought Nathan, the other players were equally deep. Nearly four hundred dollars lay in a pile of coins and bills in the center of the table. The round of betting raised the pot and required each player pay more in order to stay in the game.

"Your bet. Time to play," the drunken dealer said as he made a sweeping motion of his arm in the direction of the man whose turn it was.

"Ten to stay in the game," the man said and threw a gold coin into the center of the table.

The result was the next to quit who turned his cards face down in front of him. Following that, the man adjacent saw the last bet, raised it twenty. By the time it came to Makala, he had to meet fifty.

Clear voiced, he said, "I'll see that, raise it a hundred."

The gathered crowd murmured in awe. Nathan gulped the last swallow of beer.

Makala allowed Nathan to see what he held. Nothing, Queen high. If the remaining four players had equally bad hands, there were two cards that could beat the Queen by itself. There was the high possibility one of the four had paired up. In that case, nothing in Makala's hand would do him any good.

The man who had raised it ten and whose turn it was to meet the one hundred fifty dollar bet said, "Too rich for my blood," and folded. He threw his cards in.

The next man said nothing, stared at the cards fanned in his hands long and hard, grimaced and pushed them away.

That left two who simply declined in their turn to meet the bet. The pile of discarded cards had to be pushed aside in order for Makala to gather the money in front of him.

Eero collected his winnings. He shoved uncounted bills loosely into a pocket, held another pocket open to collect the coins which he swept uncounted off the table.

"Gennlmen, I thang yew all. Sincerely. But I b'lieve s'time t'go. 'Cn barely sit upright an' my pal an' I gotta be back afore the ship sails."

Nathan knew this was an oblique reference to the hotel, but kept his mouth shut. He had lost a good deal of respect for his new friend now that he had seen him drink too much. Still, he assisted Eero to a standing position and pulled Makala's arm over his shoulder to become a crutch while they walked. He realized how hungry he was and hoped Miss Betty would take pity on him when he strolled in this late reeking of alcohol.

Makala made a supreme effort and grabbed his distinctive wide-brimmed, high crowned hat from the rack as they passed. He fit it clumsily on his head where it hung at an angle threatening to fall with every lurching step he took.

As they stumbled through the door, Nathan feared he would have difficulty making the hike back to the hotel with this burden. Out on the street, he thought of hailing a hansom cab but did not have enough money to pay the fare. He complained out loud: "You know, you might come up with cab money out of all you took off that table!"

"That's the first sensible thing I've heard you say, my man," said Eero straightening up and removing the weight from Nathan's shoulders. He turned his wide smile toward Nathan who could only gasp in surprise. Eero adjusted his coat and tucked in his shirt, fit his hat squarely on his head and stood perfectly upright.

"Now for that meal I promised. I recommend the lobster at Tadich's. A Sacramento River sturgeon, however, may be more to your liking, Nate. What say we enjoy the rest of the night in style?"

"You're not drunk at all," the bank teller said in astonishment.

"You complaining?" Makala asked with a laugh. "Come on, let's get out of here before those boys decide to get the pot back without a deck of cards." He broke into a brisk walk, then a near run as he crossed Broadway and entered the de facto border of Chinatown. "Catch us a rickshaw. C'mon!"

Nathan followed close behind, leaped aboard a foot cab as Eero waved a bill under the nose of the runner.

"Go fast, fast. You hear? Chop, chop. I pay double you make double time. Got that?"

"Loud and clear," the man said in perfect English. He set off at a fast trot.

Dawn was squinting at San Francisco from the East as the two men made their way up the steps of the landing to their hotel. Nathan had no trouble drifting off to sleep in his basement room. But because there were no windows, he was astonished to find he slept late into Saturday by the time he finally woke to look at his clock.

And very much exactly the same thing happened the following night when he accepted another invitation from Makala to dine out.

§

Mr. Gianini was feeling rather good Monday morning. So good, in fact, he told his wife to join him in his bed when she brought morning toast and coffee. She was impressed by his ardor, which until then had been reduced to a monthly event at best over the last year or two.

She caught him examining his inner thighs in the mirror afterwards. She thought it odd, but made no remark.

Gianini was extremely delighted with himself as he directed the horse toward the bank. So delighted, he began to hum a song, an old song his mother crooned to him from her own childhood in Tuscany. He was surprised he knew the melody and a few of the words after all these years.

Upon arrival, he left word with his secretary he was expecting a visitor. He would be available at any time, do not hesitate to knock he importuned her.

Frequently that morning Gianini checked his watch. Not until late, just before noon, did his secretary finally inform him that two men were waiting to see him, one of whom was the young man he lunched with last Friday.

"Show them in."

As she opened the door Gianini beamed a smile at her which she thought was too beatific. It was quite out of character for him to be so pleasant.

Makala was accompanied by another gentleman wearing a pinstripe suit. Gianini guessed him to be the young man's senior by at least twenty years. Makala carefully closed the door behind them.

He gave the bank president a rather stern expression. It was apparent he was all business.

"Mister President, I believe you know why we are here."

Gianini said he did. He, too, assumed a more businesslike manner. It was a great test of his will, however, to control his good feelings knowing he had won the wager.

"Good. Then, Mister President, I would ask if you would please stand up and walk over here rather than sit behind your desk."

Gianini rose and did as Makala requested.

"If I may, I would like to request you remove your shoes and spats."

Gianini obliged from his standing position. He held the shoes in his right hand, the gaiters draped over his forearm.

"Mister President, could I ask you to unbuckle your pants and lower them to the floor?"

Gianini did so. Frowning, Makala first made a distant inspection of the man's legs, then bent closer.

"You might remove them all the way, sir. I'd find it more convenient if you would separate your legs."

Gianini stepped out of the garment wrapped around his feet, lifted it with one foot to grab hold of the pants at the belt line. He stood holding them in his left hand, footgear in his right.

At that moment the older fellow in the pinstripe suit who accompanied Makala into the room uttered a loud sound of disgust, then a curse. Before either the bank president or the young man could react, the door to the president's office was opened and slammed shut as the man hurriedly left. The fellow was obviously quite angry about something.

Gianini saw his secretary's surprised face taking in his pose as the door closed.

"Who was that man anyway?" asked Gianini only moderately curious. He had assumed he was there as a witness to the fact he had no rose tattoo. He still held his pants and shoes expecting Makala to continue the inspection.

"Him?" the young man said in an offhanded way. "That's the guy I bet twenty thousand dollars I could talk the pants off the bank president by Monday."

CHAPTER FIFTEEN

A DAY IN COURT

Benny Rossen was flanked by a clerk to his left and a pile of books to his right. He stood behind a table looking down at the hand held notes from which he read. Gradually his head lifted toward the judge.

"At issue is the claimed right of the salvor plaintiff, Mr. Don Worthy, and the libeled, the Boesk Corporation. Now comes the plaintiff begging the court to offer remedy in the form of a cure. It should be noted that time is of the essence and an extension is requested on behalf of Mr. Worthy in order to effect proper removal of the vessel from the tidelands in which it has become mired. The extension requested is at least six months, no longer than one year from the time of beginning of salvage. That date to be commenced at the conclusion of these proceedings this day."

Rossen looked at the judge and did his best to smile like Dustin Hoffman. "Your honor, we will show that the formal requisites of the law of salvage have been fulfilled. First, the property was in immediate peril: a danger existed to this ship which no other action could have averted. Second, the ship was abandoned and had become derelict; therefore anyone could come forward as the salvor. Third, the act of salving was totally voluntary in nature; it continues to this day. Finally, we have every reason to believe the salvage will be successful."

Rossen dropped his brief and picked up another sheaf of papers. He said, "Permission to approach."

The black robed figure in the high chair nodded. "You may approach the bench.

"Your Honor, the case law on the subject is specific. It leaves no doubt that the rights to the vessel are now Mr. Worthy's to do with as he sees fit. I lay before you copies of pertinent decisions."

There was a moment of paper shuffling as the Judge rifled the documents Rossen presented her.

"Is the salvor, Mr. Worthy in attendance today?" the Judge asked as she set the pile aright, looking at Rossen.

"As a matter of fact, no, Your Honor. As to possessory rights of the salving party, Mr. Worthy now claims he is the captain of the ship he is salving. In as much as that requires he not abandon ship lest it become derelict again, he remains in possession. On board, so to speak."

In response, the Boesk Corporation fielded a Southern California attorney whose specialty, Rossen heard in the outside hallway, was in Admiralty Court. His name was Joseph Roberts.

"Your honor, there is no reason to believe an act of salvage is in progress," Roberts began. Another attorney on the Boesk team, one of four, was seated at the table next to Roberts. He leaned toward his associate and handed him a small piece of paper on which was a hand written note. Roberts smiled, but did not miss a beat in his discourse. "It is a well known principle of maritime law that 'for property to become the subject of salvage, it must be on water (or at any rate on the beach) and not on land.' I quote from Gilmore & Black, page 539."

A rather self serving smile covered his face for an instant. Then he continued.

"Further, the property was not abandoned, merely vacated for the weekend. It was properly fenced-off from the public, of which the claimant is a member, and an act of trespassing... perhaps piracy would be a better choice of words... ," Roberts paused allowing the thought to be considered before continuing, "was committed. That would, of course, be covered by tort, and is a civil matter best taken up as soon as the current issue is laid to rest."

He waved his own sheaf of papers at the judge. A clerk took them and handed them over. "That is a counter suit for trespass with a request for general damages of $50,000 per day. This amount is based on a calculation of the cost of interest lost on the principle amount held by our banks as well as a net present value analysis of the amount of rental income lost by every day of delay. Punitive damages are herein specified as two million in this pleading. We pray for a speedy conclusion in order to continue with the project as planned."

Rossen had never felt he was on particularly solid legal ground in this case, but the last few words shook the earth under him completely. He scrambled and fumbled with the papers on his desk in an insane effort to come up with rebuttals to Roberts' arguments.

"Your Honor," he began when the judge was satisfied the defense had concluded, "this is most certainly a salvage action."

In his left hand he held a book which he waved in front of his face. He assumed an oratorical stance, his other hand on his hip.

"'A vessel under repair in dry dock was held subject to salvage' in the Jefferson case, 1909. In this instance, we have the vessel known as the *Niantic* which was a perfectly serviceable ship when she was partially destroyed by fire in 1851. The extent of damage was not known then and remains unknown, but it is Mr. Worthy's contention the value of the ship today goes beyond its utility as a boat. It has historical interest and may well provide clues in our understanding of frontier and Gold Rush era shipbuilding. I have expert witnesses from the university as well as from a private archaeology firm here in town who consult on exactly this sort of find. We ask that you quash the tort action and extend the injunction to give us time to prove the value of the discovery and to attempt a recovery of the ship. Finally, I request you restrict defendant from any cross complaint and his request for compensatory or punitive damages."

Judge Tarera joined the two masses of papers into one on her desk and smacked her gavel. There was utter silence as she stood.

"The matter is now under advisement. I shall issue my determination when we reconvene this afternoon at," she glanced at her watch, "will three o'clock be acceptable to you gentlemen?"

Both parties agreed to the time.

"Very well then, this court is adjourned until three this afternoon."

§

Don was not awake during these proceedings. He was still in his bedroll when the phone began squawking at him at 9:45. He managed to crawl out of the sack and wrestle the case open before whoever was at the other end gave up.

"Hello!" he said too loudly. Immediately he recognized his crankiness, attempted to tone it down. "Hello," he repeated in a more convivial voice before anyone at the other end could say anything.

He stood and kicked the bedroll away. He was cold. He pulled his pants on with one hand, the towel still safely buckled about his middle. He hopped on one foot and searched for a cigarette in his shirt pocket.

Finding them and his lighter, he tried to claw his way back into the bedroll.

"I wish to speak with Captain Worthy, please."

Don was momentarily disoriented by the request. He decided it had a nice ring to it.

"Speaking."

"My name is Haroldson and I wish to offer some assistance in the recovery of the Gold Rush ship on which you're sitting."

Don was naturally leery of anyone who volunteered. For anything. It was something he had learned not to do when he was in the service and the philosophy had stood him in good stead ever since.

"Assistance? What you got, a tugboat?"

"No," came the good natured response over the earpiece, "I do not have a boat of any sort with which you may be interested. It's rather complicated, my ability to help you, but suffice it to say I have an interest which is in no way contra to your own.

"Yah, what's in it for you?" Don asked in his own direct style.

"Let me assure you that you will only benefit from our meeting, Mr. Worthy. Do you mind if I visit you in person rather than discuss this over the telephone? I'm quite close. In fact, just across the street. I can take my time, however, in case you need to perform a few morning ablutions."

Don considered that he was suddenly under a microscope. How did the guy at the other end know he was just getting started for the day? It gave him a different sort of chill as he replied.

"Gimme half an hour. You know how to get here?"

The voice at the other end chuckled again in what Worthy took as a positive response, said he certainly did.

Don snapped the cell phone closed. He resigned himself to the new morning, smoked two cigarettes in a row as he buttoned his shirt, cinched his jeans and peeled a banana for breakfast. The belt of coins looked like a roll of fat under his shirt.

Half a block away and nearly two hundred feet in the air, Haroldson replaced his own telephone in its cradle. He was standing in his office window with a pair of binoculars in his hands. Next to him was Winton Chirup, a half smile on his face.

Haroldson continued to watch with interest as Don had breakfast, rummaged around his living quarters doing a small amount of tidying up and straightening out in anticipation of his guest.

Haroldson had a direct bird's eye view of the construction zone from his offices on Commercial Street. Ever since the demolition of the Niantic Hotel, Haroldson had been seeking a way to stop or at least slow the construction of Boesk's neighboring project.

Chirup placed the opportunity and the tools squarely in is lap. It was time to make his move.

§

Last night the pit worked a change on Worthy he found difficult to admit: he had to face the fact that he did not want to spend another moment below ground aboard his ship. Don did not really want the mantle of captaincy on his shoulders; it was not a comfortable coat and hat. A bad fit, he muttered to himself.

He was still concerned about what he might be giving up by leaving. He felt no particular obligation to Rossen to stay aboard, only an obligation to his own greedy self.

Yesterday was the worst so far. He spent the entire day with the retrieved earth pick, poking and prodding the ground, hoping to satisfy himself there were no more sacks of coins to be found without major earth moving. The construction crew would accomplish that a whole lot better than he. It was the Boesk offer that remained an unknown. Would it be renewed? Why had it not been left open to him?

The answer was obvious. They expected him to fail in court.

He thought briefly of calling them up and asking if they'd take fifty.

Coffee. He wanted a cup of hot coffee, but water never really boiled for him on the Coleman stove. It made a semblance of being hot by steaming in front of him. He sprinkled a tablespoon of instant crystals and prepared a cup. He had slept fitfully. The weight of the coins kept him awake most of the night. It was a burden on his mind as well as on his stomach, giving him a peculiar insomnia.

He stirred the cup, took a sip.

The pit had served its purpose in a manner he had not foreseen, now it was preventing him from experiencing a free life. This was exactly the opposite of what he should feel with his new fortune wrapped around his belly. It was more than the uncomfortable nature of the belt or the insecurity of his surroundings that kept him throughout the night, conscious in the dark, his ears cocked for any sound.

This is not the way it was supposed to be. He should not fear to look over his shoulder, should not be jumping and squirming with every imagined noise, especially when he remembered MacArthur the watch-cat was on duty. Over this first cup of coffee and third cigarette, Don had to admit there had come a dramatic change in his attitude. With a sigh, he realized he had lost his spirit to joust with the Boesk

Corporation. All he wanted now was to call Christine, tell her he was sorry he'd yelled at her, and have her come pick him up.

After he got cleaned up, he intended to rent a safety deposit box, sell a few pieces of gold and eat a cheeseburger at Howard's.

He was not interested in explaining to his attorney how he felt or in being told what his options were. He just wanted to go home. He did not even really care what Boesk did, whether or not the offer was renewed.

Then another side of his mind spoke up. It said, but wait a minute. You have no idea what the outcome of the hearing will be. Boesk could double the offer if the judge sees things our way.

Don looked up to see a man approaching, his feet making kerplop sounds as he worked his way into Worthy's domain.

Haroldson arrived precisely thirty minutes after completing their telephone conversation. He was a middle-aged business man with no outwardly distinguishing characteristics immediately noticeable to Don. If anything, the man was remarkable by his being so nondescript. He wore a three piece suit the same charcoal grey as all others Don could remember and a yellow tie spotted with black geometric figures. Haroldson had an assertive manner which was not put off by the environment. Don invited him to have a cup of coffee which he politely refused.

Don smoked and sipped in silence. He scratched occasionally at parts of his body that were fairly screaming to be soaked in soap and rinsed in water.

"Your position here only came to my attention two nights ago," the business man began. "I saw the news broadcast and contacted one of my associates to investigate and learned you've created quite a stir in that pointy-top building next door."

Don smiled without speaking. He was unsure if he was hearing a compliment or a veiled threat. He had a sudden urge to go over to the yellow tie and pull it out of its waistcoat. He managed to control himself.

The man laughed affably enough. He had the kind of easy good humor that invites others to join it.

"Believe me. We are on the same team, Captain Worthy. We both want to put a thorn in the lion's paw. To teach it a lesson. We do this, of course, for completely different reasons, from diametrically opposite directions, but with the same end in mind."

The laugh again.

"My inside information says you are merely trying to extort a considerable sum of money from H. J. Boesk, his corporations and anyone involved in this construction project," Haroldson said with the candor of a man who prefers to come to the point.

"Now just a goddam minute," Don said angrily. He rose to his feet and towered over his seated companion. "You don't come here and tell me you're on my side, then say something like that!"

Haroldson attempted to mollify Worthy by calling him by his first name. "Terribly sorry, Don. Honestly I am. Don, I do have something good to say to you so please hear me out."

Worthy managed to calm down.

"I doubt you could have precise information about your Hearing to Show Cause which is at this moment in recess."

Don's eyes lit up in surprise. This guy knew everything. Right up to what was happening in the courtroom. Don suddenly realized how closely scrutinized his life here had become. Foolish he, thinking himself alone when all along he was inside a giant fishbowl. He still had his secret wrapped around his stomach and was quite glad of his caution in keeping his gold hidden from prying eyes. It occurred to him to wonder how good Haroldson's spies really were. How had he been able to get the cellular phone's number? It was certainly not listed in Don's name. He had given it to no one but Rossen and Christine. Did this guy also know what Don found buried under his tent?

Don stared intently at his guest.

The other man took the look to mean Don was interested in how the case was proceeding. Haroldson began to fill Don in on the trial right up to the time of recess.

"Yes, I have information which is quite contemporary. That information is filtered to me within moments of the event." He looked at the fingernails of his left hand as if they had just been manicured. They had.

"I do not, of course, know the outcome, but I do know Judge Tarera has taken the matter under advisement. Already she has made several calls to government attorneys whom she considers specialized in maritime law and she has contacted the National Park Service in an apparent attempt to determine what salvage rights they have dealt with recently."

Worthy's face must have shown his lack of knowledge thereon, so Haroldson said, "To answer that, I believe there have been three recent cases — I mean within the last five years — dealing with sunken vessels here and in Florida as well as off shore which she may use as guides. Yes, your judge intends to be as informed as she can be by the afternoon deadline she set herself."

Everything the man said was news to Worthy. He perked up with Haroldson's mention of the recess. "What deadline are you talking about?" Don inquired over the lip of his cup.

"Terribly sorry. You wouldn't know yet, would you? Well, your judge informed all present that she shall end the controversy today at 3:00 p.m."

Don was surprised at the dispatch with which things were being handled.

"I have many ears, many eyes, many hands," Haroldson said smiling wryly. "Sometimes I think of myself as an insect, Mr. Worthy, with multifaceted eyes. Or I think of myself and my activities in terms of watching the symbols glide by on the big board at the exchange. I know what transactions are taking place and how they affect other activities. You, for instance. I know how you have already affected a multinational corporate giant and I can say with some certitude you have done more than I could ever have hoped to accomplish with all the resources at my disposal."

Don caught sipping, stopped mid-drink as Haroldson's attention focused on him. This talk of insect eyes was beginning to make Don think he might be dealing with a mystic. Or a madman.

"The truly valuable thing for you to realize, Mr. Worthy, is that you have become an important player in an otherwise rather pedestrian game of chess. I believe you rose to a level above a pawn by accident rather than design. But, no matter," Haroldson said in a cavalier manner, waving a hand in mid-air. "Let me tell you how things will probably proceed. During this time-out period which shall last until mid-afternoon, a judge is deciding whether or not to grant a continuance to your stay here. Please do not become upset with my frankness. I think we would both agree that you are here at sufferance and it is merely a question of time before you will be obliged to depart. This assessment is approximately correct?" he asked rhetorically.

There was little point in contradicting Haroldson. Don nodded in agreement and wished the man would make his point.

"In all likelihood the judge will grant you a little time. Perhaps a week. Perhaps two." Don's face fell visibly with this projection. He no longer wished to remain on the boat at all. The prospect of an additional week or two was more than he could stand. He wanted to take his coins and run.

Haroldson incorrectly read Don's expression to mean he wanted more than a week or two.

"I would point out, however, that an expert in matters of this nature might be able to gain even more time, might make real the request for half a year which your representative has made." Haroldson pulled an old fashioned round watch from his vest pocket and glanced at it. He replaced it without comment.

Don did not become excited with the news that some legal eagle could squeeze six months out of Boesk.

"Which brings me to my reason for visiting you here. I wish to buy your interest in those two weeks, Mr. Worthy. I wish to purchase the vessel from you. To assume your place, so to speak, in the historic past which you have discovered. I came over here today to ask what you think that is worth to you."

This surprised Don so much he nearly fell off of his perch. He saw how important this meeting could be to him. But he gritted his teeth and smiled tightly. So many offers had already been made to him that he was able to maintain an outward calm. He was becoming a practiced negotiator with billionaires.

He thought over what the man said. He was being asked to name his price to vacate at the very time Rossen might get an extension. The offer was an answered prayer, but Don did not allow his feelings to show. He willed his face to be a study in passive reflection, unaffected by the thoughts within.

Yet something nagged in the back of his mind. The question finally resurfaced.

"I already asked you on the phone, what's in it for you? You gonna tell me?"

Haroldson considered this. "After we have come to terms, I will be delighted to explain. Not before. Can we make a deal?" Haroldson was supremely polite as he put this last question to Don.

"Six figures?" Don asked this tentatively not knowing what to expect.

"I am a man of substantial means, Mr. Worthy," Haroldson said by way of agreement. "Though I shall limit myself to the low six figures."

"Does that mean three hundred thousand?"

"No, Mr. Worthy, I am afraid it does not." The formal trading had begun. Haroldson looked about the dig and clucked disapproval. "I need not point out that two weeks is hardly time to begin an excavation here. You can accomplish nothing in less than a month. So, although worthless to you, I can do something with this artifact in that length of time."

"Two hundred then?"

"Still too steep, Mr. Worthy. Though I applaud your temerity. Brashness, though, will not do well by you when you are up against me in a bargain. I offer one hundred thousand for your position with respect to this vessel. That amounts to fifty thousand dollars a week. Not a penny more."

"One seventy-five." Don knew he was not in a winning position but he could not help himself. He did not want to lose the deal, ought to keep in mind that Haroldson could withdraw his offer, just like Boesk had, at any time. But the flea market haggler inside him could not be stilled.

"We have no need to continue this discussion, I can see." Haroldson rose with finality written all over him. "You will not meet my offer, I will not meet your asking price." Haroldson turned as if to take his leave.

"Okay. Okay. Just sit down a minute, Mr. Haroldson. Let me have some time to think about it." Don did not take a second to make up his mind. He responded almost immediately. "One hundred it is. Where do I sign?"

"This is a matter on which we shall have a gentleman's agreement for the time being. May I have your hand on that, sir?"

Don extended his hand and it was taken in a strong grip, given one up and one down movement, then returned to his own use.

"Very good, sir. We shall meet again this afternoon to conclude our transaction, Mr. Worthy. I shall have the papers drawn up and a cashier's check in that sum made out to you."

"Call me Cap'n." Don looked over the rim of his mug rather sheepishly. "Unless you want to be Captain?"

"Not at all, Captain Worthy. However, there is one qualification to my offer. It is based on the successful extension of the injunction which you seek today. If the judge is unwilling to rule in your favor, I am afraid our little deal is off. Is that agreeable to you?"

Don considered the import of this last statement. "If I don't get an extension, you won't pay, is that it?"

"That is correct, sir."

"How much time does the judge have to grant?"

"I will need at least two weeks. If you get more, I shall be delighted. But in that event I shall not raise my offer. Is that satisfactory with you?"

Don nodded agreement. He was afraid to spoil things by talking.

"Good. I shall have the papers drawn up and be prepared to meet with you at that time. Um, you will accept a return visit from me?" Again the nod. "Good. I thought as much. Until then, Captain."

Haroldson rose. He extended his hand which Don shook warmly, then turned and began walking toward the ramp. Sidney Greenstreet, Don muttered to himself. That's who he reminds me of. A thin Sidney Greenstreet. Right out of *The Maltese Falcon*.

Don tossed the now cold contents of his mug on the ground in front of him. The liquid instantly melted into nothing.

§

Don's phone rang the moment Haroldson breasted the hill and disappeared from sight.

"Donald." It was Rossen. He sounded unusually bright and cheerful. His voice echoed as if he were calling from a cavern. "I have to tell you how things are going. I'm calling from right outside the courtroom. Tarera's called recess until three this afternoon. Says she'll have an answer for us then."

"That's what I heard," Worthy replied.

"Too bad you couldn't have been there. She bought the part about you being the captain and unable to abandon ship." Rossen was elated. He was prepared to launch into a blow-by-blow description of the morning's events when he arrested his speech. "What do you mean you heard? How could you? Who could have told you? It just happened, like, maybe half an hour ago. I just left the courtroom. I didn't even get cup of tea before I called you."

Worthy described his visitor and their conversation. He concluded by telling his attorney about the handshake.

"Don, how could you do such a thing without consulting me? I'm your lawyer. Your legal counsel, for crissakes. I got you this far, didn't I? I can get you all the way!"

"Yah, well Benny, it wasn't easy. I should tell you I really had to soul search before I agreed. I had to dig deep. And I thought of you and all you've done for me. I knew I could count on you to understand. But my word is my word so I intend to keep it."

"I just can't believe it, Don. We have such a strong case!" Rossen had no idea what kind of verdict the judge would return, but he couldn't tell his client that. "And you go and sell out on me."

Don suddenly felt generous. He was wearing more money than he ever expected to see in his lifetime and had just been offered an additional hundred thousand. It was exactly what he wanted out of the whole ordeal and said as much to Rossen.

"Benny, this is the best way. Believe me. I'm not up to staying in this hole any more. I feel like I'm living in a foxhole during basic training or something. Let me offer you ten percent of Haroldson's deal. How's that? But you gotta get me two weeks. Otherwise we don't have anything. Boesk is counting on us getting zip. You gotta get us the two weeks or he's right. I got us the best deal I could under the circumstances."

Rossen was silent at the other end.

"What's the matter Benny? Don't you want to take this and end it?"

A rather miffed attorney was staring at the phone in his hands. "It's usually 25% in a personal injury case, Don," he said softly.

They settled on fifteen.

§

The bailiff called the court to order. All rose and then were seated.

"I'll make this short and sweet," the judge began. "I find merit in this case. However, not for the reasons cited by plaintiff. One of the cardinal rules of salvage is that it must be at sea. I can find no circumstance where land salvage has been an operation of law. However, I intend to see this vessel excavated to the satisfaction of a court appointed archeologist. If in the course of that expert witness's findings there is reason to continue the excavation or abandon it, that shall be the decision of this court. The injunction is in effect for twenty days." She slapped the gavel twice. "Let the court adjourn."

§

Worthy packed as many things into one suitcase as would fit. He grabbed the handle and felt its weight. He discarded the telephone briefcase, slipped the phone in his pants pocket. He reached for MacArthur.

The animal was happy to be leaving. Probably as pleased as Worthy was. Haroldson stood smiling amid the camping equipment.

"The bathroom's over there, and you can't miss the coat rack at the end of the hall," Don explained the layout of his erstwhile residence with the air of a homeowner leaving on vacation.

He set the cat down on the card table that had been the centerpiece of his dining room. He stroked MacArthur gently several times and the animal lay down on its side.

"I have been informed a certified check is in the hands of my attorney," Don said. The man bowed slightly toward Don at this news. "Now it's your turn to complete the bargain."

"How do you mean?" the businessman asked quite astonished.

"Tell me what value this place has for you. Like I asked twice now, what's in it for you?"

"Oh. Right. I quite forgot, I promised you an answer to that question, didn't I?" Haroldson appeared to be sincerely apologetic for his oversight. "I don't suppose the term 'absorption rate' carries any meaning for you?" Don shook his head negative. "I thought not. Well, how about 'Present Value Analysis'?" Don's head continued in its negative arc. "The term 'vacancy factor' is a little more understandable?" Don began to nod positive.

"Yes. Well. Let me simplify. I own that building across the street." Haroldson pointed at a tall new structure nearly the equal of the Pyramid. He had the satisfied look of a proud parent on his face. "And it still has ten floors vacant." His face clouded slightly. "When Boesk began this building," Haroldson indicated the hole where they stood, "it was obvious he intended to bleed me. He made agreements with several of my potential leasees to give them rents far below mine if they would accept a date to occupy two years hence. He planned to complete this structure by then."

MacArthur was beginning to get restless. His tail was flicking the table top. Don drew a hand across the animal's back starting at the head. The creature quieted.

"It may seem like a large sum to you, ex-Captain Worthy, but for me one hundred thousand is a small price to pay for the privilege of throwing Boesk off his schedule. In fact, I believe with this hulk," he swung around in a gesture which encompassed the area occupied by the *Niantic*, "I expect to keep Boesk's tenants out of their proposed offices for three years, at least six months longer than he promised. If you really want to see what that means, you run your own NPV analysis. I think $50,000 a day is a conservative estimate of what this is going to cost H. J. Boesk."

"I still don't get how you can accomplish any more delays," Don said. "What can you do with Tarera if she doesn't offer more than twenty days?"

"Why, that's precisely the point, Mr. Worthy. We can do nothing with Tarera. It's really quite simple. We merely ask for a change of venue. To the Federal Courts. And at that point I can invoke an 'Admiralty Arrest.'"

Don had no idea what that meant and said as much.

"It has been used successfully against the state of Florida, it can be used here. Quite simply, no one can exhume the boat until all liens are removed. The 'Arrest' is a federal lien which prevents a vessel from leaving a port. In this case, it will be used to prevent it from being taken apart." Haroldson smiled broadly. "You see, Mr. Worthy, I have no more intention of excavating this relic than you had. However, in my case, I want it to stay right where it is. For weeks, months or years, if possible."

Don was glad he was not involved in this game of hardball. He lifted his cat, the suitcase containing the few items he refused to leave to Haroldson and began his final walk out of the pit.

Then a thought occurred to him.

Don Worthy turned around and said to Haroldson, "You mind fronting me bus fare?"

THE END

About the Author

H. W. Moss was born in Riverside, CA, on August 4, 1947, darn near one of the first Baby Boomers. Graduated Long Beach State, B. A. English Literature, 1970. M.B.A. San Francisco State University, 1988. He successfully avoided marriage and the military.

Discover Other Titles by H.W. Moss

Youth and Other Science Fiction Stories
Googol the Great
City At Night
Windows For Remy
Talk Show Host
Jimmie Leigh's Wild Ride Through Life

Collected Short Stories

Collected Works 2004
Collected Works 2005
Collected Works 2006

Connect Online

http://NetNovels.com
http://twitter.com/NetNovels
http://www.netnovels.com/blog/
http://www.facebook.com/NetNovels

www.ingramcontent.com/pod-product-compliance
Lightning Source LLC
Chambersburg PA
CBHW070931250626
47159CB00009B/3203